SUDDEN
FICTION

(Continued)

Also edited by Robert Shapard and James Thomas:

Sudden Fiction: American Short-Short Stories

Sudden Fiction International

Also by James Thomas:

Pictures, Moving (stories)

Flash Fiction: 72 Very Short Stories
(editor with Denise Thomas and Tom Hazuka)

*The Best of the West: Short Stories from the
Wide Side of the Missouri, Volumes 1–5*
(editor with Denise Thomas)

60 *New* Short-Short Stories

SUDDEN

FICTION

(Continued)

edited by

Robert Shapard

and

James Thomas

W. W. NORTON & COMPANY
New York
London

Since this page cannot legibly accommodate all the copyright notices,
pages 307–311 constitute an extension of the copyright page.

The text of this book is composed in Berthold Bodoni-Antiqua Regular
with the display set in Trade Gothic Light Oblique and Condensed.
Composition and manufacturing by the Maple-Vail Book Manufacturing
Company. Book design by Charlotte Staub

Library of Congress Cataloging-in-Publication Data

Sudden fiction (continued) : 60 new short-short stories / edited by
    Robert Shapard and James Thomas.
        p.   cm.
    ISBN 0-393-03830-0.–ISBN 0-393-31342-5 (pbk.)
    1. Short stories, American.   I. Shapard, Robert, date.
    II. Thomas, James, date
    PS648.S5S83   1996
    813'.0108–dc20   95-39355

W. W. Norton & Company, Inc., 500 Fifth Avenue, New York, N.Y. 10110
http://web.wwnorton.com
W. W. Norton & Company Ltd., 10 Coptic Street, London WC1A 1PU
1 2 3 4 5 6 7 8 9 0

For their invaluable assistance,
the editors would especially like to thank:

Revé Shapard, Denise Thomas,
Jerry Saviano, Charlene Gilmore,
Byron Crews, and C. J. Baker.

CONTENTS

A NOTE FROM THE EDITORS

As we complete our third collaboration as editors, and our third collection of Sudden(s), we think back to the time—more than a decade ago—when we first noticed these short fictions popping up in literary magazines and in books from small presses. Although some were showing up in well-known journals, others seemed to be thriving well outside the greenhouse of the literary establishment. Tiny kingdoms, one writer called them. A critic trying to describe them said they had "a depth and intensity of penetration into human life that was of a luminous difference in kind from the novel or the larger story." But no one, so far as we knew, had identified them as a literary form all their own.

At first curious, we began to look seriously for these stories, then decided to gather what we thought were the best and bring them together in a book. At this early stage, we had referred to them as *blasters,* but fortunately we were persuaded to abandon this term. It was pointed out to us that some of the most quiet short fictions were the most powerful. "They don't all blast," one correspondent wrote, "but they *all* are suddenly just there." And so *Sudden,* from the Latin *subire* (to steal upon, unforeseen, swift), seemed an absolutely appropriate name for this form.

Sudden Fiction: American Short-Short Stories, the first volume published in 1986, was followed in 1989 by *Sudden Fiction International.* Then, taking a break to explore an even shorter form, one of us, James Thomas, became co-editor of *Flash Fiction,* stories of no more than 750 words. Reader response to all these volumes, and the reception from colleges and universities, where course adoptions reached more than two hundred, indicated that the time was right for this third collection. Because the form itself endures, we decided to call the new volume *Sudden Fiction (Continued).*

As before, we chose to limit the number of stories to sixty, and the length to two thousand words. Each story had to be complete, and if in translation, the translation should be excellent. We consulted nearly two hundred magazines, including issues over a five-year period for each, plus new book collections and unpublished manuscripts. As we read, it seemed to us that the spirit of experimentation continues to be most alive these days in the shorter forms. No longer relegated to special sections, they are scattered as regular fare throughout the pages of an even larger number of magazines, including the larger-circulation magazines. But one thing remains constant: each story revels in its own elements of surprise; each, whether traditional or experimental, proves that a tale told quickly offers pleasure long past its telling. This is serious fiction that's fun to read.

Perhaps Charles Baxter, in introducing *Sudden Fiction International,* best captured the protean quality of the Sudden form when he said, "I suspect that these stories appeal to readers so much now because the stories are on so many various thresholds: they are between poetry and fiction, the story and the sketch, prophecy and reminiscence, the personal and the crowd."

Helping us in our selection for this volume was an enthusiastic and opinionated "staff" of readers: friends who are writers, editors, and—not least—students in our respective writing programs who sometimes raucously gave thumbs up or thumbs down to stories we had ranked otherwise. We listened to them all, and while we cannot claim unanimity of opinion on every story in this book, we do know that the process was democratic. All the stories were considered with care and debated with passion. Now we offer them to you, our reader and final arbiter.

Robert Shapard
James Thomas

SUDDEN
FICTION
(Continued)

Margaret Atwood

MY LIFE AS A BAT

1. Reincarnation

In my previous life I was a bat.

If you find previous lives amusing or unlikely, you are not a serious person. Consider: A great many people believe in them, and if sanity is a general consensus about the content of reality, who are you to disagree?

Consider also: Previous lives have entered the world of commerce. Money can be made from them. *You were Cleopatra, you were a Flemish duke, you were a Druid priestess,* and money changes hands. If the stock market exists, so must previous lives.

In the previous-life market, there is not such a great demand for Peruvian ditch-diggers as there is for Cleopatra; or for Indian latrine-cleaners, or for 1952 housewives living in California split-levels. Similarly, not many of us choose to remember our lives as vultures, spiders or rodents, but some of us do. The fortunate few. Conventional wisdom has it that reincarnation as an animal is a punishment for past sins, but perhaps it is a reward instead. At least a resting place. An interlude of grace.

Bats have a few things to put up with, but they do not inflict. When they kill, they kill without mercy, but without hate. They are immune from the curse of pity. They never gloat.

2. Nightmares

I have recurring nightmares.

In one of them, I am clinging to the ceiling of a summer cottage while a red-faced man in white shorts and a white V-necked T-shirt jumps up and down, hitting at me with a tennis racquet. There are cedar rafters up here, and sticky flypapers attached with tacks, dangling like toxic seaweeds. I look down at the man's face, foreshortened and sweating, the eyes bulging and blue, the mouth emitting furious noise, rising up like a marine float, sinking again, rising as if on a swell of air.

The air itself is muggy, the sun is sinking; there will be a thunderstorm. A woman is shrieking, "My hair! My hair!" and someone else is calling, "Anthea! Bring the stepladder!" All I want is to get out through the hole in the screen, but that will take some concentration and it's hard in this din of voices, they interfere with my sonar. There is a smell of dirty bathmats—it's his breath, the breath that comes out from every pore, the breath of the monster. I will be lucky to get out of this alive.

In another nightmare I am winging my way—flittering, I suppose you'd call it—through the clean-washed demilight before dawn. This is a desert. The yuccas are in bloom, and I have been gorging myself on their juices and pollen. I'm heading to my home, to my home cave, where it will be cool during the burnout of day and there will be the sound of water trickling through limestone, coating the rock with a glistening hush, with the moistness of new mushrooms, and the other bats will chirp and rustle and doze until night unfurls again and makes the hot sky tender for us.

But when I reach the entrance to the cave, it is sealed over. It's blocked in. Who can have done this?

I vibrate my wings, sniffing blind as a dazzled moth over the hard surface. In a short time the sun will rise like a balloon on fire and I will be blasted with its glare, shriveled to a few small bones.

Whoever said that light was life and darkness nothing?

For some of us, the mythologies are different.

3. Vampire Films

I became aware of the nature of my previous life gradually, not only through dreams but through scraps of memory, through hints, through odd moments of recognition.

There was my preference for the subtleties of dawn and dusk, as opposed to the vulgar blaring hour of high noon. There was my déjà vu experience in the Carlsbad Caverns—surely I had been there before, long before, before they put in the pastel spotlights and the cute names for stalactites and the underground restaurant where you can combine claustrophobia and indigestion and then take the elevator to get back out.

There was also my dislike for headfuls of human hair, so like nets or the tendrils of poisonous jellyfish: I feared entanglements. No real bat would ever suck the blood of necks. The neck is too near the hair. Even the vampire bat will target a hairless extremity: by choice a toe, resembling as it does the teat of a cow.

Vampire films have always seemed ludicrous to me, for this reason but also for the idiocy of their bats—huge rubbery bats, with red Christmas-light eyes and fangs like a saber-toothed tiger's, flown in on strings, their puppet wings flapped sluggishly like those of an overweight and degenerate bird. I screamed at these filmic moments, but not with fear; rather with outraged laughter, at the insult to bats.

O Dracula, unlikely hero! O flying leukemia, in your cloak like a living umbrella, a membrane of black leather which you unwind from within yourself and lift like a stripteaser's fan as you bend with emaciated lust over the neck, flawless and bland, of whatever woman is longing for obliteration, here and now in her best negligée. Why was it given to you by whoever stole your soul to transform yourself into bat and wolf, and only those? Why not a vampire chipmunk, a duck, a gerbil? Why not a vampire turtle? Now that would be a plot.

4. The Bat as Deadly Weapon

During the Second World War they did experiments with bats. Thousands of bats were to be released over German cities, at the hour of noon. Each was to have a small incendiary device strapped onto it, with a timer. The bats would have headed for darkness, as is their habit. They would have crawled into holes in walls, or secreted themselves under the eaves of houses, relieved to have found safety. At a preordained moment they would have exploded, and the cities would have gone up in flames.

That was the plan. Death by flaming bat. The bats too would have died, of course. Acceptable megadeaths.

The cities went up in flames anyway, but not with the aid of bats. The atom bomb had been invented, and the fiery bat was no longer thought necessary.

If the bats had been used after all, would there have been a war memorial to them? It isn't likely.

If you ask a human being what makes his flesh creep more, a bat or a bomb, he will say the bat. It is difficult to experience loathing for something merely metal, however ominous. We save these sensations for those with skin and flesh: a skin, a flesh, unlike our own.

5 . B e a u t y

Perhaps it isn't my life as a bat that was the interlude. Perhaps it is this life. Perhaps I have been sent into human form as if on a dangerous mission, to save and redeem my own folk. When I have gained a small success, or died in the attempt—for failure, in such a task and against such odds, is more likely—I will be born again, back into that other form, that other world where I more truly belong.

More and more, I think of this event with longing. The quickness of heartbeat, the vivid plunge into the nectars of crepuscular flowers, hovering in the infrared of night; the dank lazy half-sleep of daytime, with bodies rounded and soft as furred plums clustering around me, the mothers licking the tiny amazed faces of the newborn; the swift love of what will come next, the anticipations of the tongue and of the infurled, corrugated and scrolled nose, nose like a dead leaf, nose like a radiator grill, nose of a denizen of Pluto.

And in the evening, the supersonic hymn of praise to our Creator, the Creator of bats, who appears to us in the form of a bat and who gave us all things: water and the liquid stone of caves, the woody refuge of attics, petals and fruit and juicy insects, and the beauty of slippery wings and sharp white canines and shining eyes.

What do we pray for? We pray for food as all do, and for health and for the increase of our kind; and for deliverance from evil, which cannot be explained by us, which is hair-headed and walks in the night with a single white unseeing eye, and stinks of half-digested meat, and has two legs.

Goddess of caves and grottoes: bless your children.

Luis Arturo Ramos

UNDERWATER

The trick turned out to be very simple; it consisted of holding onto the rope and letting yourself swing, using the
momentum from your run up. Then, some twenty meters
from the edge of the river, when the dizziness from your
flying leap had stopped and your wrist muscles had twisted,
you only had to let go of the rope, flip forward a few times—
a couple would be enough—and go knifing straight into the
water.

Several boys have already done it, and although some of
them—most, in fact—left a lot to be desired, no one was
denied applause or some yell of encouragement. Raul waits
his turn with his hands on his hips, the sunlight through
the branches of the trees barely warming the drops of water
scattered over his body. His feet feeling the dry and broken
bark of the enormous tree trunk, fallen forward over the
river. From there, the liquid surface is a constant and tran-
quil mirroring.

Raul was recognized as the best. They all knew it. However, he was already calculating the kind of flip he was going

to use to impress them: two turns in the air, his head nestled in his chest, and then knife very straight into the flexible green coating of the river.

His eyes went over the surface again. On the riverbanks the girls were putting their feet into the water and shielding their eyes with their hands to avoid the glare. Some of the boys took turns helping each acrobat gather up the momentum necessary to perform the trick. In the water, the heads of friends slide by like large fruits adrift. The sunlight models geometric figures, which then shatter and explode at the slightest movement.

When he takes the rope into his hands, they all cheer and heckle him, joking; someone calls him "Champ." The girls jump up and down and cheer again. Raul runs along the trunk of the tree with the rope in his hands, and then the turning stomach, the world incomprehensible, upside down.

The trees whizzed by. Needles of light pierced the blurry green of the bottom. He let go of the rope, drew himself together in the air to help the spin: one, two turns; tensed like a nail, the water down below like a necessary and undulating moss that opens when he enters with his arms and head and entire body, and Raul manages to feel for a few seconds the sensation of two worlds: the sun out there with its last brush strokes on his legs, the yelling of his buddies . . . and the river here inside, sucking him down with its fresh and greenish vapor.

Raul opens his eyes and feels around with his hands to keep from reaching the river bottom. Everything around him becomes like the inside of a lemon. Long leafy stalks arch overhead in the water and, at the bottom, the jaws of the trees and branches are like dogs barking at the sky of the river.

Before reaching bottom, he turned over and, after lashing out with his legs, began the ascent. He thought of the girls' faces, imagined the smiling and envious looks of his friends. Of the hurrahs that would flood his ears almost before they were out of the water. He started to release air through his mouth, and the bubbles fluttered in his face; his legs flailed and he could see there, behind the opaque crystal of the river, blades of light stirred up by the current.

The first one to feel uneasy is Ricardo. From the tree where Raul had been a few moments earlier, Ricardo tries to get to where his friend will come out. Some of the girls stand up and go into the river up to their waists. It was then that he threw himself into the water. While Ricardo swims towards the point where Raul had gone under water, two other boys are already diving in.

Raul was sure that he was moving forward very slowly. The light seemed as far away as ever, and the water that surrounded him, and its inhabitants, proved to be the same. Nothing indicated that he had moved. However, his lungs were releasing oxygen and that was convincing proof that time had not passed at the speed that he wanted. He concentrated on observing around him the shadows from beyond the water. The massive forms that changed their shapes but never their color. Everything was green, as only the inside of a river can be.

Some of the girls cry. Ricardo shows a boy he's never met the place where Raul should have come out. Someone said that maybe he's on the other bank of the river, peeing with laughter. Several of them said that Raul wasn't like that. They appealed to reason: his swimming ability, his knowledge of the river, the fact that nobody has ever drowned in this place. The sunlight slowly leaves the river until it strikes the hill on the other side. The green of the surface becomes opaque.

Raul began to feel uneasy when the holes of light in the roof of the river disappeared. The inside became dark, cozier and closer. He kicked with his legs faster and this time helped himself along with his arms. The bubbles choked his mouth and bothered his face. He told himself that it was all because of the tricks the water was playing; because of the light and the afternoon underneath the river. Because everything is different under water; that the air in his lungs proved the impossibility of such slowness.

They divide into groups. One stays there, on watch. The other has gone to town for help. One of the boys stretches a rope from one bank to the other and ties a red kerchief at the exact spot where Raul has disappeared. Ricardo, crying, hacks the other rope to pieces with a knife. The rest don't say anything. They look at the river and the gradual disappearance of highlights on the water. A slight breeze hits them from upriver and speeds up the flow of the current, ruffles the surface, touches the shoulders of the friends.

The lack of light frightened him a little. He asked himself if he might not be dead; drowned. Possibly, going down, he had not flipped over and had hit something hard with his head: a rock, a tree trunk, maybe. And now he was dead and drowned, floating inside the water, assessing his new situation. He would never again come out to the surface, which seems each minute to close in more, to darken.

Nobody wanted to leave; they all sat on the promontory, next to the immense tree, and watched what was going on. Three men with aqualungs dove down more than three times at the spot marked by the red kerchief. Then, in concentric circles that grew larger each time, they continued the search. They began to light oil lamps on one bank, and then on the other. They threw the lights of reflectors onto the river. Then, when the light swelled the water and the river fattened up like a serpent, it seemed as if nothing had happened, as if it all were a party. The next day the friends heard that a machine was coming to drag that part of the river.

It seemed as if he had had his eyes closed and had suddenly opened them. Or as if a third eye, more powerful and sensitive than the other two, had sprouted in his forehead because, all of a sudden, the roof of the river lit up as if someone had set it on fire. Raul kicked harder to reach the light, but up there, like a fading noon, the light fled into opaqueness until not even a ray of light could get through the water. This frightened him. Not weariness nor lack of oxygen. Only fear at not being able to get out.

The men took down their tents. The dredge sailed down the river toward the town pier. The friends had left long before. The river remained alone, extinguished. The lights slipped away behind the dredge, and the water became like silk until there was silence. The only thing that remained was the rope with the kerchief, its shadow cutting the width of the river.

Raul slowly climbed the branches that had fallen into the river. Now the horizontal light of the day and even sounds that could be of wind or of animals filtered through the cobweb of water and became distorted below into guttural echoes. He noticed that the temperature of the water was becoming a little warmer and that he could see enormous blotches beyond the surface. He smiled; he was about to come out. It had all been a bad joke. Panic had overcome him and made him confused about time, things.

He stuck one hand out, and the air and warmth trapped it outside. Then appeared the face and the agitated chest. The wind began to dry him, and the sun was on his body again. He opened his eyes: there wasn't anyone on either bank. He didn't hear cheers or hurrahs; not even laughter. From the surface, Raul recognized that the joke was a pretty good one.

Lunging, Raul gets more than halfway out of the water and calls his friends. Moments later he does it again; but this

time he doesn't get to call out because he feels a blow: he is
hit by the flapping of a bird's wing against his forehead. He
looks up and sees a kerchief, bleached by the sun, tied to a
rope that splits the river in two. He starts to swim, following
the direction of the rope, and wondering where the devil
they could be hiding.

Translated from the Spanish by
Robert Kramer and Gloria Nichols

Andrew Lam

GRANDMA'S TALES

The day after Mama and Papa took off to Las Vegas, Grandma died. Nancy and I, we didn't know what to do, Vietnamese traditional funerals with incense sticks and chanting Buddhist monks not being our thing. We have a big freezer, Nancy said. Why don't we freeze her. Really. Why bother Mama and Papa. What's another day or two for Grandma now anyway?

Nancy's older than me, and since I didn't have any better idea, we iced her.

Grandma was 94 years, 8 months, and 6 days old when she died. She lived through three wars, two famines, and a full hard life. America, besides, was not all that good for her. She had been confined to the second floor of our big Victorian home, as her health was failing, and she did not speak English, only a little French, like *Oui monsieur, c'est evidemment un petit monstre*, and, *Non, Madame, vous n'etes pas du tout enceinte, je vous assure.* She was a head nurse in the maternity ward of the Hanoi hospital during the French colonial time. I used to love her stories about delivering all these strange two-headed babies and Siamese triplets connected at the hip whom she named Happy, Liberation, and Day.

Grandma's death came when she was eating spring rolls with me and Nancy. Nancy was wearing a nice black mini-skirt and her lips were painted red, and Grandma said you look like a high-class whore. Nancy made a face and said she was preparing to go to one of her famous San Francisco artsy cocktail parties where waiters were better dressed than most upper-class Vietnamese men back home, and there were silver trays of duck paté and salmon mousse, and ice sculptures with wings and live musicians playing Vivaldi.

So get off my case, Grandma, because I'm no whore.

It was a compliment, Grandma said, winking at me, but I guess it's wasted on you, child. Then she laughed, as Nancy prepared to leave. Child, do the cha-cha-cha for me. I didn't get to do it when I was young, with my clubbed foot and the wars and everything else.

Sure, Grandma, Nancy said, and rolled her pretty eyes.

Then Grandma dropped her chopsticks on the hardwood floor—clack, clack, clatter, clack, clack—closed her eyes, and stopped breathing. Just like that.

So we iced her. She was small, the freezer was large. We wrapped her body in plastic wrap first, then sent a message to Circus-Circus, where Mama and Papa were staying.

Meanwhile Nancy had a party to go to, and I had to meet Eric for a movie.

I didn't care about the movie, but cared about Eric. He's got eyes so blue you can swim in them, and a warm laugh, and is really beautiful, a year older than me, a senior. Eric liked Grandma. Neither one knew the other's language, but there was this thing between them, mutual respect, like one cool old chic to one cool young dude. (Sometimes I would translate but not always 'cause my English is not all that good and my Vietnamese sucks.) What was so cool about

Grandma was she was the only one who knew I'm bisexual. Even though she was Confucian bound and trained and a Buddhist and all, she was really cool about it.

One night, we were sitting in the living room watching a John Wayne movie together, *The Green Berets*, and Eric was there with me and Grandma. (Mama and Papa had just gone to bed and Nancy was at some weird black and white ball or something like that.) And Eric leaned over and kissed me on the lips and Grandma said, That's real nice, and I translated and we all laughed and John Wayne shot dead five guys. Just like that. But Grandma didn't mind, really. She's seen Americans like John Wayne shooting her people in the movies before. She always thought of him as a bad guy, uglier than a water buffalo's ass. And she'd seen us more passionate than a kiss on the lips and didn't mind. She used to tell us to be careful and not make any babies—obviously a joke— 'cause she'd done delivering them. So you see, we liked Grandma a lot.

Anyway, after Nancy and I packed Grandma down into the 12 degree Fahrenheit, I went out to meet Eric, and later we came back to the house. We made out on the couch. After a while I said, Eric, I have to tell you something. Grandma's dead. You're kidding me, he whispered, with his beautiful smile. I kid you not, I said. She's dead, and Nancy and me, we iced her. Shit! he said. Why? 'Cause otherwise she would start to smell, duh, and we have to wait for my parents to perform a traditional Vietnamese funeral. We fell silent. Then Eric said, can I take a peek at Grandma? Sure, I said, sure you can, she was as much yours as she was mine, and we went to the freezer and looked in.

The weird thing was the freezer was on defrost and Grandma was nowhere in sight. There was a trail of water and plastic wrap leading from the freezer to her bedroom. We followed it. On the bed, all wet, sat Grandma, counting her Buddhist rosary and chanting her diamond sutra. What's weirder is that she looked real young. I mean around 54 now, not 94, the high cheeks, the rosy lips. When she saw us she smiled and said: "What do you say we all go to one of those famous cocktail parties that Nancy's gone to, the three of us?" I wasn't scared because she said it in English, I mean accentless, Californian English.

Wow, Grandma, Eric said, your English is excellent.

"I know," Grandma said, "that's just a side benefit of being reborn. But enough with compliments, we got to party."

Cool, said Eric. Cool, I said, though I was a little jealous 'cause I had to go through junior high and high school and all those damn ESL classes and everything to learn the same language while Grandma just got it down cold because she was reborn. Grandma put on this nice brocaded red blouse and black silk pants and sequined velvet shoes and fixed her hair real nice and we drove off downtown.

Boy, you should've seen Nancy's face when we arrived at her cocktail party. She nearly tripped over herself. She laid her face against the wing of an ice sculpture to calm herself. Then she walked straight up to us, haughty, and said, It's invitation only, how'd ya'll get in?

"Calm yourself, child," said Grandma, "I told them that I was a board member of the Cancer Society and flashed my jade bracelet and diamond ring and gave the man a forty dollar tip."

Nancy had the same reaction Eric and I had: Grandma, your English is flawless! Grandma was oblivious to compliments. She went straight to the punch bowl for some spirits. Since her clubbed foot was cured she had an elegant grace about her. Her hair floated like gray-black clouds behind her. Everyone stared, mesmerized.

Needless to say Grandma was the big hit of the party. She had so many interesting stories to tell. The feminists, it seemed, loved her the most. They crowded around her as she told them how she'd been married early and had eight children while being the matriarch of a middle-class family during the Viet Minh uprising. She told them about my grandfather, a brilliant man who was well versed in Molière and Shakespeare and who was an accomplished violinist but who drank himself to death because he was helpless against the colonial powers of the French. She told everyone how single-handedly she had raised her children after his death and they all became doctors and lawyers and pilots and famous composers. Then she started telling them how the twenty-four-year-old civil war divided her family up and brothers fought brothers over ideological notions that proved bloody pointless. Then she told them about our journey across the Pacific Ocean in a crowded fishing boat where thirst and starvation nearly did us all in until it was her idea to eat some of the dead and drink their blood so that the rest of us could survive to catch glimpses of this beautiful America and become Americans.

She started telling them, too, about the fate of Vietnamese women who had to marry and see their husbands and sons go to war and never come back. Then she recited poems and told fairy tales with sad endings, fairy tales she herself had learned as a child, the kind she used to tell me and my cousins when we were young. There was this princess, you see, who fell in love with a fisherman and he didn't know about her 'cause she only heard his beautiful voice singing from a distance, so when he drifted away downriver one day she died, her heart turning into this ruby with the image of his boat imprinted on it. (In Grandma's stories, the husbands and fishermen always come home, but they come home always too late and there was nothing they could do but mourn and grieve.)

Grandma's voice was sad and seductive and words came

She knew her history. Or at least a version, one that I had never heard before.

"And now you're coming forward."

"We've always been here," she said. "You've never noticed."

I wanted to believe her, but I was having a little difficulty. "So for the last fourteen hundred years . . ."

"That's right," she said. "Oh, we've intermarried some, but we've kept our traditions alive." She started to wail. Her eyes were closed and her mouth was stretched in an unnatural grimace. After a minute of this, she stopped, opened her eyes, and wiped her brow.

"Birth song," she announced.

"It's very different," I said. "Haunting."

She seemed pleased that I'd said this. She bowed her head. "For over a millennium our voices have been silenced. No one wanted to hear the Vandal songs. No one cared, though I suppose we were lucky. In some ways, we prefer the world's indifference to its attention. As soon as you're recognized, you're hunted and destroyed. So we waited. And now we're back."

My shoulders tensed and I rubbed my neck where the muscle had popped.

"Thank you for coming forward," I told her. "I know how hard it must be for you. I'm sure there are many things you could teach me."

She smiled at me again and all the anger seemed to be gone. "About the paper that's due?" she said.

"What?"

"Lies are the province of Romans and writers."

At first I didn't get it, but then I saw what she was telling me. "Oh, right," I said. "I guess you can't write it, can you?"

"No, I'm sorry," she said.

"No, don't be sorry," I said, reaching over and nearly touching her shoulder, but not quite. "I understand. I understand completely. It's part of your tradition."

"The Vandal tradition," she said. "Thanks, Dr. Radlisch. I knew you'd understand."

"That's my middle name."

"It is?"

"No, Amy. It's just a turn-of-phrase."

"Oh," she said, and she smiled. She liked me now. I could tell.

But I felt saddened. I was so used to teaching my subject a certain way. I had found a strange comfort in Lucan's quote, but now his question seemed unanswerable, at least by me. "Where shall strength be found?" How was I going to learn the new ways?

That night, I dreamed about my student who had killed himself. He was accusing me of something. He told me I was going to flunk out. I panicked and shot him. That was the dream. Ludicrous, but when I awoke, it felt so real that I nearly cried with relief. When I went to my office that day, I almost expected to see graffiti scrawled on the walls, "Death to All Vandals." But there was none. The walls were clean. No one had defaced them. What's more, Amy never showed up in class again. On the final transcript beside her name there was simply a blank, no "Withdrawn" as I'd hoped. It was up to me. I didn't know what to do. I couldn't give her an "A." But I couldn't flunk her. She knew her history. So I settled on a "B." But why had she stopped coming to class? Was it me? I thought we understood one another now. As I always told my students, they should come see me, no matter what the problem, before they just disappear.

WHAT HE WAS LIKE

He kept a diary, for his own pleasure. Because the days passed by so rapidly, and he found it interesting to go back and see how he had occupied his time, and with whom. He was aware that his remarks were sometimes far from kind, but the person they were about was never going to read them, so what difference did it make? The current diary was usually on his desk, the previous ones on a shelf in his clothes closet, where they were beginning to take up room.

His wife's uncle, in the bar of the Yale Club, said, "I am at the age of funerals." Now, thirty-five years later, it was his turn. In his address book the names of his three oldest friends had lines drawn through them. "Jack is dead," he wrote in his diary. "I didn't think that would happen. I thought he was immortal. . . . Louise is dead. In her sleep . . . Richard has been dead for over a year and I still do not believe it. So impoverishing."

He himself got older. His wife got older. They advanced deeper into their seventies without any sense of large changes but only of one day's following another, and of the days being full, and pleasant, and worth recording. So he went on doing it. They all got put down in his diary, along with his feelings about old age, his fear of dying, his declining sexual powers, his envy of the children that he saw running down the street. To be able to run like that! He had to restrain himself from saying to young men in their thirties and forties, "You do appreciate, don't you, what you have?" In his diary he wrote, "If I had my life to live over again— but one doesn't. One goes forward instead, dragging a cart piled high with lost opportunities."

Though his wife had never felt the slightest desire to read his diary, she knew when he stopped leaving it around as carelessly as he did his opened mail. Moving the papers on his desk in order to dust it, she saw where he had hidden the current volume, was tempted to open it and see what it was he didn't want her to know, and then thought better of it and replaced the papers, exactly as they were before.

"To be able to do in your mind," he wrote, "what it is probably not a good idea to do in actuality is a convenience not always sufficiently appreciated." Though in his daily life he was as cheerful as a cricket, the diaries were more and more given over to dark thoughts, anger, resentment, indecencies, regrets, remorse. And now and then the simple joy in being alive. "If I stopped recognizing that I want things that it is not appropriate for me to want," he wrote, "wouldn't this inevitably lead to my not wanting anything at all—which as people get older is a risk that must be avoided at all costs?" He wrote, "Human beings are not like a clock that is wound up at birth and runs until the mainspring is fully unwound. They live because they want to. And when they stop wanting to, the first thing they know they are in a doctor's office being shown an X-ray that puts a different face on everything."

After he died, when the funeral had been got through, and after the number of telephone calls had diminished to a point where it was possible to attend to other things, his wife and daughter together disposed of the clothes in his closet. His daughter folded and put in a suit box an old, worn corduroy coat that she remembered the feel of when her father had rocked her as a child. His wife kept a blue-green sweater that she was used to seeing him in. As for the rest, he was a common size, and so his shirts and suits were easily disposed of to people who were in straitened circumstances and grateful for a warm overcoat, a dark suit, a pair of pigskin gloves. His shoes were something else again, and his wife dropped them into the Goodwill box, hoping that somebody would turn up who wore size-9A shoes, though it didn't seem very likely. Then the two women were faced with the locked filing cabinet in his study, which contained business papers that they turned over to the executor, and most of the twenty-seven volumes of his diary.

"Those I don't know what to do with, exactly," his wife said. "They're private and he didn't mean anybody to read them."

"Did he say so?" his daughter asked.

"No."

"Then how do you know he didn't want anybody to read them?"

"I just know."

"You're not curious?"

"I was married to your father for forty-six years and I know what he was like."

Which could only mean, the younger woman decided, that her mother had, at some time or other, looked into them. But she loved her father, and felt a very real desire to know what he was like as a person and not just as a father. So she put one of the diaries aside and took it home with her.

When her husband got home from his office that night, her eyes were red from weeping. First he made her tell him

45

what the trouble was, and then he went out to the kitchen and made a drink for each of them, and then he sat down beside her on the sofa. Holding his free hand, she began to tell him about the shock of reading the diary.

"He wasn't the person I thought he was. He had all sorts of secret desires. A lot of it is very dirty. And some of it is more unkind than I would have believed possible. And just not like him—except that it *was* him. It makes me feel I can never trust anybody ever again."

"Not even me?" her husband said soberly.

"Least of all, you."

They sat in silence for a while. And then he said, "I was more comfortable with him than I was with my own father. And I think, though I could be mistaken, that he liked me."

"Of course he liked you. He often said so."

"So far as his life is concerned, if you were looking for a model to—"

"I don't see how you can say that."

"I do, actually. In his place, though, I think I would have left instructions that the diaries were to be disposed of unread. . . . We could burn it. Burn all twenty-seven volumes."

"No."

"Then let's put it back," he said, reaching for the diary. "Put it back in the locked file where your mother found it."

"And leave it there forever?"

"For a good long while. He may have been looking past our shoulders. It would be like him. If we have a son who doesn't seem to be very much like you or me, or like anybody in your family or mine, we can give him the key to the file—"

"If I had a son, the *last* thing in the world I'd want would be for him to read this filth!"

"—and tell him he can read them if he wants to. And if he

doesn't want to, he can decide what should be done with them. It might be a help to him to know that there was somebody two generations back who wasn't in every respect what he seemed to be."

"Who was, in fact—"

"Since he didn't know your father, he won't be shocked and upset. You stay right where you are while I make us another of these."

But she didn't. She didn't want to be separated from him, even for the length of time it would take him to go out to the kitchen and come back with a Margarita suspended from the fingers of each hand, lest in that brief interval he turn into a stranger.

Terese Svoboda

SUNDRESS

It's a terrible thing to be kicked out. I hold the kicked-out birdcage, the kicked-out double geranium, and the kicked-out dog. But after we look at all this kicked-out stuff, there really isn't much we want. I mean, those pillows have seen heads. So we leave the birdcage and flower with the ironing board in the hope of Stayprest and recycling, and go for a walk, Ernie in his most impressive Just-A-Moment-Sir suit, which he put on as a sort of armor this morning, and I in my sundress, off-the-shoulder, with a pattern swirly and close, one that if you look too long at it, well, instead of thanked, you get kicked out.

The walk goes into the subway and out to the suburbs. Ernie walks with the leash held high and his saggy chin tilted, scenting promise because what else? I bring up the rear with the two mostly empty bags bumping syncopated on a carrier up and down the high curbs they have here. We don't go far. Ernie comes up with a couple of nearly last bills and buys sodas, something with a lot of escape, he says, and we sip them outside the store, looking at wide lawns and white houses.

We don't talk. I know Ernie from the beginning, from

when we crossed twice in foster homes. We had luck and not luck after leaving fifty years between us and them, and now I can see, even with dime-store bifocals, Ernie is already thinking up some new way, taking in the neighborhood with his careful old-man looks over soda.

After a while he calls a taxi. I am not surprised at the why, not to mention the where, for those are the very, very last bills he is now waving. This Ernie is quick as well as silent. I am seated inside before I hear him say: Three times around the block and make it snappy.

We stop in front of the house we'd stared at over sodas and pull right into the driveway. Ernie pops out and surveys the short walk to the door, all mystery and smiles. The driver says as I whip out the two suitcases, They're not home, and slips his gear into reverse.

We are, says Ernie and pays him.

The driver looks at me in my sundress, then he takes his time backing out but finally does gun off when Ernie settles the bags on the front step. Then Ernie pats me on my bare shoulder and says, I'll be just a minute, and ducks out to the stucco-front neighbors.

But what exactly does he say to the blonde with curls down to here and a face of collapsed Saran Wrap to have her hand over the house keys? To me not more than a minute later he says, We're the Olsens' first cousins, and tosses his almost white, anybody-cousin hair out of his part to open the door with the key.

While he gets the bags, I like it. I like the dark wood, the books, the lot of things to dust. There is a place for the rag under the sink, and secret spots for the laundry. When I open the fridge, it is so empty it's like a bulldozed half building, but the pantry is walk-in, olives and sherry. Not like the last with its locks, with its May-I-this-and-that, its curtsey and shuffle.

Being help is the foster home forever.

Hey, Ernie, I yell, handling a quart of homemade picca-lilli. But Ernie is out.

From the picture window I catch him, changed into his only other outfit, patched dungarees, wringing a wrench against the neighbor's stuck x. The woman of the stucco waves at me as soon as Ernie fixes it, wiping his hands and wrench on his clean shirt front, then accepting her invite to come in, wash up, and no doubt eat cookies. The woman at the window has cookie in her Saran Wrap face, not sex, which is flatter.

He goes in.

I don't panic at being so elsewhere so fast. I know Ernie. Ernie will talk us up. We will stay the night. The night is something. I open cocktail weiners and feed them singly to the dog, who likes the smell of dark wood and low books but does not mark anything, not once. When Ernie comes back, we agree: night is something.

But we are there weeks and weeks. I take out videos on Saturdays from the pack of coupons I find by the console and make popcorn for the neighborhood kids, who don't even put their feet on the sofa. Right by the video is the Olsens' address in France which I keep clean, in a sort of shrine, away from the butts. I also take good care of the lawn, and I ask, Did Olsen really mean water three times a week, like it is on a list? To the boy who does have a list, I feed Oreos and we never see him again, except once, riding his bike and waving while Ernie's getting at the cracks in the driveway and scrubbing the oil spots. For everyone else Ernie fixes dishwashers, radiators, computers, any of those -er things. And takes nothing for it. I have words with him as usual, but he says, Give and it will come back. It is true we get invitations nearly daily in lieu, and two old fridges which we sell as if unused. And when we visit, Ernie smokes out the boy-part in each husband where the talk locks on small parts or their dads' cars.

The ladies love the dog. All grin and no bite, it lures them off a lawn they are dressing or, even while tuning a headset, makes them bend at the knees and pet it. All I have to do is stand by that dog and they forgive my sundress with that pattern and its troubles.

It is on a Friday, a big day for waving and helping, for parading the dog and going to dinner, with the sun outside so hot in the late afternoon the neighbors have their blinds down and so don't see Ernie puttering and me dusting, when the phone rings.

Now we don't answer the phone ever. We tell people they have the machine on and we don't want to lose messages so it is just us, listening. But this is the ring we'd been expecting, a Mina something saying how she looks forward to seeing Mr. Olsen on Monday.

I haven't mentioned how little the neighbors look forward to seeing their neighbors. I try always to stay positive, people can feel it. But the Olsens are so unlike us, they say, you two are really so nice and how did they, they wonder, get so different. They even suggest we rent a bungalow just blocks off that would do so well, they say, for a couple active like us so we don't have to go back to Florida, where we live in one of those wretched old-people condos. Condos, I snort. But I let Ernie talk, just as I memorize the albums of pictures on the dresser and can speak on them. It is clear it is us the neighbors want, not them, the ones who are coming.

We drop off handwritten notes at all the doors Ernie has fixed and more, the ones who have asked for him but can't as yet be fit in, and we put out potato chips and tonic I find in the basement closet. Then we make up a sheet with SURPRISE! across it, a twin of one I'm making another sundress from.

All the kids come and watch what they want on video and all the adults clutch their last-minute repairs, small items like clocks and candy thermometers. And the man with the now-blinking electric eye brings liquor that goes with the tonic.

Then the driveway is parked full, and the car that stops across the street and the bewildered couple who slam it shut are the right ones to greet the silence of the hidden crowd with the banners unfurling WELCOME HOME, COUSIN! and of course our SURPRISE! but we don't see it, me in my gloves from wiping down doorknobs and Ernie with the suitcases still quite light settled on the street with his hand out for a taxi that is sure to come.

Just the dog doesn't want to.

Denis Johnson

OUT ON BAIL

I saw Jack Hotel in an olive-green three-piece suit, with his blond hair combed back and his face shining and suffering. People who knew him were buying him drinks as quickly as he could drink them down at the Vine, people who were briefly acquainted, people who couldn't even remember if they knew him or not. It was a sad, exhilarating occasion. He was being tried for armed robbery. He'd come from the courthouse during the lunch recess. He'd looked in his lawyer's eyes and fathomed that it would be a short trial. According to a legal math that only the mind of the accused has strength to pursue, he guessed the minimum in this case would have to be twenty-five years.

It was so horrible it could only have been a joke. I myself couldn't remember ever having met anybody who'd actually lived that long on the earth. As for Hotel, he was eighteen or nineteen.

This situation had been a secret until now, like a terminal disease. I was envious that he could keep such a secret, and frightened that somebody as weak as Hotel should be gifted with something so grand that he couldn't even bring himself to brag about it. Hotel had taken me for a hundred dollars once and I always talked maliciously about him behind his back, but I'd known him ever since he'd appeared, when he was fifteen or sixteen. I was surprised and hurt, even miserable, that he hadn't seen fit to let me in on his trouble. It seemed to foretell that these people would never be my friends.

Right now his hair was so clean and blond for once that it seemed the sun was shining on him even in this subterranean region.

I looked down the length of the Vine. It was a long, narrow place, like a train car that wasn't going anywhere. The people all seemed to have escaped from someplace—I saw plastic hospital name bracelets on several wrists. They were trying to pay for their drinks with counterfeit money they'd made themselves, in Xerox machines.

"It happened a long time ago," he said.

"What did you do? Who did you rip off?"

"It was last year. It was last year." He laughed at himself for calling down a brand of justice that would hound him for that long.

"Who did you rip off, Hotel?"

"Aah, don't ask me. Shit. Fuck. God." He turned and started talking to somebody else.

The Vine was different every day. Some of the most terrible things that had happened to me in my life had happened in here. But like the others I kept coming back.

And with each step my heart broke for the person I would never find, the person who'd love me. And then I would remember I had a wife at home who loved me, or later that my wife had left me and I was terrified, or again later that I had a beautiful alcoholic girlfriend who would make me happy forever. But every time I entered the place there were veiled faces promising everything and then clarifying quickly into the dull, the usual, looking up at me and making the same mistake.

That night I sat in a booth across from Kid Williams, a former boxer. His black hands were lumpy and mutilated. I always had the feeling he might suddenly reach out his hands and strangle me to death. He spoke in two voices. He was in his fifties. He'd wasted his entire life. Such people were very dear to those of us who'd wasted only a few years. With Kid Williams sitting across from you it was nothing to contemplate going on like this for another month or two.

I wasn't exaggerating about those hospital name-bands. Kid Williams was wearing one on his wrist. He'd just come over the wall from Detox. "Buy me a drink, buy me a drink," he said in his high voice. Then he frowned and said in his low voice, "I come down here for just a short time," and brightening, in his high voice: "I wanted to see you-all! Buy me one now, because I don't have my purse, my wallet, they took all my money. They thiefs." He grabbed at the barmaid like a child after a toy. All he was wearing was a nightshirt tucked into his pants and hospital slippers made of green paper.

Suddenly I remembered that Hotel himself, or somebody connected with him, had told me weeks ago that Hotel was in trouble for armed robbery. He'd stolen drugs and money at gunpoint from some college students who'd been selling a lot of cocaine, and they'd decided to turn him in. I'd forgotten I'd ever heard about it.

And then, as if to twist my life even further, I realized that all the celebrating that afternoon hadn't been Hotel's farewell party after all, but his welcome home. He'd been acquitted. His lawyer had managed to clear him on the curious grounds that he'd been trying to defend the community against the influence of these drug dealers. Completely confused as to who the real criminals were in this case, the jury had voted to wash their hands of everybody and they let him off. That had been the meaning of the conversation I'd had with him that afternoon, but I hadn't understood what was happening at all.

There were many moments in the Vine like that one—where you might think today was yesterday, and yesterday was tomorrow, and so on. Because we all believed we were tragic, and we drank. We had that helpless, destined feeling. We would die with handcuffs on. We would be put a stop to, and it wouldn't be our fault. So we imagined. And yet we were always being found innocent for ridiculous reasons.

Hotel was given back the rest of his life, the twenty-five years and more. The police promised him, because they were so bitter about his good luck, that if he didn't leave town they would make him sorry he'd stayed. He stuck it out a while, but fought with his girlfriend and left—he held jobs in Denver, Reno, points west—and then within a year turned up again because he couldn't keep away from her.

Now he was twenty, twenty-one years old.

The Vine had been torn down. Urban renewal had changed all the streets. As for me, my girlfriend and I had split up, but we couldn't keep away from each other.

One night she and I fought, and I walked the streets till the bars opened in the morning. I just went into any old place.

Jack Hotel was beside me in the mirror, drinking. There were some others there exactly like the two of us, and we were comforted.

Sometimes what I wouldn't give to have us sitting in a bar again at 9:00 a.m. telling lies to one another, far from God.

Hotel had fought with his girlfriend, too. He'd walked the streets as I had. Now we matched each other drink for drink until we both ran out of money.

I knew of an apartment building where a dead tenant's

had to hold his hand over his mouth like he was going to call a duck, but he was breathing in through the tube his fingers made instead of blowing out with his tongue. That was when the Brahma bull went by backwards. The way it went past, with just its head out of the water holding up its long, flat horns, my uncle said it looked like a big brown bird made of solid wood, gliding over the boiling waters for its breakfast. My uncle drove his boat alongside the Brahma bull and he looped some ski rope around the long, flat horns, but he said it did not work too well trying to pull the animal back to the barge because sometimes the ski rope pulled down on the Brahma bull's head so that its long, thin horns dipped into the water, and sometimes the Brahma bull's nose blew out water instead of breath, and by the time my uncle got over to where the barge seemed to be moving toward him, the ski rope was going straight down into the water by my uncle's boat like it held an anchor my uncle could not pull up. When the men in the green uniforms asked my uncle what it was, he said it was nothing, and he cut the ski rope loose from his boat and set out over the boiling waters again.

When it was supposed to be noon my uncle said he found the baby on the rope. He said it looked like somebody had tied a strong rope around the baby's waist and was still holding on, because the other end seemed deep down in the water. The baby was cutting through the current with its arms and head thrown back like it had just broken up to the surface to take a long deep breath that it was still taking. My uncle said when he pulled the rope from where it went deep into the water, it did not feel like it gave as much as it felt like it was being let go of. When my uncle got back to the barge with the baby on the rope, the men in the green uniforms gave him some coffee and a doughnut and a Spam sandwich. He said the doughnut dissolved and the sandwich washed away and the coffee tasted like rain.

My uncle said the girl swimming on the barbed-wire fence had skin that did not come off in his hands like the skin on some of the others did. He said when he first saw her, her right arm was crooked over her head and her left arm was following, with her head turned like she was a swimmer in the boiling waters, making it look like she was stroking away from where everything was being boiled off the face of the earth. He said he was shouting at her, Swim, come on and swim! as he drove his boat over to her. He said even as he unstuck her from the barbed-wire fence he talked to her and looked away from her modesty, because her clothes had been boiled away, so he just focused on a little mark on her cheek like a snakebite the barbed wire had made that did not bleed because all her blood had boiled away, too. He made over her, protecting her modesty until they got back to the barge and the men in the green uniforms helped him hand her up from his boat so they could lay her on top of the other boiled-over people they had stacked at one end of the barge like corded wood.

My uncle said that after three days, when the only sun was just the amber light, the barge was full. The men in the green uniforms headed it back up the bayou, and even though sometimes they would see things hung up in the trees and caught along the fences they would not stop. The men in the green uniforms spread white powder out of green barrels on the people stacked under big green tarps. Men's boats like my uncle's were laid helter-skelter on the barge, all banged up like a lot of toys some bullies had come along and played too rough with. All the men like my uncle who had the boats stood around the edges of the barge away from the big green tarps, away from their boats they could not look at, and as far away from each other as they could without falling over into the boiling water. They stood watching for faces of boiled-over people to come up to just below the surface like they sometimes did, like they just wanted to sneak a peek before slipping back under. Then the men stood looking away to the trees and to the fences along the bayou that caught the boiled-over people. They stood looking, giving good hard long looks, because they knew, like my uncle knew, that once they were back up the bayou home they would never be able to watch a stew pot boil, or look at something caught on barbed wire ever the same again, even with someone like me coming in to show it is nothing but a piece of nothing thrown up on the fence by the wind.

David Leavitt

WE MEET AT LAST

They decided to meet in a park—a small, verdant park near Stewart's office where there were iron benches and a duck pond. Jack got there early so he'd have time to arrange himself, so that when Stewart strolled in he'd see a good-looking man wearing jeans and a white shirt, his tie loosened, his jacket on his lap, one leg crossed over the other in the masculine fashion. He'd be reading the newspaper, the Metro—not the Business—section, and would give off an aura of devil-may-care casualness.

They had known each other eight weeks but they'd never met. Well—"met." What does it mean, to "meet?" Their relationship—begun as a routine business transaction that required negotiation by telephone—had evolved, with alarming speed, into something else, something neither of them felt quite prepared to name, much less trust: was it a love affair? A love affair of voices? All they could say was that since that first call they'd been compelled to call each other dozens more times; that they'd told each other every detail of their histories and shared dangerous secrets; that they'd even been brought, each by the other's voice, to heights of pleasure achieved only rarely with corporeal lovers. It was this erotic aspect to their relationship they found most bewildering—bewildering, and at the same time, cause for celebration. Still, they couldn't help but feel there was something wrong with it. All their friends laughed when they told them. No one took them seriously. So they agreed to meet, over Stewart's objections—he'd been afraid that whatever fragile thing they'd constructed would bow and sunder under the weight of physical proximity. Jack, however, had insisted; things couldn't go on the way they'd been going on for much longer, he reasoned. Shouldn't they at least see? And Stewart had relented, primarily because he too, though by nature more skeptical than Jack, wanted so badly for the thing to translate into the physical world.

Now it was two minutes past the hour agreed upon for their appointment. Moving his eyes only (he didn't want to corrupt the careful positioning of himself on the bench) Jack watched as a variety of men entered the park, either to sit on the grass or benches, or because the diagonal pathways provided a shortcut to somewhere else. His heart pounded each time one neared but unfortunately none of them matched the description Stewart had given of himself—a description now burned into Jack's brain. Stewart, Stewart said, was about six foot two inches tall, with brown hair and mottled green eyes. Clean-shaven. Hair wavy, longer in the front than in the back. Average WASP nose. A thick beard that usually manifested itself as a kind of brown sheen on the lower half of his face by midday; large, veiny hands. Pants size? Thirty-four. Shoe size? Eleven-and-a-half. A list of particulars, specs, if you will, like for a television set or computer; nonetheless, from these details Jack had composed an image of Stewart over which his mind's eye labored a good part of every day, especially when they were on the phone and Stewart's voice was leading him on an erotic voyage for which the word "masturbatory" seemed insufficient; Jack preferred "onanistic," which had an air about it of paganism, of ritual.

Suddenly he was there. Stewart was there. They were looking at each other, blinking. Jack's posture broke. He uncrossed his legs and stood up, inadvertently dropping his paper, which scattered in the breeze. "Hello, Jack," Stewart said—his voice coming from this stranger's mouth. What was so dreadfully wrong? Stewart hadn't lied—he was everything he'd said he'd be—and yet he was someone Jack wouldn't have looked at twice on the street.

"We meet at last," Jack said—a rehearsed line. But Stewart turned away. "You're disappointed," he said. "I knew it. I knew you would be."

"No, it's not that, I'm just—"

Stewart closed his eyes. "It's over," he said. "Of course it would have burned itself out anyway. It just seems such a shame we had to end it like this—spoiling it. Instead of just cutting it off, sealing it off. A whole, perfect thing."

Jack only looked at the ground. "It doesn't have to be over," he said, suddenly wanting to be hopeful, to resist the urge to flight. "We could start again, from step one." And to himself: I could will myself to be attracted to him.

"It's no good," Stewart said. "We went too far—the other way. For it to have worked, you'd have to have wanted me. And clearly you don't."

Sometimes there just isn't anything more to say than that. Still they didn't move. If we could only get out of this moment, Jack was thinking, we could go back to our offices; we could go back to our lives and pretend none of it ever happened. And yet they could not—they were not willing—to get out of this moment. Meanwhile, the wind picked up, driving pages of Jack's newspaper against their legs, across the lawn, into the duck pond: black and white tumbleweeds that seemed to take flight.

Jack looked up at Stewart. "Well, good-bye," he said, offering his hand.

"Sorry," Stewart said, backing off, his hands in the air as if Jack—holding a gun—had ordered him to put them there.

Stephen Dixon

FLYING

She was fooling around with the plane's door handle. I said "Don't touch that, sweetheart, you never know what can happen." Suddenly the door disappeared and she flew out and I yelled "Judith" and saw her looking terrified at me as she was being carried away. I jumped out after her, smiled and held out my arms like wings and yelled "Fly like a bird, my darling, try flying like a bird." She put out her arms, started flying like me and smiled. I flew nearer to her and when she was close enough I pulled her into my body and said "It's not so bad flying like this, is it? It's fun. You hold out one arm now and I'll hold out one of mine and we'll see where we can get to." She said "Daddy, you shouldn't have gone after me, you know that," and I said "I wouldn't let you out here all alone. Don't worry, we'll be okay if we keep flying like this and once we're over land, get ourselves closer and closer to the ground."

The plane by now couldn't be seen. Others could, going different ways, but none seemed to alter their routes for us no matter how much waving I did. It was a clear day, blue sky, no clouds, the sun moving very fast. She said "What's that?" pointing down and I said "Keep your arm up, we have to continue flying." She said "I am, but what's that?" and I said "Looks like a ship but's probably an illusion." "What's an illusion?" and I said "What a time for word lessons; save them for when we get home. For now just enjoy the flying and hope for no sudden air currents' shifts." My other arm held her tightly and I pressed my face into hers. We flew like that, cheek to cheek, our arms out but not moving. I was worried because I hadn't yet come up with any idea to help us make a safe landing. How do we descend, how do we land smoothly or crash-land without breaking our legs? I'll hold her legs up and just break mine if it has to come to that. She said "I love you, Daddy, I both like you and love you and always will. I'm never going to get married and move away from home." I said "Oh well, one day you might, not that I'll ever really want you to. And me too to you, sweetie, with all that love. I'm glad we're together like this. A little secret though. For the quickest moment in the plane I thought I wouldn't jump out after you, that something would hold me back. Now nothing could make me happier than what I did."

We left the ocean and were over cliffs and then the wind shifted and we were being carried north along the coast. We'd been up at almost same distance from water and land for a long time and I still had no idea how to get down. Suddenly along the coastal road I saw my wife driving our car. Daniel was in the front passenger seat, his hand sticking out the window to feel the breeze. The plane must have reported in about the two people sucked out of the plane, and when Sylvia heard about it she immediately got in the car and started looking for us, thinking I'd be able to take care of things in the air and that the wind would carry us East.

"Look at them, sweetheart, Mommy and Daniel. He should stick his arm in; what he's doing is dangerous." She said "There aren't any other cars around, so it can't hurt him." "But it should be a rule he always observes, just in case he forgets and sticks it out on a crowded highway. And a car could suddenly come the other way. People drive like maniacs on these deserted roads and if one got too close to him his arm could be torn off." "But the car would be going the other way, wouldn't it? so on Mommy's side, not his," and I said "Well, the driver of another car going their way could suddenly lose his head and try and pass on the right and get too close to Daniel's arm. —Daniel," I screamed, "put your arm back right now. This is Daddy talking." His arm went back in. Sylvia stopped the car, got out and looked up and yelled "So there you are. Come back now, my darlings; you'll get yourselves killed." "Look at her worrying about us, Judith—that's nice, right? —Don't worry, Sylvia," I screamed, "we're doing just fine, flying. There's no feeling like it in the world, we're both quite safe, and once I figure out a way to get us down, we will. If we have to crash-land doing it, don't worry about Judith—I'll hold her up and take the whole brunt of it myself. But I think it's going to be some distance from here, inland or on the coast, so you just go home now and maybe we'll see you in time for dinner. But you'll never be able to keep up with us the way this wind's blowing, and I don't know how to make us go slower." "You sure you'll be all right?" she yelled and I said "I can hardly hear you anymore, but yes, I think I got everything under control."

We flew on, I held her in my arm, kissed her head repeatedly, thinking if anything would stop her from worrying, that would. "You sure there's nothing to worry about, Daddy?—I mean about what you said to Mommy," and I said "What are you doing, reading my mind? Yes, everything's okay, I'm positive." We continued flying, each with an arm out, and by the time night came we were still no closer or farther away from the ground.

Margaret Broucek

ALVIN JONES'S IGNORANT WIFE

I work with a young gal who don't think her husband is gon fool around, hmmm? She's not a stupid gal, just ignorant. I know he will. But she ain't married yet, not even a boyfriend around, so she's got this vision, see, how it's gonna be for her.

She cornered me and Alice and Yvonne in the emulsion room one day and I knew she was gon bring it up again. She says to us, "Hey now, here's my point—you all haven't fooled around on your husbands, have you?" She didn't get an answer right off, so she asked Yvonne—"Yvonne, see I know you haven't fooled around." Yvonne was standing at the counter next to me and I see her pocked chin's hanging lower than usual. Well, Alice pipes right up. "Let's all say we have!" And me and Yvonne didn't have a choice, had to go along with that. Girl's eyes peeled open, slow, and she looked so she like to had a baby! I sure felt bad for her—just dropped her big lip, turned around and left. And I know what'll happen to her. She'll be running round in her yard; she'll draw a crowd, like that woman we all saw dancing with the gun.

I messed with Alvin Jones a while back, when my kids was young. He lived across the street with his string bean, Carla? Karen? Don't know what it was. Alvin was a big man, see, and built so nice. I could make an afternoon watching him wax his car in his small shorts and nothing else. And he always had a good word for me. Well it didn't last long, now, and really I just wanted to smell him up close (didn't Yvonne laugh when I told her that). He helped me in with my grocery bags one day. That was the start. I told him "just set them on the kitchen counter and thanks a lot." But he wanted a powdered doughnut out of one of those long boxes with the cellophane window. *That* was the start.

Those months we carried on I don't guess I ever asked him about his skin-and-bones wife. I just remember it was a summer of flies, hot houses and hot car seats, and a summer you could never get the film off your skin. God knows why Alvin wanted my doughnuts. I had been with my husband seven years then. I smelled like my husband, wore his shirts since I never left the house. I looked like my husband, but Alvin gave me open-mouth kisses. He'd come over midday with those five-pound bags of ice that he'd dump in the bathtub. Then we'd run a bit of cool water over them and slide in howling. Yes I do remember that ice clinking around and bumping 'gainst my numb skin, and Alvin rubbing me warm after. I figured his wife was at work, and he wasn't gon be no worse for wear when she got home, not that big old man, naah.

Mondays, in August, Alvin would pull in my drive with his top down and I'd come out the door with my head silk-wrapped and sunglasses on with rhinestones set in. "Why Miss Aretha Franklin!" he'd say. He'd put a towel on the seat where I was to sit. Once we drove in the country, and it was all steam. And the only trees, there, were the ones what sat in rows on both sides of the road and hung over you with those humming bugs nesting thick in the leaves. Gawd! I was scared they was gonna drop in the car with Alvin and me. That day he was singing blues, "I wish it would rain." Felt like we was sitting in front of one of those big clothes dryers with the door open, only not really, because our clothes was wringing wet and my scarf was ruint. Sounds like a bad day, hmm? I liked the time Alvin was singing.

Wasn't long then—Uh uuh. Two days, three days, a few days passed—before he was mowing Widow Timm's yard. He even bagged all the grass and set it by the drive real nice. Got so I missed him quite a bit around mid-morning. I'm shamed to admit it, but I'd linger by the front window about an hour a day. He'd stop me in the street every once in a while, tell me, "Why Mrs. Otis, every time I see you I'm falling in love again, prettier every day." Once, when he happened to have a glass of tea along, he fished around in it and brought out a small ice piece to slip in the neck of my dress. It slid so slow down my back, and I stood there 'till I couldn't feel it sting, and he was back at his door.

Now, I did envy the man's wife. She got to see his big teeth all the time and live in that split-level with the iceman. After a while, half the women on the block had been with her husband and we didn't none of us pity her. We marveled at her, how she was so quiet—not ranting and raving like so many do, you know. Every time I laid eyes on his gal she was to and from the car, kind of running up on her toes and not looking to see what the neighbors was about.

This one evening, late, I was picking up bits of cake out the backyard 'cause James, my husband, threw half his dinner onto the grass, didn't want that corn bread that come in a box and tossed the pan out the kitchen door. It was too sweet, see, got to make it all by hand. Well, I got about all the pieces back in the pan when I heard a radio blasting across the street. Wasn't like Alvin to turn his music up so I walked around to see. I was hearing someone singing along too and I thought, "Lord, that wife of his sure can't carry a tune." First person I saw was Widow Timms pressed up against her window, sliding herself around to get a good look at something, then Ginny Meyer and all her children sitting in their parked car, rolling up the windows, poking the locks down. Then I make it around to see the show: Alvin's gal swinging her hair, leaping about that yard with a gun above her head. She fired the whole round off before the police came, put her in their car.

Well, she didn't kill Alvin. He was gone, with some woman from two blocks down who won money suing the police. And either Alvin left a note or somebody told his wife what she never suspected. She hadn't known any of it, see.

And this young gal I work with had two men in mind that she was sure would never fool around. Her father, she said, and her brother-in-law, that was her list, and she nodded as if to say the case was closed. She'd met my husband at a company picnic and wanted to add him to her list too, asked me, "Uh, does your husband go out on you?"

Girl, we're lucky to see him home one night a week, and his women call the house.

I didn't tell her that about him, 'cause I'm not one to be pitied, you know. She's the one. She'll be running around in her yard, draw a crowd—entire families watching her from the car.

Ricardo Pau-Llosa

THE UNLIKELY ORIGIN OF METAPHOR

One morning during a particularly cold winter Jesus came out of the house where he had spent the night and, to his surprise, a crowd of people had been standing outside for hours, waiting for him. "We don't understand the parable of the whale, master," said one of the fishermen of the village. "What's a whale?" said another, "And what parable was that? I couldn't come to hear him yesterday."

Jesus looked at them, sorry he had not explained the parable. He thought that because they lived in a coastal town, they would understand it alright. "Well, it goes like this. The sinner is like the whales that sometimes wash up on the shore. Haven't you ever seen one, still half alive, lifting its tail slightly, more and more weakly as it nears death, occasionally letting out this gross and pathetic squeak-belch while nervously turning one decrepit, sandy fin in the air before letting it thud anemically on the dirt? You see, whales are not fish. They are mammals, pretty much like you and me. They breathe air, unlike fish. You may have also noticed that whales don't have scales. Neither do sharks, though, and they are fish. Anyway, whales breathe, so they can live a bit longer on the shore than a fish that flaps around on deck like lost money. In the way they seem to breathe on shore, whales are like sinners who are dead to the spirit but seem to live, indeed to enjoy themselves, in this life. Eventually, their inability to live on solid ground, although they breathe our air too, kills them. They cannot live in the kingdom of heaven because they cannot breathe its air, which is a metaphor here for the spirit. Granted, it is a complex metaphor, a tricky bit of trope-turning here, because 'air' is a symbol for spirit—you have all heard the Greeks call it pneuma. So the whale breathes and doesn't breathe, lives and doesn't live, is in its element and is not in its element, looks saved but is damned, is huge and powerful but is helpless in a thin, transparent element—the spirit—in which it cannot exist. I guess you could also say the sinner can only take in small gulps of the spirit while he is in his ocean of sin, but if exposed to a full dose of it he will perish, he will see his guilt and die spiritually. So water is a symbol of evil here, but only here, because my disciples and John's are baptizing people all over the place and in those rituals water is the symbol of purity. So don't get confused."

"O," said the bewildered fisherman politely, "We see now." His wife stepped forward to ask, "Is this the same whale that swallowed Jonah?"

"Yes, the same," said Jesus.

Thomas McGuane

WAR AND PEACE

My son, Clay, is at the car lot in town and my daughter, Karen, is way off to Powderville. But they talk on the phone a lot and I know that's how they cooked up this business with the Indian. They concluded that my attitude was from being by myself so much. In other words, no contact with my own past, which at this point is my life. Karen arranged to bring the Indian to the house for a visit. She stood in my kitchen and told me what she was going to do, period. I didn't say a word. I just lit a cigarette and looked at her.

It so happens that I know this Cheyenne quite well—John Red Wolf, or, as he was known in the service, John R. Wolf. He was my friend. Even though we had gone from Montana to Alameda, California, then to the Solomon Islands on the same cruiser, we only met after I had ridden half the 40-mm gun mount over the side in the wake of an attack by a suicide plane. I remember it was an overcast day and we had reason to fear Japs coming in from the low cloud cover. We never heard this one. Or at least I didn't, after what living between the two five-inch guns had done to my eardrums. The Jap plane dropped like a rock and blew up about a city block in front of me and took my gun mount into pieces. I went over the side with a bunch of dead and dying guys who had been passing shells from the ammunition bay. The minute I knew I was alive and floating in the big ground swell from the Philippines, I'm thinking about the sharks that shadowed the ship from about mid-Pacific until we got to Saipan—big pets of the cruiser, that looked like submarines. As a matter of fact, they got right into the dead guys and were cleaning them up when Mr. Red Wolf pulled me into the lifeboat.

The next day, we were playing catch on the stern. I had loaned my glove to an officer and he never returned it. John Red Wolf just went up and recovered it straight out of the officer's quarters so we could play catch together—two guys from Montana anchored off a little island covered with abandoned Jap bunkers and a blown-up ammo dump that looked like a hole right in the middle of the world. The Indian wasn't particularly afraid of officers.

We almost got used to the kamikazes, they were such a regular feature there toward the end, when the Emperor knew he'd had the course. Every now and then something would happen you couldn't forget, though, like the Zero that came from between the two little islands near Jolo and Tawi Tawi, about five feet off the water, weaving with amazing skill. Then he elevated and just caught the stern catapult, and blew up. Before the firemen could move and before we even had time to admire the skill of this pilot, a hand came whistling down the deck and stopped next to the sick-bay ventilator. We went over to look at it: this little brown Jap hand. It really shook us up. Isn't that something? That air show was right out of the Olympics, and here was this loose hand.

When we resumed boxing matches on the fantail for the first time since the New Hebrides, I attended with my new friend Red Wolf. This big farm kid from Indiana put on the gloves with a smaller but more experienced Mexican from California. The Mexican danced around until some of the guys started booing, but he kept it up till the farm boy was out of gas. Then the Mexican began wailing on his head. It wasn't good. We kept seeing his face flatten, with hair all pointed one way and sweat drops flying out over the ocean. Red Wolf remarks, "Yes sir, this makes a lot of sense." We began to feel we'd helped the Mexican arrange an assassination. It must've been catching, because even though there was an enthusiastic crowd, by the Marianas boxing on the ship was kaput. For months afterward, anytime we were on the fantail Red Wolf would remember it and say, "That made a lot of sense, didn't it?"

The ship smelled, because the captain didn't want subs following our garbage. Therefore, we kept our garbage and the ship smelled like a dump. Red Wolf says, "I'll take the subs." It was hot. We slept on deck with seabags for pillows and had big theories about the stars, which swarmed right down onto the surface of the sea. Sometimes, when it was too hot to sleep, like on our way down to Borneo, me and Red Wolf we talked about home.

I told him I ranched a little, and he told me he was an auto mechanic and a medicine man. He said, "That'd be like a preacher man to you, only my religion ain't the same as your religion."

At first, it made it look like we had less in common than I thought. But the more we talked we realized we had the land we lived on, which I guess neither one of us owned, though at one point Red Wolf made a joke about how he really owned my ranch. This kind of talk was so much like the talk we had with the Southern rebels on the ship, about the War Between the States, that we dropped it, a way of saying, What the fuck, this is war. By the time the Japs were backing down toward the mainland, the only country we had was this light cruiser. At first, guys would show off, reciting every state of the union and its capital, but that gave out long before the equator. By Subic Bay, the only country we had was the ship.

One of the last things our task force took on was the shelling of a bunch of islands near New Georgia, if I remember right, where we succeeded in setting off a Jap ammunition dump. What fireworks! During this bombardment, Red Wolf showed one and all what kind of stuff he was made out of. To wit: a five-inch shell hung fire in the gun, and while the whole crew waited for this horror to discharge and blow a hole in the side of our ship, Red Wolf worked alone to free the shell, after which it was dumped over the side. The Navy should have cited him for bravery but never did. We sailors won't forget, for whatever that's worth. They said it was humanly impossible to remove that shell by yourself. Red Wolf said that being a medicine man gave him extra powers where required.

Sometimes, when Roosevelt was being broadcast to all hands over the loudspeakers, Red Wolf and me would find a quiet spot to visit about some of the things that were so amazing, or worse, to young fellows from the sagebrush such as us. Like when a Jap torpedo bomber crippled us in '43 and we had to seal off a flooded compartment with seventeen of our buddies still inside. Funny thing was, we shot that plane down after he cut his torpedo loose. The pilot bailed out and we turned him to hamburger with the 20-mm. Later, we heard that was against the rules of war. Tell it to our buddies. We discussed other close calls, like seeing a periscope on a moonlight night and our ship zigzagging all over the ocean to keep from getting sunk. We discussed guys that couldn't take the heat and concussion and boredom and finally went Asiatic and had to be sent home.

I'd like to have a nickel for every time we looked out there at all the flying death and said to each other, "It's like a movie!" For example, the big powder magazine that went up on Tarawa—a rolling ball of smoke and flame, full of dead Japs. Other stuff going up: pill-boxes, assembly areas, truck depots. Never a dull moment. Only Hollywood could come close to what we went through. Or like at Magicienne Bay when Jap shore batteries opened up on the battleship *California*. Or when we'd watch those dark hillsides with the little tongues of light from the flamethrowers. Bodies were always floating past us, Japs and Americans, just bobbing meatballs that used to have moms and home towns. One time the ship got caught in a gigantic oceanic whirlpool. Bing Crosby was on the air from Radio Tokyo. The ship swinging in huge circles toward a hole in the center, and we're listening to this crooner and basically saying, Fuck the consequences. It was something, that war. Like I say, never a dull moment. You don't hear much about it anymore. Vietnam captured the country's imagination. Guys like me and Red Wolf, we don't exist. Don't exist.

One day, another suicide plane came in, lost its bombs before it reached us, then the canopy peels away, then a wing, it came in over the stern, bounced sideways. The motor came loose and slid across the ship, killing the mount captain on another 40-mm. They found his earphones wrapped around a roll of his scalp about a hundred feet away. We were getting pretty squirrelly every time they called general quarters. We were getting worn out by having to be so good in the clutch every time the Nips were in the mood to play ball.

But it didn't matter. The war was over. Truman said so on the radio. Hi, I'm Harry. The war is over. Next thing, the Japs signed the peace papers on board the *Missouri*. We let them keep their little fucking emperor. Red Wolf and I are standing on the fantail. Two nobodies from the boonies. We're waving goodbye to the enemy and all the dead, who-ever the hell they were.

John Red Wolf and I were discharged from the United States Navy at the Navy receiving station in San Diego, Cali-fornia. Red Wolf asks this blue-eyed twenty-one-year-old officer if he had a good idea how we could get to Montana. The officer said, "That's your problem, sailor." It was obvi-ous to both of us this character hadn't been west of Califor-nia, much less Leyte Gulf or the Solomons, where the lead really flew.

Red Wolf remarked, "I ain't a sailor anymore, Shit-for-brains. I'm an Indian trying to get back to the reservation. Care to step outside and help me with the directions?" The officer froze where he's at and we went out into the Califor-nia sunshine. It seemed like everybody and his dog wanted to welcome us home. Something about that didn't set right.

When you've been through a lot of things with someone that are hard to understand, maybe too big to understand, you get fairly close to that person without having to say too much. Then you get someplace where there is less happen-ing and you start to feel like you ought to say something but nothing comes to you.

That's what took place on the bus ride to Montana.

"You think this desert will ever end?" I asked Red Wolf.

"How should I know?"

About fourteen hours later, Red Wolf says, "It looks a lot better with a few hills."

By this time I was in on it, whatever it was: I just grunted. When we hit that first "Welcome to Montana" sign, we were staring out the window like we were stuck with this scenery.

I remember I wanted to ask John what he was going to do with the rest of his life. I just didn't dare. The last place I really knew that Cheyenne was on the Inland Sea of Japan.

You don't realize how much you miss your own life until something brings it back. The *Gazette* had a picture of a battleship graveyard near Mobile, Alabama, and I recognized our little cruiser in the pack of wrecked ships. I had to go out in the yard so the kids didn't see me.

I'm not all that worried anymore what anybody sees me do or don't do. But when Karen comes down the driveway I really feel like I'm afraid. She stops her car under the China willow across from the porch. I can tell exactly who is with her. I'm having to tell myself to breathe out. I'm watching Karen. She's moving her hands a lot. She's having to talk to Red Wolf. He's looking down and listening. He's scared, too.

W. S. Merwin

TERGVINDER'S STONE

One time my friend Tergvinder brought a large round boulder into his living room. He rolled it up the steps with the help of some two-by-fours, and when he got it out into the middle of the room, where some people have coffee tables (though he never had one there himself) he left it. He said that was where it belonged.

It is really a plain-looking stone. Not as large as Plymouth Rock by a great deal, but then it does not have all the claims of a big shaky promotion campaign to support. That was one of the things Tergvinder said about it. He made no claims at all for it, he said. It was other people who called it Tergvinder's Stone. All he said was that according to him it belonged there.

His dog took to peeing on it, which created a problem (Tergvinder had not moved the carpet before he got the stone to where he said it belonged.) Their tomcat took to squirting it, too. His wife fell over it quite often at first and it did not help their already strained marriage. Tergvinder said there was nothing to be done about it. It was in the order of things. That was a phase he seldom employed, and never when he conceived that there was any room left for doubt.

He confided in me that he often woke in the middle of the night, troubled by the ancient, nameless ills of the planet, and got up quietly not to wake his wife, and walked through the house naked, without turning on any lights. He said that at such times he found himself listening, listening, aware of how some shapes in the darkness emitted low sounds like breathing, as they never did by day. He said he had become aware of a hole in the darkness in the middle of the living room, and out of that hole a breathing, a mournful dissatisfied sound of all absence waiting for what belonged to it, for something it had never seen and could not conceive of, but without which it could not rest. It was a sound, Tergvinder said, that touched him with fellow-feeling, and he had undertaken—oh without saying anything to anybody—to assuage, if he could, that wordless longing that seemed always on the verge of despair. How to do it was another matter, and for months he had circled the problem, night and day, without apparently coming any closer to a solution. Then one day he had seen the stone. It had been there all the time at the bottom of his drive, he said, and he had never really seen it. Never recognized it for what it was. The nearer to the house he had got it, the more certain he had become. The stone had rolled into its present place like a lost loved one falling into arms that had long ached for it.

Tergvinder says that now on nights when he walks through the dark house he comes and stands in the living room doorway and listens to the peace in the middle of the floor. He knows its size, its weight, the touch of it, something of what is thought of it. He knows that it is peace. As he listens, some hint of that peace touches him too. Often, after a while, he steps down into the living room and goes and kneels beside the stone and they converse for hours in silence—a silence broken only by the sound of his own breathing.

Don DeLillo

VIDEOTAPE

It shows a man driving a car. It is the simplest sort of family video. You see a man at the wheel of a medium Dodge.

It is just a kid aiming her camera through the rear window of the family car at the windshield of the car behind her.

You know about families and their video cameras. You know how kids get involved, how the camera shows them that every subject is potentially charged, a million things they never see with the unaided eye. They investigate the meaning of inert objects and dumb pets and they poke at family privacy. They learn to see things twice.

It is the kid's own privacy that is being protected here. She is twelve years old and her name is being withheld even though she is neither the victim nor the perpetrator of the crime but only the means of recording it.

It shows a man in a sport shirt at the wheel of his car. There is nothing else to see. The car approaches briefly, then falls back.

You know how children with cameras learn to work the exposed moments that define the family cluster. They break every trust, spy out the undefended space, catching Mom coming out of the bathroom in her cumbrous robe and turbaned towel, looking bloodless and plucked. It is not a joke. They will shoot you sitting on the pot if they can manage a suitable vantage.

The tape has the jostled sort of noneventness that marks the family product. Of course the man in this case is not a member of the family but a stranger in a car, a random figure, someone who has happened along in the slow lane.

It shows a man in his forties wearing a pale shirt open at the throat, the image washed by reflections and sunglint, with many jostled moments.

It is not just another video homicide. It is a homicide recorded by a child who thought she was doing something simple and maybe halfway clever, shooting some tape of a man in a car.

He sees the girl and waves briefly, wagging a hand without taking it off the wheel—an underplayed reaction that makes you like him.

It is unrelenting footage that rolls on and on. It has an aimless determination, a persistence that lives outside the subject matter. You are looking into the mind of home video. It is innocent, it is aimless, it is determined, it is real.

He is bald up the middle of his head, a nice guy in his forties whose whole life seems open to the handheld camera.

But there is also an element of suspense. You keep on looking not because you know something is going to happen—of course you do know something is going to happen and you do look for that reason but you might also keep on looking if you came across this footage for the first time without knowing the outcome. There is a crude power operating here. You keep on looking because things combine to hold you fast—a sense of the random, the amateurish, the accidental, the impending. You don't think of the tape as boring or interesting. It is crude, it is blunt, it is relentless.

It is the jostled part of your mind, the film that runs through your hotel brain under all the thoughts you know you're thinking.

The world is lurking in the camera, already framed, waiting for the boy or girl who will come along and take up the device, learn the instrument, shooting old Granddad at breakfast, all stroked out so his nostrils gape, the cereal spoon baby-gripped in his pale fist.

It shows a man alone in a medium Dodge. It seems to go on forever.

There's something about the nature of the tape, the grain of the image, the sputtering black-and-white tones, the starkness—you think this is more real, truer to life than anything around you. The things around you have a rehearsed and layered and cosmetic look. The tape is superreal, or maybe underreal is the way you want to put it. It is what lies at the scraped bottom of all the layers you have added. And this is another reason why you keep on looking. The tape has a searing realness.

It shows him giving an abbreviated wave, stiff-palmed, like a signal flag at a siding.

You know how families make up games. This is just another game in which the child invents the rules as she goes along. She likes the idea of videotaping a man in his car. She has probably never done it before and she sees no reason to vary the format or terminate early or pan to another car. This is her game and she is learning it and playing it at the same time. She feels halfway clever and inventive and maybe slightly intrusive as well, a little bit of brazenness that spices any game.

And you keep on looking. You look because this is the nature of the footage, to make a channeled path through time, to give things a shape and a destiny.

Of course if she had panned to another car, the right car

at the precise time, she would have caught the gunman as he fired.

The chance quality of the encounter. The victim, the killer, and the child with a camera. Random energies that approach a common point. There's something here that speaks to you directly, saying terrible things about forces beyond your control, lines of intersection that cut through history and logic and every reasonable layer of human expectation.

She wandered into it. The girl got lost and wandered clear-eyed into horror. This is a children's story about straying too far from home. But it isn't the family car that serves as the instrument of the child's curiosity, her inclination to explore. It is the camera that puts her in the tale.

You know about holidays and family celebrations and how somebody shows up with a camcorder and the relatives stand around and barely react because they're numbingly accustomed to the process of being taped and decked and shown on the VCR with the coffee and cake.

He is hit soon after. If you've seen the tape many times you know from the handwave exactly when he will be hit. It is something, naturally, that you wait for. You say to your wife, if you're at home and she is there, Now here is where he gets it. You say, Janet, hurry up, this is where it happens.

Now here is where he gets it. You see him jolted, sort of wireshocked—then he seizes up and falls toward the door or maybe leans or slides into the door is the proper way to put it. It is awful and unremarkable at the same time. The car stays in the slow lane. It approaches briefly, then falls back.

You don't usually call your wife over to the TV set. She has her programs, you have yours. But there's a certain urgency here. You want her to see how it looks. The tape has been running forever and now the thing is finally going to happen and you want her to be here when he's shot.

Here it comes, all right. He is shot, head-shot, and the camera reacts, the child reacts—there is a jolting movement but she keeps on taping, there is a sympathetic response, a nerve response, her heart is beating faster but she keeps the camera trained on the subject as he slides into the door and even as you see him die you're thinking of the girl. At some level the girl has to be present here, watching what you're watching, unprepared—the girl is seeing this cold and you have to marvel at the fact that she keeps the tape rolling.

It shows something awful and unaccompanied. You want your wife to see it because it is real this time, not fancy movie violence—the realness beneath the layers of cosmetic perception. Hurry up, Janet, here it comes. He dies so fast. There is no accompaniment of any kind. It is very stripped. You want to tell her it is realer than real but then she will ask what that means.

The way the camera reacts to the gunshot—a startle reaction that brings pity and terror into the frame, the girl's own shock, the girl's identification with the victim.

You don't see the blood, which is probably trickling behind his ear and down the back of his neck. The way his head is twisted away from the door, the twist of the head gives you only a partial profile and it's the wrong side, it's not the side where he was hit.

And maybe you're being a little aggressive here, practically forcing your wife to watch. Why? What are you telling her? Are you making a little statement? Like I'm going to ruin your day out of ordinary spite. Or a big statement? Like this is the risk of existing. Either way you're rubbing her face in this tape and you don't know why.

It shows the car drifting toward the guardrail and then there's a jostling sense of two other lanes and part of another car, a split-second blur, and the tape ends here, either because the girl stopped shooting or because some central authority, the police or the district attorney or the TV station, decided there was nothing else you had to see.

This is either the tenth or eleventh homicide committed by the Texas Highway Killer. The number is uncertain because the police believe that one of the shootings may have been a copycat crime.

And there is something about videotape, isn't there, and this particular kind of serial crime? This is a crime designed for random taping and immediate playing. You sit there and wonder if this kind of crime became more possible when the means of taping and playing an event—playing it immediately after the taping—became part of the culture. The principal doesn't necessarily commit the sequence of crimes in order to see them taped and played. He commits the crimes as if they were a form of taped-and-played event. The crimes are inseparable from the idea of taping and playing. You sit there thinking that this is a crime that has found its medium, or vice versa—cheap mass production, the sequence of repeated images and victims, stark and glary and more or less unremarkable.

It shows very little in the end. It is a famous murder because it is on tape and because the murderer has done it many times and because the crime was recorded by a child. So the child is involved, the Video Kid as she is sometimes called because they have to call her something. The tape is famous and so is she. She is famous in the modern manner of people whose names are strategically withheld. They are famous without names or faces, spirits living apart from their bodies, the victims and witnesses, the underage criminals, out there somewhere at the edges of perception.

Seeing someone at the moment he dies, dying unexpectedly. This is reason alone to stay fixed to the screen. It is instructional, watching a man shot dead as he drives along on a sunny day. It demonstrates an elemental truth, that every breath you take has two possible endings. And that's another thing. There's a joke locked away here, a note of cruel slapstick that you are completely willing to appreciate. Maybe the victim's a chump, a dope, classically unlucky. He had it coming, in a way, like an innocent fool in a silent movie.

You don't want Janet to give you any crap about it's on all the time, they show it a thousand times a day. They show it because it exists, because they have to show it, because this is why they're out there. The horror freezes your soul but this doesn't mean that you want them to stop.

Charles Baxter

SCHEHERAZADE

She leaned down to adjust his respirator tube and the elastic tie around his neck that kept it in place. "Don't," he said, an all-purpose warning referring to nothing in particular, and she heard Muzak from down the hall, a version of "Stardust" that made her think of cold soup. A puddle outside his window reflected blue sky and gave the ceiling of his room a faint blue tint.

He was looking sallow and breathing poorly; she would have to lie again to perk him up.

"Do you remember," she said, sitting in the chair next to his chair, "my goodness, this would have been fifty years ago, that trip we made to Hawaii?"

"Don't remember it," he said. "Don't think I've been there."

"Yes, you have," she said, patting his hand where the wedding ring was. "We took the train, it had 'Zephyr' in its name somewhere, one of those silver trains that served veal for dinner. We had a romantic night in the Pullman car; I expect you don't remember that."

"Not just now," he said.

"Well, we did. We took it to Oakland or San Francisco, I forget which, and from there we took the boat to Honolulu."

"What boat? I don't remember a boat. Did it have a name?"

She leaned back and stared at the ceiling. Why did he always insist on the names? She couldn't invent names; that always caused her trouble. And her bifocals were hurting her. She would have to see that nice Dr. Hauser about them. "The name of the ship, dear, was *Halcyon Days*, not very original, I must say; we were on the C deck, second-class. The first night out you were seasick. Then you were all right. The ship had an orchestra and we danced the fox-trot. You flirted with that woman whose room was down the hall. You were quite awful about it."

The outline of a smile appeared on his face. "Who?"

She saw the smile and was pleased. "I don't remember," she said. "Why should I remember her name? She was just a silly woman with vulgar dark-red hair. She let it fly all over her shoulders."

"What was her name?"

"I told you I don't remember."

"Please," he said. His mouth was open. His filmy eyes looked in her direction.

"All right," she said. "Her name was Peggy."

"Peggy" he said, briefly sighing.

"Yes, Peggy," she said, "and you made yourself quite ridiculous around her, but I think she liked you, and I remember I once caught you two at the railing, looking at the waters of the Pacific go by as the ship churned westward."

"Was I bad?"

"You were all right, dear. You were just like any man. I didn't mind. Men are like that. You bought her drinks."

"What did she drink?"

"Old-fashioned," she said, but she felt herself going too

98

far and hauled herself back in. "What *I* minded was that she would not always close the door to her stateroom. You would look in, and there she was."

"Yes," he said. "There she was."

"There she was," she continued, "in her bathrobe, or worse, with that terrible red hair of hers billowing down to her shoulders. In her white bathrobe, and you, standing in the hallway like any man, staring at her."

"You caught me."

"Yes, I did, but I didn't blame you. You were attractive to women."

"I was?"

"Yes, you were. You were so handsome in those days, and so witty, and when you sat down at the piano and sang those Cole Porter tunes, it was hard for women to resist."

"Could I play the piano?" He was smiling, perhaps thinking of the Pacific, or Peggy.

"Very well, dear. You could play and sing. Though I've heard better, I have certainly heard worse. You sang to me. You'd sing to anybody."

"To Peggy?"

"To anyone," she said. When she saw his smile fade, she said, "And to her, too. In an effort to charm. You sang 'You're the Top.' I daresay she liked it. Who knows what trouble you two got into? I was not a spy. All I know now is, it's been over fifty years."

He closed his eyes and stretched his thin legs. She saw a smile cross his face again and was pleased with herself.

"In Hawaii," she said, "we stayed at the Royal Palm Hotel." Although she had once been on a ship, she had never been in Hawaii and was speaking more slowly now as she tried to see the scene. "It was on the beach, the famous one with the name, and the sands were white, as white as alabaster. We played shuffleboard."

"I remember that," he said.

"Good. We drove around the island and climbed the extinct volcano, Mount Johnson. There's a lake inside Mount Johnson, and you went swimming in it, and there were large birds, enormous blue birds, flying over our heads, and you called them the archangel birds and said that God had sent them to us as a sign."

"A sign of what?"

"A sign of our happiness."

"Were we happy?"

"Yes," she said. "We were."

"Always?"

"It seems so to me now. Anyway, Mount Johnson was one day, and on another day we went diving for pearls. You found an oyster with a pearl in it. I still wear it on a pin."

He looked over at her and searched her face and chest and arms.

"Just not today," she said. "I'm not wearing it today."

The sound of the oxygen hissing out of the respirator tube fatigued her. She would not be able to continue this much longer. It was like combat of a subtle kind. She hurried on. "On the island we picked enormous flowers, and every evening we sat down for dinner by the water, and you put a gardenia in my hair one night. We ate pineapples and broke open coconuts, and at moonrise the sea breezes came in through the window of our room where we were lying on the bed. We were so in love. We had room service bring us champagne and you read poetry to me."

"Yes," he said. "What did you look like?"

She clasped her hands in her lap. "I was beautiful." She paused. "You said so."

"The sound," he said.

"What sound?"

"There was a sound."

"I don't remember a sound," she said.

"There was one," he insisted.

"Where?"

"In the room."

"Yes?"

"It came in through the window," he whispered.

"From where?"

"From the sea. Do you hear it?"

"No."

"Listen."

She sat listening. The Muzak from the hallway had fallen silent. From outside there was a faint, low humming.

"Hear it?"

"Yes," she said faintly.

"I heard it first there. In Hawaii."

"So did I."

"I feel a little better," he said. "I feel sleepy."

"Go to sleep, dear," she said. "Take a little nap."

"You'll be back?"

"Yes, tomorrow."

"Where else did we go?"

"We went," she said, "to Egypt, where we crawled through the pyramids. We went through the fjords in Norway. We saw wonders. We saw many wonders."

"Tell me tomorrow."

"I will." She kissed him on the forehead, stood up, and walked to the doorway. She looked back at him; he seemed to be about to fall asleep, but he also seemed to be listening to the sound. She gazed at him for a moment, and then went down the hallway, past the nurses, bowing her head for a moment before she went out the front door to the bus stop, thinking of tomorrow's story.

Miloš Macourek

JACOB'S CHICKEN

A chicken is a chicken, you all know how a chicken looks, sure you do, so go ahead and draw a chicken the teacher tells the children, and all the kids suck on crayons and then draw chickens, coloring them black or brown, with black or brown crayons, but wouldn't you know it, look at Jacob, he draws a chicken with every crayon in the box, then borrows some from Laura, and Jacob's chicken ends up with an orange head, blue wings and red thighs and the teacher says that's some bizarre chicken, what do you say children, and the kids roll with laughter while the teacher goes on, saying, that's all because Jacob wasn't paying attention, and, to tell the truth, Jacob's chicken really looks more like a turkey, but then not quite, for it also resembles a sparrow and also a peacock, it's as big as a quail and as lean as a swallow, a peculiar pullet, to say the least, Jacob earns an F for it and the chicken, instead of being hung on the wall, migrates to a pile of misfits on top of the teacher's cabinet, the poor chicken's feelings are hurt, nothing makes it happy about being on top of a teacher's cabinet, so, deciding not to be chicken, it flies off through the open window.

But a chicken is a chicken, a chicken won't fly too far, hence it ends up next door in a garden full of white cherries and powder-blue currants, a splendid garden that proudly shows its cultivator's love, you see, the gardener, Professor Kapon, a recognized authority, is an ornithologist who has written seven books on birds and right now is finishing his eighth, and as he puts the last touches to it, he suddenly feels weary, so he goes out to do some light gardening and toss a few horseshoes, which is easy and lets him muse over birds, there are tons of them, so many birds, Professor Kapon says to himself, but there isn't a single bird that I discovered, he feels down, flips a horseshoe and dreams a love-filled dream about an as-yet-unknown bird when his eye falls on the chicken picking the baby-blue currants, the rare blue currants that dammit he didn't grow for chicken feed, now that would make anyone's blood boil, the professor is incensed, he is furious, he seems unable to zap the chicken, so in the end he just catches it, flings it over the fence, the chicken flies off, and voilà, Professor Kapon follows, he flies over the fence in pursuit of the chicken, grabs it and carries it home, quite an unusual chicken, that one, bet nobody has seen one quite like it, an orange head, blue wings and red thighs, the professor jots it all down, looks like a turkey, but then not quite, reminds one of a sparrow but also of a peacock, it's as big as a quail and as lean as a swallow, and after he has written it all down for his eighth book, the professor, all quivers, bestows upon the chicken his own name and carries it to the zoo.

A chicken is a chicken, who would fuss over a chicken, you think, but this one must be well worth the bother for the whole zoo is in an uproar, such rarity turns up perhaps once in twenty years, if that often, the zoo director is rubbing his hands, the employees are building a cage, the painter has his hands full and the director says the cage must sparkle and make the bed soft, he adds, and already there appears a nameplate, Kapon's chicken, *Gallina kaponi,* it sounds lovely, doesn't it, what do you say, it sounds, actually, how about it, the chicken is having the time of its life, it's moved to tears by all this care, it really can't complain, it has become the zoo's main attraction, the center of attention, the zoo has never had so many visitors, says the cashier, and the crowds are growing larger by the minute, wait, look, there is our teacher with the whole class standing in front of the cage, explaining, a while ago you saw the Przewalski horse and here you have another unique specimen, the so-called Kapon's chicken or *Gallina kaponi* that looks some-what like a turkey but not quite, resembles a sparrow and also a peacock, it's as big as a quail and as lean as a swallow, why, look at that gorgeous orange head, the blue wings, the scarlet thighs, the children are agog, they sigh, what a beau-tiful chicken, ain't that right, teacher, but Laura, as if struck by lightning, pulls on teacher's sleeve and says, that's Jacob's chicken, I bet you it is, the teacher becomes irked, this silly child's ridiculous notions, what Jacob's chicken is she prat-tling about and, come to think of it, where is Jacob anyhow, again he is not paying attention, now, wouldn't you know, there, just look at him, there he is, in front of an anteater's cage, watching an anteater when he is supposed to be look-ing at Kapon's chicken, Jacob, the teacher yells at the top of her lungs in a high-pitched voice, next time you'll stay home, Jacob, I've had enough aggravation, which shouldn't surprise anyone, for something like that would make any-body's blood boil.

Translated from the Czech by Dagmar Herrmann

DEEP END

Sally noticed that a man stood in the section of the pool roped off for water aerobics class. She set the plastic infant chair at the poolside and, bending down with her baby Linda, belted her into the chair. Nice-looking guy, she thought. About sixty. Not balding, gray-haired—hair on his chest—not fat, robust. His pleasant eyes glinted humorously as the women shivered slowly into the water. They always felt cold at first, even in this Indian summer air. The man rubbed his own arms briskly, smiling at them in a friendly manner. Sally drew her towel robe around her swimsuit and glanced off toward the last sunlight shimmering behind the stand of redwoods at the edge of the park. The fog had begun its evening drift across Monterey Bay. Greg waved to her from the redwood lifeguard chair. The clock behind him said six.

Sally called out: "Okay, let's start with a run in place!" She thought: I love these women. None of the twenty or so who came regularly was under fifty. Gingerly, they sank into the pool with their teeth chattering. The oldest, who wore a black wetsuit for her thin skin and cold bones, had told Sally she was eighty.

Soon the women were smiling as if aware of how silly they appeared, bobbing and splashing alongside the lap swimmers making their sleek, even strokes in the adjacent lanes. But they need aerobics, and they didn't have the endurance for laps. Some of the women gossiped together—about restaurants, clothes, shows, some just bent and reached, hopped and kicked. "Pick up your legs, let's really run now!" Sally called.

Usually she got into the water and worked out with the class as she called the moves. But today she had to bring the baby. Her sitter had a cold, and her dad had gone to his barbershop quartet convention. Sometimes he would stay with Linda but sometimes, Sally knew, her situation stressed him out. When he did his single-mother number, she didn't even want him to be around Linda. Usually he did his best. After all, one day he would need Sally's help. He was single too since her mom died, and so full of quirks no other woman'd have him. She felt grateful that he at least still enjoyed singing with his cronies. Such a curious mixture, her dad, singing those sentimental songs and grumping about the shortcomings of politicians and anchor teams.

She bent down and tucked a blanket around Linda's feet, as the group ran in place. A baby and a man at class—what a difference! The women cooed over the baby, of course. Who wouldn't—three months old and a perfect doll, asleep in her chair. They were less overt in their attention to the man. Men had come before; a couple of the women brought their husbands from time to time, but most didn't have husbands. Like me, Sally thought. And this man was alone. Too old for her, of course, older than her dad probably.

He stood in the deep end, shoulders above the water, and so everyone could see he was tall as well as nice-looking. And he went through all the moves as she called them: frog leaps, karate kicks, puddle jumpers, even the ballerina leg lifts. He smiled as he followed her calls, stretch and pull, row and lean. Sally could feel how his presence animated everyone. What a charge in the air!

She called out: "Let's do the CanCan! Double kick!" A blonde named Mary Lou spoke in a low voice to the red-headed woman at her side: "I used to do this for real in school days."

One of the women said, "A friend of mine just installed one of those motorized lap pools where you swim in place. It's really tough, and she's sixty-five!" Swimming against the current of age, Sally thought, feeling a wave of sadness.

Secret gazes darted toward the deep end from two of the women especially. Mary Lou, the realtor, was more obvious; she had a naturally affectionate nature, hair colored a pretty ash, with wide blue eyes grown a little watery. The other woman, lean and reserved, with hair colored dark red, seldom talked, and so Sally didn't know her name. When she did speak she was sly and witty, offering a remark about a play or a book. Usually she wore a cap, but today her longish hair hung to her shoulders; the water dampened its tips and short wisps framed her face attractively.

"She's awake," the man called out. Linda had kicked the blanket off her toes. "So tiny," said Mary Lou. "So quiet," the redhead said. "Doesn't cry when she wakes up." It was true; Linda sat there kicking and smiling. I'm a lucky mother, Sally thought. Of course, taking care of her alone was no clambake, and she'd had to drop out of college. But she preferred it this way to hanging on to slaphappy-Hal, just waiting for the inheritance from his still-healthy grandmother instead of getting a job. Unlucky in love, she had become a lucky mother. And she had friends, like Greg, the lifeguard, and others on the pool staff, real friends she could talk to, not agonize over. People she did Master's Swim with, and her support group of single mothers. "Bend forward, rowing arms!" she called. "Pull back."

The fog was lifting, someone observed, unusual for Santa

Cruz evenings. "Maybe it's the moon," the eighty-year-old said. "Full moon rising." When the time changed, would it mean class before dark or after? another woman wondered. Would we spring forward or fall back? Kick back, rock forward. Rocking horse, switch legs, then volcano, jump up, arms in the air, explosions of water—maybe the goofiest-looking of all the exercises.

Sally called for the striding tread: "Cross Country!" This took them to the deep end of the pool for a strenuous stomach workout. Her eighty-year-old, as always, stayed behind in the shallow water, stretching.

The move to the deep end gave Mary Lou and the redhead a chance to draw nearer to the man; they treaded across the pool close to him during Cross Country. She heard the redhead speak directly to him. "I'd rather be skiing." He laughed.

Mary Lou, striding on the other side, said, "I like the Can-Can better."

The man said, "I like that too. It was in the ballet I saw in Cleveland last night. *Gaieté Parisienne.*"

Next Sally gave everyone styrofoam floats to loop over their shoulders for the stomach exercises. She saw that the man took note of the good figures of the two women on either side of him, as they lifted their knees to split their legs wide apart in the stomach tensions. And they couldn't fail to see that he also had a fairly flat stomach.

"You went to the ballet in *Cleveland* last night?" asked Mary Lou, moving into the Accordion exercise, knees lifted to chest, then legs straight out.

"Yes," he said. "They're coming to San Francisco. You can see it in a week or two."

"I'd rather tango than CanCan," said the redhead.

"How about that new tango?" Sally said to encourage her, as she called for them to do Jaws, legs spread forward, wide open, then spread back.

The man smiled. "I read about the new tango in *The New Yorker.*"

So—Sally thought, info as concise as a singles ad: a traveler, if only to Cleveland, a concert-goer, a music lover, a reader of sophisticated literature—all in a few comments. He was also knowledgeable about the moon, which rose in the branches of distant trees along the eastern side of the bay. In just a few minutes the full yellow sphere became visible against the darkening sky and seemed very close.

"Is it a harvest moon, do you think?" asked Mary Lou, eyes very wide, her question directed to Sally. Sally didn't know, but the man did.

"The harvest moon is an aberration," he told everyone. "You see it against the trees, and so it looks very large as it rises. But if you take a small tube and look at the moon through it without including the trees, it is reduced immediately to its usual size."

"Disillusioning," the redhead murmured.

Mary Lou groaned in mock sorrow. "All these years I've had a romance with the harvest moon," she said, a little too exaggerated. Sally began to root for the redhead.

There were only a few more minutes of class. Sally wanted to hug the baby, awake now for almost twenty minutes, merely smiling and chirping in her chair. Maybe the chlorine gas rising from the water had drugged her—she wasn't usually *this* quiet. While everybody did the final stretches, Sally released the baby's strap, lifted her from the chair and tucked her inside her rope. The baby's breath made a warm stream at her shoulder. "Hold onto the side of the pool, one leg forward and stretch out the opposite calf; change, stretch the other."

As they finished and the women started to rush from the pool for the warm showers, Mary Lou and the redhead glanced back at the man. Standing alone in the center of the pool, he lifted his arms and stretched them languidly, turning his chest toward the moon. Sally could see why anyone might want to rush into his arms. He began to sing in a warm baritone. Not a trained voice, but the voice of a man who enjoyed his life.

> *Overhead the moon is beaming*
> *Bright as blossoms in the air*
> *Nothing is heard but the song of a bird*
> *Filling all the night with music . . .*

"That was a wonderful class," he said, making a little applause sign to Sally. The two women, lingering as casually as possible, joined in the gesture. Sally remembered her dad singing that old song. Its next words floated into her mind: "Only you can ease this longing, only you . . ."

Then as he waded to the shallow end of the pool, the man spoke to Sally again. "Next time I'll bring my wife. She'd love it."

Mary Lou crossed her arms over her chest and grasped her shoulders, shivering as she followed the other women inside. The redhead took one of the lap lanes to do the backstroke until the showers cleared. Her arms stretched out behind her and Sally could see the moonlight play on her breasts as she swam. Sally hugged her baby inside her robe and stared after the man as he went into the men's shower room alone, where it was never crowded.

Kenneth Bernard

SISTER FRANCETTA AND THE PIG BABY

Let me get right into it. When Sister Francetta was a little girl she looked into a baby carriage one day and saw a baby with a pig head. It wore dainty white clothes, had little baby hands and feet, a baby's body. Of course the sounds it made were strange, but the main thing was the pig head. It lay there on its back, kicking its feet, waving its arms, and staring at the world through a pig head. Now Sister Francetta taught us her morality through stories. For example, little boys and girls who put their fingers in forbidden places sometimes found that their fingers rotted away. That was the moral of a story about a boy who picked his nose. However, rotting fingers were a comparatively mild consequence. Sister Francetta's childhood world was filled with sudden and horrible attacks of blindness, deafness, and dumbness. Ugly purple growths developed overnight anywhere inside or outside of people's bodies. Strange mutilations from strange accidents were common. It absolutely did not pay to be bad. Sinful thoughts were the hardest to protect against. Prayer and confession were the surest remedies. As I grew older, Sister Francetta's tales gradually subsided into remote pockets of my mind, occasionally to crop up in dream or quaint reminiscence. Except for the pig baby. The pig baby is still with me. It was different from her other stories. For example, it had no moral, it was just there: there had once been a baby with a pig head. Also, whereas Sister Francetta told her other stories often, and with variations, she told the story of the pig baby only once. And she told it differently, as if she herself did not understand it but nevertheless felt a tremendous urgency to reveal it. The other stories she told because they were *useful*. The story of the pig baby she told because she had *faith* in it. It captured my imagination totally. I tried to find out more, but she usually put me off. And I thought a great deal about it. Since Sister Francetta is dead now, I suppose I am the only expert in the world on the pig baby, and what I know can be listed very quickly:

1. The pig baby was apparently Caucasian.
2. Its parents were proud of it and in public seemed totally unaware of its pig head.
3. I do not know how long it lived. It apparently never went to school.
4. It always snorted noticeably but never let out any really piglike sounds like *oink*.
5. It ate and drank everything a regular baby ate and drank.
6. Its parents were not Catholic.
7. Everyone pretended not to notice that the baby had a pig head. For some reason it was not talked about either.
8. At some early point the family either moved away or disappeared.
9. No one said anything about that either.

Sister Francetta died a few years after I had her as a teacher. She was still young. It was whispered among us that she had

horrible sores all over her body. I became an excellent student and went on to college. There I developed more sophisticated ideas about the pig baby, the two most prominent of
which were 1. that Sister Francetta herself was the pig baby,
and 2. that the pig baby was Jesus Christ. There is no logic
to either conclusion. Since college I have more or less given
up the pig baby. Nevertheless it is a fact that I never look
into a carriage without a flush of anxiety. And I cannot get
rid of the feeling that Sister Francetta is angry with me.

Joy Harjo

THE FLOOD

It had been years since I'd seen the watermonster, the snake who lived in the bottom of the lake, but that didn't mean he'd disappeared in the age of reason, a mystery that never happened. For in the muggy lake was the girl I could have been at sixteen, wrested from the torment of exaggerated fools, one version anyway, though the story at the surface would say car accident, or drowning while drinking, all of it eventually accidental. But there are no accidents. This story is not an accident, nor is the existence of the watersnake in the memory of the people as they carried the burden of the myth from Alabama to Oklahoma. Each reluctant step pounded memory into the broken heart and no one will ever forget it. When I walk the stairway of water into the abyss, I return as the wife of the watermonster, in a blanket of time decorated with swatches of cloth and feathers from our favorite clothes. The stories of the battles of the watersnake are forever ongoing, and those stories soaked into my blood since infancy like deer gravy, so how could I resist the watersnake, who appeared as the most handsome man in the tribe, or any band whose visits I'd been witness to since

childhood? This had been going on for centuries: the first
time he appeared I carried my baby sister on my back as I
went to get water. She laughed at a woodpecker flitting like
a small sun above us and before I could deter the symbol we
were in it. My body was already on fire with the explosion
of womanhood as if I were flint, hot stone, and when he
stepped out of the water he was the first myth I had ever
seen uncovered. I had surprised him in a human moment. I
looked aside but I could not discount what I had seen. My
baby sister's cry pinched reality, the woodpecker a warning
of a disjuncture in the brimming sky, and then a man who
was not a man but a myth. What I had seen there were no
words for except in the sacred language of the most holy
recounting, so when I ran back to the village, drenched in
salt, how could I explain the water jar left empty by the river
to my mother who deciphered my burning lips as shame?
My imagination had swallowed me like a mica sky, but I
had seen the watermonster in the fight of lightningstorms,
breaking trees, stirring up killing winds, and had lost my
favorite brother to a spear of the sacred flame, so certainly I
would know my beloved if he were hidden in the blushing
skin of the suddenly vulnerable. I was taken with a fever and
nothing cured it until I dreamed my fiery body dipped in
the river where it fed into the lake. My father carried me as
if I were newborn, as if he were presenting me once more to
the world, and when he dipped me I was quenched, pronounced healed. My parents immediately made plans to
marry me to an important man who was years older but
would provide me with everything I needed to survive in
this world, a world I could no longer perceive, as I had been
blinded with a ring of water when I was most in need of a
drink by a snake who was not a snake, and how did he know
my absolute secrets, those created at the brink of acquired
language? When I disappeared it was in a storm that

destroyed the houses of my relatives; my baby sister was found sucking on her hand in the crook of an oak. And though it may have appeared otherwise, I did not go willingly. That night I had seen my face strung on the shell belt of my ancestors, and I was standing next to a man who could not look me in the eye. The oldest woman in the tribe wanted to remember me as a symbol in the story of the girl who disobeyed, who gave in to her desires before marriage and was destroyed by the monster disguised as the seductive warrior. Others saw the car I was driving as it drove into the lake early one morning, the time the carriers of tradition wake up, before the sun or the approach of woodpeckers, and found the emptied six-pack on the sandy shores of the lake. The power of the victim is a power that will always be reckoned with, one way or the other. When the proverbial sixteen-year-old woman walked down to the edge of the lake to call out her ephemeral destiny, within her were all sixteen-year-old women from time immemorial; it wasn't that she decided to marry the watersnake, but there were no words describing the imprint of images larger than the language she'd received from her mother's mouth, her father's admonishments. Her imagination was larger than the small frame house at the north edge of town, with the broken cars surrounding it like a necklace of futility, larger than the town itself leaning into the lake. Nothing could stop it, just as no one could stop the bearing-down thunderheads as they gathered for war overhead in the war of opposites. Years later when she walked out of the lake and headed for town, no one recognized her, or themselves, in the drench of fire and rain. The children were always getting ready for bed, but never asleep, and the watersnake was a story that no one told anymore. She entered a drought that no one recognized as drought, the convenience store a signal of temporary amnesia. I had gone out to get bread, eggs and the newspaper before breakfast and hurried the cashier for my change as the crazy woman walked in, for I could not see myself as I had abandoned her some twenty years ago in a blue windbreaker at the edge of the man-made lake as everyone dove naked and drunk off the sheer cliff, as if we had nothing to live for, not then or ever. It was beginning to rain in Oklahoma, the rain that would flood the world.

Ursula Hegi

DOVES

Francine is having a shy day, the kind of day that makes you feel sad when the elevator man says good afternoon, the kind of day that makes you want to buy two doves.

Her raincoat pulled close around herself, Francine walks the twelve blocks to Portland Pet And Plant. She heads past the African violets, past the jade plants and fig trees, past the schnauzers and poodles, past the hamsters and turtles, past the gaudy parrot in the center cage who shrieks: "Oh amigo, oh amigo . . ."

What Francine wants are doves of such a smooth gray that they don't hurt your eyes. With doves like that you don't have to worry about being too quiet. They make soft clucking sounds deep inside their throats and wait for you to notice them instead of clamoring for your attention.

Six of them perch on the bars in the tall cage near the wall, two white with brownish speckles, the others a deep gray tinged with purple. Above the cage hangs a sign: Ring Neck Doves $7.99. Doves like that won't need much; they'll turn their heads toward the door when you push the key into the lock late in the afternoon and wait for you to notice them instead of clamoring for your attention.

"Oh amigo, oh amigo . . . ," screeches the parrot. Francine chooses the two smallest gray doves and carries them from the store in white cardboard boxes that look like Chinese takeout containers with air holes. The afternoon has the texture of damp newspaper, but Francine feels light as she walks back to her apartment.

In her kitchen she sets the boxes on top of her counter, opens the tops, and waits for the doves to fly out and roost on the plastic bar where she hangs her kitchen towels. But they crouch inside the white cardboard as if waiting for her to lift them out.

She switches on the radio to the station where she always keeps it, public radio, but instead of Tuesday night opera, a man is asking for donations. Francine has already sent in her contribution, and she doesn't like it when the man says, "None of you would think of going into a store and taking something off the shelves, but you listen to public radio without paying . . ." The doves move their wing feathers forward and pull their heads into their necks as if trying to shield themselves from the fund-raising voice.

Francine turns the dial past rock stations and commercials. At the gaudy twang of a country-western song, the doves raise their heads and peer from the boxes. Their beaks turn to one side, then to the other, completing a nearly full circle. Low velvet sounds rise from their throats. Francine has never listened to country-westerns; she's considered them tacky, but when the husky voice of a woman sings of wanting back the lover who hurt her so, she tilts her head to the side and croons along with the doves.

Before she leaves for her job at K-Mart the next morning, Francine pulls the radio next to the kitchen sink and turns it on for the doves. They sit in the left side of her double sink which she has lined with yellow towels, their claws curved around folds of fabric, their eyes on the flickering

light of the tuner that still glows on the country-western station. When she returns after working all day in the footwear
department, they swivel their heads toward her and then
back to the radio as if they'd been practicing that movement
all day.

At K-Mart she finds that more people leave their shoes. It
used to be just once or twice a week that she'd discover a
worn pair of shoes half pushed under the racks by someone
who's walked from the store with stolen footwear. But now
she sees them almost every day—sneakers with torn insoles,
pumps with imitation leather peeling from the high heels,
work shoes with busted seams—as if a legion of shoe thieves
had descended on Portland.

Francine keeps the discarded shoes in the store's lost and
found crate out back, though no one has ever tried to claim
them. But some are still good enough to donate to Goodwill.
She murmurs to the doves about the shoes while she refills
their water and sprinkles birdseed into the porcelain soap
dish. Coming home to them has become familiar. So have
the songs of lost love that welcome her every evening. A few
times she tried to return to her old station, but as soon as
the doves grew listless, she moved the tuner back. And lately
she hasn't felt like changing it at all. She knows some of the
lines now, knows how the songs end.

Francine has a subscription to the opera, and after feeding
the doves, she takes a bubble bath and puts on her black
dress. In the back of the cab, she holds her purse with both
hands in her lap. Sitting in the darkened balcony, she feels
invisible as she listens to *La Traviata,* one of her favorite
operas. For the first time it comes to her that it, too, is about
lost love and broken hearts.

In the swell of bodies that shifts from the opera house,
Francine walks into the mild November night, leaving

behind the string of waiting taxicabs, the expensive restaurants across from the opera house, the stores and the bus station, the fast-food places and bars.

A young couple saunters from the Blue Moon Tavern hand in hand, steeped in amber light and the sad lyrics of a slow-moving song for that instant before the door closes again. Francine curves her fingers around the doorhandle, pulls it open, and steps into the smoky light as if she were a woman with red boots who had someone waiting for her. Below the Michelob clock, on the platform, two men play guitars and sing of betrayed love.

On the bar stool, her black dress rides up to her knees. She draws her shoulders around herself and orders a fuzzy navel, a drink she remembers from a late night movie. The summer taste of apricots and oranges soothes her limbs and makes her ease into the space her body fills.

A lean-hipped man with a cowboy hat asks Francine to dance, and as she sways in his arms on the floor that's spun of sawdust and boot prints, she becomes the woman in all the songs that the men on the platform sing about, the woman who leaves them, the woman who keeps breaking their hearts.

Ron Carlson

THE TABLECLOTH OF TURIN

*A man, anywhere from forty to sixty, comes onto the stage. He wears
glasses, a white shirt with the sleeves rolled up, wool slacks, and shined
black shoes. He carries under his arm: a folded tablecloth. It is very
large. He is also carrying a folding desk lamp, a pointer, and a packet
of other small gear. The man, Leonard Christofferson, pins the tablecloth to the backdrop, sets up the desk lamp to illuminate the tablecloth, lifts the pointer and steps toward the audience.*

This is the seventy-first public appearance of the famed
Tablecloth of Turin. My name is Leonard Christofferson, and
the tablecloth and I have been traveling for almost three
months now. I am an insurance investigator by trade from
Ann Arbor, Michigan, but I've pretty much let that all go.
After all, it is my tablecloth, and it is my wish to share it and
show it to as many folks as I can.

In the last three months, I've been met with a lot of skepti-
cism about the authenticity of the cloth, but most people,
when they hear the story and see the evidence, come to
know as well as I do that this is the tablecloth of the Last
Supper, the very cloth depicted in so many famous paintings,
including Leonardo da Vinci's, the very tablecloth over
which Christ broke that bread and poured that wine.

I want to say right here: as an insurance investigator, I had
many years experience with and exposure to frauds, some of
them silly, some of them so well constructed as to seem gen-
uine. We had homicides made to look like drunk driving and
a bad curve; we had grand larcenies perpetrated by neph-

ews, nieces, wives, and sons, all in cahoots with the "victim"; we had an insured Learjet go down to the bottom of Lake Michigan which upon salvage turned out to be a junked box-car, the jet having been sold in Mexico. In my experience as a detective, I learned slowly over the years to trust nothing, nobody. It's a terrible profession, picking through death cars and the ashes of every dry cleaner that burns up. The owner stands there hating you and you don't trust him, a guy you never met before in your life. The twelve years I worked for Specific Claims in Ann Arbor were hard years on me, and they destroyed my faith in the human race.

And when I went to Italy with the Art Guild and I found, well, I was offered, this piece of white cloth, I saw my chance to turn my life around. I do not now, nor have I ever spoken Italian, but I could see from the glistening ardor in the man's eyes that he too had recovered his faith and he wanted me to take care of this sacred emblem in a way that he, working in his brother's restaurant, could never do. I paid him, left the Art Guild's Renaissance trip early, flew back to Ann Arbor, quit my job, and I have been sharing my good fortune ever since.

Enough about me. Let me show you my tablecloth.

As you can see, it's a large one: six foot five by twenty-three feet. We have had it all chemically analyzed and I want to share our findings with you tonight. The cloth itself is constructed of rough linen, approximately fourteen threads per inch, woven in a single piece on a hand loom, we esti-mate, about twenty-nine A.D. The X rays have revealed thir-teen place settings, most of them three-piece settings of an iron clay material, which means there were over forty dishes on the table and possibly fifty depending on how many carafes of wine were out.

This is where Christ sat. We know this not only from his-torical and artistic record, but also from the fact that this one space, this seat of honor, is unmarked. All the other places have revealed, under the spectrometer, bread crumbs, spilled wine, palm prints (the oil of the human hand), in one place elbow prints (someone, possibly James the Lesser, had his sleeves rolled up), but Christ's place is untainted. He not only was a careful eater, he probably didn't have that much to eat, knowing what he knew.

Examination has also revealed some shocking new evidence: *the apostles didn't all sit on one side of the table.* Three of the places, including the place where Judas Iscariot sat, were opposite Jesus. So: sorry, Leonardo, thanks for giving us all their faces, but the truth has three backs to the camera. We suspect that Judas sat opposite Jesus for the reasons that science has supplied. In fact, science, the ultimate detective, has unraveled the whole story of the Last Supper from this humble tablecloth.

Listen: *it was a nervous dinner.* We know this from the number of wine glass rings in the cloth itself. The men were picking up their glasses and setting them down more frequently than for just drinking. They were playing with their glasses as if they were chess pieces. They would have been nervous for a number of reasons. None of the thirteen men in that room (with the possible exception of Jesus, who somehow knew the host) had ever eaten there before. Imagine it: you go to a new city, find a man carrying a pitcher of water down the street as Jesus had instructed you, and *ask him to have you* to Passover Dinner. It's an upstairs room with a limited view. Your host, whoever he is, doesn't eat with you. It is a bit of a strange setup. So, you're nervous. You sit there. You'd tap your glass too, maybe as many as seventy times, like Andrew, who sat here, did.

Then during dinner, your leader starts in on some topics which anyone of us might think inappropriate for the supper table. Instead of the usual reaffirming and pleasant messages, the conversation becomes hostile assertions, statements of doom and gloom. Jesus says, "Verily, I say unto you, that one of you shall betray me." Try that at home sometime, see if somebody doesn't spill the wine. Which, our spectrometer shows, every one of the twelve disciples did, the largest spill being here, where Judas sat. In addition, traces of bread crumbs were found here, as we found everywhere, but these were partially decomposed via the starch-splitting enzymes found in human saliva, so we know almost certainly that Mr. Iscariot, almost two thousand years before the Heimlich maneuver, choked on his bread when Jesus said that. We don't know who patted him on the back.

There is another large spill here. (Thirty-six square centimeters), and we theorize that Peter was still sitting when told he would deny Jesus thrice before dawn. From the shape of the spill, something like a banana, it seems that Peter stood to protest, and dragged his glass with him.

Other evidence in this sacred cloth suggests that besides bread and wine, the attendees at the Last Supper enjoyed a light salad with rich vinegar and some kind of noodle dish. There was no fish. The wine was a seasoned, full-bodied red wine, which our analysis has revealed to be a California wine. This last bit of evidence has given the skeptics great joy, but I've got news for you. That it is a California wine does not mean that this is not the Tablecloth of Turin; it simply means that civilization in California is older than some people now think.

When I look at this magnificent cloth and see its amazing tale of love and faith and betrayal written for all to see in wine, bread, and prints of human hands, I'm suddenly made glad again that I went to Turin last fall with the Art Guild, that I met Antony Cuppolini in his brother's restaurant, and that for some strange reason known only to God, Antony made me caretaker of this, the beautiful Tablecloth of Turin.

Mary Swan

WHERE YOU LIVE NOW

Now that you've been dead for weeks instead of days, I find I'm scanning headlines at the checkout once again. Cures for cancer in every issue and Siamese twins delivering each other's babies. A caveman's skull bears an uncanny resemblance to Elvis, who has recently been spotted in Jessup, Georgia. But what makes me stop and stare is a blurred photograph, a story about astronauts finding the footprint of a child on the surface of the moon. It reminds me of that time we sat on the back steps, eating something sticky. How we wondered about the moon, a smudgy print in a hard blue sky, and could it be the same one we saw at night? I thought not.

And then you told me about your favourite aunt, the one with the earrings shaped like broken hearts, the one with the sweet breath. How she'd been driving in her car one day, how she'd driven up the steep hill at the edge of town and ended up in heaven. This did not seem impossible, although I did wonder how she got back.

"Reverse," you said.

*　　*　　*

Where I'm living now there are no trees. Dan says I lack imagination; he can look at the spindly things surrounded by hoops of wire and see a forest, in time, lush and over-hanging and shading the back patio where he and I will read books in our retirement. I can't even see the back patio, just a churning mass of mud on a pale spring day. The boys love it, of course. They tie faded scarves about their heads and wear their coats like capes; they are superheroes doing con-stant, complex battle. At times I eavesdrop shamelessly.

That summer there was a strike at the mill and we walked by the white house on the way to the pool and someone had sprayed *Scab* in shaky letters all over the side. We couldn't work that out. And once we stood at the edge of a field; I saw a fat brown slug on your shoulder, inching its way toward your bare arm. And you screamed and I screamed and we ran across the whole field and when we got to the other side it was gone but we took off our clothes and shook them out, to make sure. After that we always ran screaming across that field, holding hands.

That summer your brothers made us their slaves, and we had to get up at six o'clock to do their paper route. They said if we didn't they would flush us down the toilet and once they even dragged us down the hall, kicking and shrieking, until your mother shouted up the stairs. We did the route for a few days because we both remembered get-ting stuck when we were small and the seat was up, how we went right down, just our calves and shoes kicking above the rim, and how both our mothers laughed in the doorway before they lifted us out. That was one of the first bonds between us.

We weren't clever enough to do it on purpose, but we must have made a terrible mess of the papers because after a few days your mother started getting calls and you told her the whole story and when your father came home your brothers got the belt and lost their allowances for a long time. We thought we were safe for a little while but sometimes they would sneak up behind you and make swooshing noises no one else could hear. Then we were sure they would come for us those times we slept in the tent in my backyard, but all we heard were the loud voices going on and on.

And that was the summer my father left and I sacrificed Becky in the river above the dam. Threw her in and watched her torn dress billow out, her yarn braids twist and flip as she was swept along. Now that you're dead there's no one else who knows how much I cried.

It was from my mother that I first heard you were sick. She's retired now; she keeps track of people. In the beginning things were hopeful and it reminded me, and I thought I would write you a letter, make some kind of contact, but it was hard after so much time.

"Oh sure," I imagined you saying, letting a page flutter toward the wastebasket.

I did mean to come and see you in the hospital, that last long time. I got as far as checking the bus schedule, working out the times so I could make the trip there and back in a day. But something happened just before I planned to leave, I can't even remember what, and I never did go. And I thought maybe it was better that I didn't. I thought maybe it wouldn't help at all if I came breezing through the door, too much flesh on my bones and a wallet stuffed with pictures of my sons. I had heard by then how you longed for a child, how you prayed for a clean checkup, just one time.

I went to your funeral though, I did manage that. Disguised as my present self. Your brothers are losing their hair; you knew that, of course, but I was not prepared. We talked about the threat of the toilet and laughed, and then they coughed and touched the corners of their eyes. I didn't show them the pictures I had brought in my purse. You and I on the back steps, squinting into the sun. And dressed as fairy princesses on skates for the carnival. During our big number you had to go to the bathroom and suddenly skated toward the exit. And I, of course, followed, and so did the other princesses, the frogs, the teddy bears and the two-person dragon. The music played on and soft red and green lights bathed the cardboard castle on the empty ice; our teacher wept with her face in her hands.

Out of nowhere your father decided to go to England for a few years; you cried and cried but there was no getting out of it. You came back tall, with an accent I didn't believe for a moment. Talking about the cinema, the ballet.

"Nothing's changed here," you kept saying, and I thought I heard my own sneer, grew prickly because of it. Maybe if you'd stayed then we would have found a new place to start from, but you were all living in the city, only coming for a visit once or twice. Talking then about the Third World, talking about becoming a nurse so you could help somewhere. You were only three months older but you grew up so much faster and we let each other go without even noticing. I'd hear things once in a while; you were in Guatemala, in Africa; you were married, then you weren't. But I didn't pay much attention. Years went by when I didn't think of you at all.

Where I live now there are no trees—I think I told you that. I wash the dishes and look out on a sea of mud, my boys now joined by other ragged heroes. They run and jump and fall, soundlessly. I keep waiting for the quiet moments, I keep waiting for the questions I've worked out answers to. If the earth is really spinning, then why aren't we dizzy? If we dig a hole to China, will the people be upside down? Where do you go when you die?

I didn't think I would mind so much, but I keep *remembering*. Twisted red letters on the side of a white house, and Becky tossing in the cold river. That time your aunt cried in the kitchen because she was thirty and your mother gave us money to go to the store. How we sat on the curb and thought that we would never be that old. You weren't.

And I wonder sometimes if you had some inkling, because what I really can't stand is the randomness of it. We stood together at the edge of a field; it smelled like summer and the sun beat down. I was so close that your hair flicked my cheek as you turned your head to see the fat brown slug that inched down your arm, not mine.

On the surface of the moon there is no gravity. No wind, no rain. The footprint could have been there for thousands of years, undisturbed. But I like to think that it is more recent. I like to think that your child self is dancing there. Or that maybe you touched down briefly, shedding years, on your way to some other place.

I OWNED VERMONT

As I remember it, we were fighting again. Probably about money, though I'm not sure. Money was something we fought a lot about then. Or maybe it was some guy I'd seen her talking with when I visited her at the department store the night before. Regardless, we were fighting again.

She said, "Do you want a divorce? Do you want a divorce?" She pulled off her wedding rings and tossed them in her ring tray on the dresser. I followed her into the bathroom, where she started to brush her hair. Her teeth were clenched.

"Listen," I said. "Listen." But then I stopped. "You don't even understand," I said. I took off my ring then, too, and threw it in the bathroom trash. I looked down into the garbage but couldn't see the ring for the Kleenex and Q-Tips there.

I turned and went into the living room, took the car keys from on top of the television, and slammed the door behind me.

That is how the battle finished. I won.

I got into the car and raced the engine as if the sound were some sort of victory cry. I knew she heard it, the apartment being only one floor up and the bathroom window facing the parking area. And so, for greater effect, I shoved the car into reverse, backed out, and did the best I could to squeal the tires as I took off. They didn't.

We'd been married a little over two years. I worked at a restaurant breakfast and lunch, Ann at a department store in Holyoke. We lived in Springfield in an old brick apartment building behind the Motor Vehicle Registry.

So we married too young. So we hardly ever saw each other, what with our schedules the way they were. I've known lots of people who've made bigger mistakes. But those are things that have been gone over time and again. It was this fight. This fight in particular.

This fight in particular because I just took off, drove north on the Interstate, not knowing if or when I'd turn around and go home to fish through the Kleenex and Q-Tips. Sometimes you need to be by yourself for a while, and north seemed best. We had been living in Springfield for over two years, but neither of us had ever been north of Greenfield, never been to Vermont or New Hampshire, not to mention Maine. We once made it to Albany, for what reason I can't remember, but never north.

And so I headed that way. Ann had never been to Vermont. Ann had never set foot in that state, and I won the fight. I would go and claim it for my own.

There was not much to be seen in the way of civilization along the Interstate between Springfield and Vermont. There was the mill in Holyoke, some houses, billboards, etc., around Northampton, the Motel-6 in Deerfield, some more buildings near Greenfield. Still, the closer I got to Vermont the more anxious I became, until when I finally crossed the border I nearly laughed out loud.

At that moment anything was possible. There was a car in front of me, a girl driving. I thought, I can seduce that girl. I can pull up next to her, roll my window down, ask her to coffee in Brattleboro, and the rest would be easy. I own Vermont, I thought. It belongs to me and Ann will never have it. I glanced at the girl as I passed. She didn't even look at me. But then, why should she have?

Like the drive up, Brattleboro, too, was nothing much to shout about. At least what I saw of it. I drove down the main street off the Interstate, past a used car dealer, a shopping center, convenience stores, bars and what-have-you you find in these small towns. I stopped the car at a package store and bought a single bottle of one of those expensive imported dark beers, and used the inside lip of the ashtray to open it up. Some of the beer spilled into the ashtray, but I didn't mind. I laughed a little.

I started home, there not being much gas left, maybe enough to get me back to the apartment and Ann to work and back the next day, and I realized I was thinking about her and knew I would have to face her when I got home. As I crossed the border I thought, I will have to walk up those stairs and open the door, set the keys back on the TV, and face Ann. I pictured her still brushing her hair, teeth still clenched, and her hand pulling the brush back through her hair with quick strokes like it was a knife. She tilted her head down and to one side, looked out the corners of her eyes to the reflection of her hair, and stabbed me, stabbed me. If she felt like that, I thought, I would dig my ring out of the trash and drop it into the garbage disposal and turn it on. To hell with her.

I got home near nine o'clock and, it being one of Ann's nights off, found her sitting on the sofa watching television. She ignored me and stared at the set. I dropped the keys on the set and waved at her, the empty beer bottle in my hand.

She did not blink. I just sort of laughed at her then and made a hissing sigh. Once I was in the kitchen, though, she spoke.

"Where have you been?" she said. "Wasting money, I suppose."

She couldn't break me. "Nowhere. Around." I looked for something to eat, opened the refrigerator and nosed around. I found some egg salad in a Tupperware dish and some bread and closed the door.

She said, "And drinking. Driving and drinking. Smart."

I set the dish and bread on the counter, opened the kitchen garbage can and dropped the beer bottle in, making sure to strike it on an empty jelly jar at the bottom. Both the bottle and jar broke. "Smart enough to know when to get away from you," I said. I was in rare form.

After I made my sandwich I heard her get up from the sofa. She turned the television off and came into the kitchen. I walked back into the bedroom and sat on the bed with my sandwich. I wanted her to follow me this time. I took a bite and noticed that her rings were no longer in the tray. "Where are your rings?" I called out. "In the garbage disposal?"

She came into the bedroom and crossed her arms and leaned against the closet door. The rings were back on her finger, and it looked like tears were in her eyes.

"Look," she said. "Look, stop it. Let's stop it. Let's stop fighting."

I set the sandwich down on the night stand and stood up, put my arms around her. "I'm sorry," I said. "I'm sorry we fight. You're right. We have to stop. Don't cry." She leaned against me and I felt her tears through my shirt. "Don't cry," I said. I think I meant it, too.

"I can't help it," she said into my shoulder, then pulled away and wiped her eyes with the back of her hand.

"Here," I said, and held her face in my hands and wiped a tear with my thumb. "Let's go find my ring." I led her out of the bedroom and into the bathroom. I sat on the toilet and put the trash basket on my lap and started fishing through the garbage. Ann sat on the edge of the tub and wiped her nose with a Kleenex.

I poked around for a few minutes looking for that ring, and then I said it. Why, I do not know. Maybe because I wanted her to feel better. Maybe I just wanted to talk.

I said, "You know, I wasn't going to tell you this, but I own Vermont." I looked up from the garbage to Ann. She blinked a couple of times, her eyes still red.

"What?" she said.

I went back to the garbage. "I said I own Vermont. That's where I went tonight. To Vermont. You've never been there before, so I claimed it for myself." I found the ring at the bottom of the basket and pulled it out. "Here it is," I said. I smiled and slipped the ring on my finger. "You know what I mean?"

She looked at me. "You shouldn't have told me," she said.

I said, "Why not?" but by that time I think I already had an idea.

"You told me," she said. "You told me, and you shouldn't have. Now I know."

She took it from me just like that.

She stood up and held out her hand to me, and I remember looking up at her and thinking. That close. That close, but I knew she was right, and that I had lost.

Marcel Marien

THE I IS NEVER ALONE

Suna Siriak had just turned fifteen when he was hired as a cabin boy on board the SS *Max Havelaar,* a barge of light tonnage which navigated among the islands of the Sonde. The ship had just left Makassar for the isle of Timor when an atrocious drama completely changed the fate of its crew.

Siriak replaced Morok at the helm while he had his evening meal with the three other mates and the captain. Generally he was never gone for more than fifteen minutes. But after an hour he still hadn't come back, so Siriak went down to the mess to see what was going on. He found his five companions crippled with pain, poisoned by some preserved meat. They all died together before sunset.

The adolescent was too inexperienced to steer the ship. During the night he vainly tried to fight against sleep, but by the next day he had passed Timor, and the ship headed out into the Indian Ocean. Three days passed. He had to get rid of the cadavers which were putrifying in the heat. Then, in the middle of the fifth night, while he was sleeping, the little boat hit a reef. A jet of water shot into it, and the condemned vessel soon sank. Siriak threw himself into the

ocean and floated on a trunk which he had hastily filled with
various tools.

At dawn he set foot on an isle. It didn't take long for him
to see it was deserted. Twenty minutes was enough to walk
to the other side. There was no trace of human habitation
that could let him hope the isle was known to sailors. On the
other hand, he did find a spring, and coconut, mango, and
banana trees grew in abundance and would make it possible
for him to survive.

Siriak hadn't read *Robinson Crusoe*, but there aren't very
many ways to make do after a shipwreck. He took an inven-
tory of his trunk and gathered up the bits of flotsam which
the sea had thrown up on the sand. This harvest was meager
except for a large box which contained nothing but mirrors.
Siriak sat down on the shore and began to organize his life.

A few days had to pass before he truly understood the
depth of the solitude to which he was condemned. Except
for birds and insects there were no animals on the island.
Siriak managed to capture several parrots which he tied to
a branch with some rope. He let them struggle there until
evening. As the sun was setting, he went up to them, stared
at them with insistence, and pronounced his name, "Siriak,"
a great number of times in a clear voice. Attentive, the parrots looked and listened without moving. Siriak gave them a
few seeds and the next day repeated the lesson. After he had
pronounced his name fifty times, he fed them again and let
them go. Nothing happened for a few days, then one beautiful morning Siriak woke up, surprised to have heard himself
called by his name. Perched on a branch a few meters away,
one of the parrots called out the boy's name several times.
As one might guess, the outcome was everything Siriak
might have hoped for, if not foreseen. By instructing one
another, soon all the parrots on the isle were repeating Siriak's name from dawn until dusk.

137

In spite of the continual presence of his self which he was confined to by solitude, he struggled to remember that he also existed outside of his self, even though this might be as a mere object on the island.

And so the weeks and months flew by. Nothing came to trouble his solitary life. Sometimes in the distance he thought he saw a passing ship or an airplane, but these were nothing but mirages. Then one day he noticed the useless trunk that had floated onto the island, the one that contained only mirrors. There had to be a thousand of them, all cut up in the same shape. According to the barely legible words on the lid, they were being shipped to a framing shop called Melville. Siriak took out a half dozen and leaned them against some coconut trees. He saw himself reflected six times. Partly out of despair and partly out of boredom, he scattered them about the entire island. Leaning them against whatever he could, against trees, against rocks, between branches and leaves, he told himself that these mirrors might perchance be seen in the distance and catch the attention of a boat. Of course, nothing of the kind occurred.

Time passed and each day Siriak walked about his miniscule empire and saw in passing his omnipresent reflection at every turn in the path. Meanwhile, his parrots proclaimed his name in the perfumed breeze and the hot scent of the sun.

He died a few years later, perhaps of boredom. The mirrors which multiplied the island and its sole inhabitant had little left to reflect. But even when his body had entirely decomposed, and his bones mixed with the sand on the beach, for a long time afterwards on the entire island, generations and generations of parrots continued to cry out his name, and it reverberated forever.

Translated from the French by Kim Connell

SKETCH

Morning, on the terrace. Can hear Jean Baptiste Quenin crooning "Veilleur de toutes les nuits." Radio in the kitchen. Middle of February. New Grumbacher French Portable easel out here on the terrace. A sketch-pad against my hip. A particular pen. A particular brush. Things changed.

Things continue to change. Here, we are somewhere else, knotted, unknotted, and the wallpaper, the sky, everything is different. If this is doppelgänger-time, you are not my uncle, not my brother, not my Other but me. I can't capture you in lines. We live in the spasm of each other's sagging lives. While shopping at the old market today I saw you look suspiciously at me (in a mirror) the same way you looked suspiciously at the onions, the red fish, the aged cheese. How are we sleeping these days? Orthodox or paradox? I'm the ox but I'm also the bull.

My wife? She's in there, in the cool house, sitting up in bed reading a magazine, no, reading a novel. We have a particular morning ritual. We donate time to thoughts like clouds, they linger over our heads, mackerel-sky stuff, then I'm up and the coffee is going, and she's up too. But this morning, she's hanging out, coffee at bedside. Marie-Paule Belle singing "Les Petits Paletlins." Is that really our kitchen radio or the neighbor's?

Running out of things to sketch? View from café-bar at corner of rue Alphonse Karr and rue de la Liberté. Quick action of people walking. Juxtaposition. Traffic jam. Noise into the clashing of lines. The rue de la Liberté traffic is hectic with honking and fumes, shouting hot, shouting cold. Four fingers of the left hand. Flower spikes.

The view from the mall with its potted tropical shrubbery at Palais de Quency against the gray of the old apartment buildings. Concentrate on this. Where are all my Arab friends this morning? Insults floating over their heads—no grass grows under foot—like scripture in a Negro church. *Une negresse morte*, or should I say dead soldiers? But my Arab friends don't drink red wine, and empty bottles are as taboo as, uh, a *sheygget* (disgusting!) to Behane, my friend from North Africa, born to a Jewish mother, which is all that counts, so they count him in. High place. A firebrand. Son of sorrow. To Behane I'm as clear as Running Water, so he never calls me *shokher*, no sir.

But the question arises: What else is there to draw here? I've done the faces—spirited, noble, valorous, comely, harmonious, bright, lily-like, hospitable, fair, helmeted, feminine, animated, veiled, pleasant, blooming, wise and unwise—and though I know there are still endless uncharted faces, all different, damsel and gaselle, I'm sagging like a palm tree with face-boredom.

So go home. What's home? Whose home?

At the end of February. A bar across from Hall du Voyage. The crowd is younger here. Motorbikes crowding the curb. British music French kids jukebox screams. Yet moderation,

moderation. The Russian with his coffee at the back table. Tatiana in apron. Sidonia in the doorway. Tara coming in with a shoe box under arm. My sketch-pad on table. My hand waiting for a jewel, a sea, a prosperous moment, the tip-off for the right motif. A thick forest of ideas floating just out of reach. Outside, a double-parked delivery truck. That's good enough for the moment, but move fast. Girl with white mane blocks view. (So stick her in.)

The lycee crowd, this. View of street construction crew and triphammer, drill-noise creating gems of terror, rosemary-throbbings. But any of this could be anywhere, in the City of Light or the Eternal City. Nice is nice. I nickname it Salty, Reborn, Without Fault, The Happy Peaceful Place, Patrician, Nymph of Ageless Lust, Opal. Café across from Hôtel Vendome on Pastorelli? Orange plastic chairs, white metal tables. This is the right stuff, the honored model, no, ideal model, the archetypal—simple things. Metal tables. Chairs.

Sit here as in a dream house, dazed but alive as Mars. Sketch the Arab street sweeper washing and sweeping the sidewalk with fire-hydrant water, cleaning the street of its unending string of dog turds and piss.

Keep the hand moving. Care not to knock over the coffee. Coffee. Two francs, not three. An old woman in a third-floor window as she opens her shutters with a bang. Her eyes connect with mine, she draws back as though slapped. Rebellion-face, a face belonging to Bitterness, to the Ill-Tempered Kingdom. Seventy different meanings for such a face, Mary, Mary, quite contrary. Touch it with a laurel, cast it in a battle, under a lime tree or keep it with the barren, the diseased. Find the right motif to move with the hand, as now the voice of Catherine Ferry singing "Bonjour, Bonjour," in the spirit of the Roman goddess of spring or the Serpent of Light.

Even this late in February, the cozy, translucent, ceramic-white sunlight, multicolored sunlight pours down in the nickname of Joy, on my sketch-pad. And page after page, I am filling it. Fulfilling it, like a promised oath. A name, a bond, a lilac in a meadow. Before leaving for Old Town, I do this: My Wife Sunbathing, her bra beside her on the towel.

Sitting with coffee. Artist with Coffee and Sketch-Pad.

Across from the Palais du Justice where the fisherman parked his pushcart. Early, old shoppers trudging into rue du Marche. Three young girls skittering by in *les jambieres* and shiny boots. Ambulances from Saint-Roch Hospital. Delivery boy unloading bottled water.

Along Jean Medicin. Panoramic. Like a staircase of tinsel sweethearts, complex crisscrossing, violent black-and-white, red-and-white forces—sound, light, supplanted, protected by its own wild goat-spirit, its vine-like network reaching out from some absolute Wrathful but Gracious Sanity.

Along the Promenade. A medley of TV antennas over on the roofs of the big hotels, roosting pigeons. Winter sky, winter light, February strife, unsurpassed. Skyline, bathers, strollers, supplanted strollers, supplanted bathers, supplanted delivery boys. Thirst. A burst of rain shoots down from the splendid sky with its hedgerow-shaped clouds out over the sea.

Run across the wide boulevard. Brightness and simplicity follow me all the days of my uncluttered life.

Pivot, enter a small street. I wear a mask of comfort, pass doors I will never knock on, draped windows through which other lives peer in the same wonderment I have known since the beginning of Human Time. Clothes strung on short lines drying between buildings not more than ten feet apart. The Palais parking lot and the big clock in the beige bell tower. I've done that before, done it from three different angles.

Rushing walkers under umbrellas and snug in raincoats. How come I didn't know? Two women talking Dali.

Brazzerie le Liberté. A seat at the bar. Overhearing a conversation, in French, of course. He wanted her to do this unmentionable act with another woman and himself. She got sick of the whole affair. Nothing to sketch in such a Post-Modernist moment. It's a verbal corridor leading to an architectural disaster, partitions of pain and staircases of desire, gifts, habitation, the archer's arm stretched, the gap.

Sunday morning. Walking along rue Pastorelli. At Gubernatis, stop. A cloudy day. Strange, powerful forces at work. Keep moving. Something is bound to give. You're on to something, something like you've never captured before. I can taste it, hear it. It's flourishing, animating me. I know for the first time I was never a Tower Dweller, always an earth-level observer of the Mighty Moment, the Silent Splash. Cross Square Dominique Durandy. A river crosser, this ancient resolution. Even today the mood as Crosser remains that of a wolf or a raven. There is resolution in crossing. Firmly I cross Square Dominique Durandy.

Cross and enter a crowd. Crowd gathered around philatelists huddled over their precious, beautiful stamps. In each tiny stamp I am somewhere different, on a carpet flying over India, in a California gold rush, on a Mediterranean island, a dairy farm, a homestead, with a prince, gazing into the eye of a conqueror. These stamps Teutonic and Anglo-Saxon gaze back, occasional disquisitions of brilliant design—in fern green, mosaics, in golds, in stairway blues, in nineteenth-century bordeaux reds. Wonderment stamped, stilled, held down with ink. Clustered narrowly, spinning in the spacious eye. And seagulls coming overhead from the slap of the sea, circling, nosy, checking us out.

I'm looking slowly, looking. And when there's this much already accomplished, when you see its Power even in miniature, it's hard to raise the rooftop from inspiration, to let it soar, to give Nature undivided attention or to take it. So you move on. Wading, as one who moves homeward, a full sketch-pad under arm, the known plot of What Comes Next already thick with afterthought.

Salarrué (Salazar Arrué)

WE BAD

Goyo Cuestas and his youngster pulled up stakes and lit out for Honduras with the phonograph. The old man carried the works over his shoulder, the kid the bag of records and the beveled trumpet element, tooled like a monstrous tin-plated bellflower that gave off the fragrance of music.

"They say there's money in Honduras."

"Yeah, Dad, and they say they've never heard of phonos there."

"Get a move on, boy—you've been dogging it since we left Mepatán."

"It's just that this saddle's about worn my crotch raw!"

"That's enough—watch your tongue!"

They laid up for a nap under the whistling and aromatic pines. Over an ocote-wood fire they warmed up coffee. Rabbits huddled in an uneasy quiet in the *sapote* grove, browsing. Goyo and the boy were approaching the wild Chamelecón. Twice they saw traces of the *carretía* snake, thin as the track of a belt. When they stopped to rest, they put on a fox trot and ate tortillas with Santa Rosa cheese. For three days they made their way through mud up to their

145

knees. The boy broke down crying; the old man cursed and laughed at him.

The priest in Santa Rosa had cautioned Goyo not to sleep in the shelters, because gangs of thieves constantly patrolled for travelers. So at nightfall Goyo and the boy went deep into the underbrush; they cleared a little spot at the foot of a tree and there they spent the night, listening to the singing of cicadas and the buzzing of blue-tailed mosquitoes as big as spiders, not daring to breathe hard, trembling with cold and fear.

"Dad, you seen *tamagases* snakes?"

"No, boy, I checked the trunk when we turned in, and there weren't any hollows."

"If you smoke, pull down your hat, Dad. If they see the embers they'll find us."

"OK, take it easy, man. Go to sleep."

"It's just I can't sleep all bunched up."

"Stretch out, then."

"I can't, Dad, it's freezing."

"The devil with you! Curl up against me then!"

And Goyo Cuestas, who had never in his life hugged his son, took him against his foul skin, hard as a rail, and, circling his arms around him, warmed him until he was sleeping on top of him, while he, his face twisted in resignation, waited for daybreak to be signaled by some far-off rooster.

The first daylight found them there, half frozen, aching, worn out with fatigue, with ugly mouths open and driveling, half folded up in their ragged blankets, dirty, and striped like zebras.

But Honduras is deep in the Chamelecón. Honduras is deep in the silence of its rough, cruel mountains; Honduras is deep in the mystery of its terrible snakes, wildcats, insects, men. Human law does not reach to the Chamelecón; justice does not extend that far. In that region, as in primitive times, it is up to men to be good- or bad-hearted, to be cruel or magnanimous, to kill or to spare according to their own free will. Clearly the right belongs to the strong.

The four bandits entered through the fence and then settled in the little square of their camp, that camp stranded like a shipwreck in the wild cane plantation. They put the phonograph works between them and tried to connect the trumpet element. The full moon made flashes of silver appear on the apparatus. From a beam of their lean-to hung a piece of stinking venison.

"I tell you it's a phonograph."

"You seen how it works?"

"Yeah! In the banana plantations I seen it."

"Youdunnit!"

The trumpet worked. The highwaymen cranked it up and then opened the bag of records and lifted them to the moonlight like so many other black moons.

The bandits laughed, like children from an alien planet. Their peasant clothes were stained with something that looked like mud and that was blood. In the nearby gully, Goyo and his youngster fled bit by bit in the beaks of vultures; armadillos had multiplied their wounds. Within a mass of sand, blood, clothing, and silence, their illusions, dragged there from far away, remained only as fertilizer, perhaps for a willow, perhaps for a pine.

The needle touched down, and the song flew forth on the tepid breeze like something enchanted. The coconut groves stilled their palm trees and listened in the distance. The large morning star seemed to swell and shrink, as if, suspended from a line, it was moistening itself by dipping into the still waters of the night.

A man played the guitar and sang a sorrowful song in a clear voice. It had a tearful accent, a longing for love and glory. The lower strings moaned, sighed with desire, while the lead strings hopelessly lamented an injustice.

When the phonograph stopped, the four cutthroats looked at one another. They sighed.

One of them took off, sobbing into his poncho. Another bit his lip. The oldest looked down at the barren ground, where his shadow served as his seat, and, after thinking hard, he said:

"We bad."

And the thieves of things and of lives cried, like children from an alien planet.

Translated from the Spanish by Thomas Christensen

Robert Olen Butler

RELIC

You may be surprised to learn that a man from Vietnam owns one of John Lennon's shoes. Not only one of John Lennon's shoes. One shoe that he was wearing when he was shot to death in front of the Dakota apartment building. That man is me, and I have money, of course, to buy this thing. I was a very wealthy man in my former country, before the spineless poor threw down their guns and let the communists take over. Something comes into your head as I speak: this is a hard man, a man of no caring, how can he speak of the "spineless poor." I do not mean to say that these people are poor because they are cowards. I am saying that being poor can take away a man's courage. For those who are poor, being beaten down, robbed of rights, repressed under the worst possible form of tyranny is not enough worse than just being poor. Why should they risk the pain and the maiming and the death for so little benefit? If I was a poor man, I too would be spineless.

But I had wealth in Vietnam and that gave me courage enough even to sail away on the South China Sea, sail away from all those things I owned and come to a foreign country and start again with nothing. That is what I did. I came at last to New Orleans, Louisiana, and because I was once from North Vietnam and was Catholic, I ended up among my own people far east in Orleans Parish, in a community called Versailles, named after an apartment complex they put us in as refugees. I lived in such a place for a time. The ceilings were hardly eight feet high and there was no veranda, nowhere even to hang a wind chime. The emptiness of the rooms threatened to cast me down, take my courage. In Saigon, I owned many wonderful things: furniture of teak, inlaid with scenes made of tiles of ivory and pearl, showing how the Trung sisters threw out the Chinese from our country in the year 40 A.D.; a part of an oracle bone from the earliest times of my country, the bone of some animal killed by ritual and carved with the future in Chinese characters; a dagger with a stag's antler handle in bronze. You might think that things like this should have protected me from what happened. There is much power in objects. My church teaches that clearly. A fragment of bone from a saint's body, a bit of skin, a lock of hair, all of these things have great power to do miracles, to cure, to heal.

But you see, though the Trung sisters threw the Chinese out, just one year later the Chinese returned and the Trung sisters had to retreat, and finally, in the year 43, they threw themselves into a river and drowned. And the oracle stone, though I did not know exactly what it said, probably dealt with events long past or maybe even foresaw this very world where I have ended up. And the dagger looked ceremonial and I'm sure was never drawn in anger. It would have been better if I had owned the tiniest fragment of some saint's body, but the church does not sell such things.

And here I sit, at the desk in the study in my house. I am growing rich once more and in the center of my desk sits this shoe. It is more like a little boot, coming up to the ankle and having no laces but a loop of leather at the back where John Lennon's forefinger went through to pull the shoe onto his foot, even that morning which was his last morning on this earth. Something comes into your head when I tell you this. It is my talent in making wealth to know what others are thinking. You wonder how I should come to have this shoe, how I know it is really what I say it is. I cannot give away the names of those who I dealt with, but I can tell you this much. I am a special collector of things. A man in New York who sells to me asked if I was interested in something unusual. When he told me about this shoe, I had the same response—how can I know for sure? Well, I met the man who provided the shoe, and I have photographs and even a newspaper article that identifies him as a very close associate of John Lennon. He says that certain items were very painful for the family, so they were disposed of and he was in possession of them and he knew that some people would appreciate them very much. He too is a Catholic. The other shoe was already gone, which is unfortunate, but this shoe was still available, and I paid much money for it.

Of course, I have made much money in my new country. It is a gift I have, and America is the land of opportunity. I started in paper lanterns and fire crackers and *cay neu*, the New Year poles. I sold these at the time of Tet, our Vietnam New Year celebration, when the refugees wanted to think about home. I also sold them sandwiches and drinks and later I opened a restaurant and then a parlor with many video games. Versailles already has a pool hall, run by another good businessman, but I have video games in my place and the young men love these games, fighting alien spaceships and wizards and kung-fu villains with much greater skill than their fathers fought the communists. And I am now doing other things, bigger things, mostly in the shrimp industry. In ten years people from Vietnam will be the only shrimp fishermen in the Gulf of Mexico. I do not need an oracle bone to tell you this for sure. And when this is so, I will be making even more money.

I may even be able to break free of Versailles. I sit at my desk and I look beyond John Lennon's shoe, through the window, and what do I see? My house, unlike the others on this street, has two stories. I am on the second story at the back and outside is my carefully trimmed yard, the lush St. Augustine grass faintly tinted with blue, and there is my brick barbecue pit and my setting of cypress lawn furniture. But beyond is the bayou that runs through Versailles and my house is built at an angle on an acre and a half and I can see all the other backyards set side by side for the quarter mile to the place where the lagoon opens up and the Versailles apartments stand. All the backyards of these houses— all of them—are plowed and planted as if this was some provincial village in Vietnam. Such things are not done in America. In America a vegetable garden is a hobby. Here in Versailles the people of Vietnam are cultivating their backyards as a way of life. And behind the yards is a path and beyond the path is the border of city land along the bayou and on this land the people of Vietnam have planted a community garden stretching down to the lagoon and even now I can see a scattering of conical straw hats there, the women crouched flat-footed and working the garden, and I expect any moment to see a boy riding a water buffalo down the path or perhaps a sampan gliding along the bayou, heading for the South China Sea. Do you understand me? I am living in the past.

I have enough money to leave Versailles and become the American that I must be. But I have found that it isn't so simple. Something is missing. I know I am wrong when I say that still more money, from shrimp or from whatever else, will finally free me from the past. Perhaps the problem is that my businesses are all connected to the Vietnam community here. There was no way around that when I started. And perhaps it's true that I should find some American business to invest in. But there is nothing to keep me in this place even if my money is made here. I do not work the cash registers in my businesses.

Perhaps it is the absence of my family. But this is something they chose for themselves. My wife was a simple woman and she would not leave her parents and she feared America greatly. The children came from her body. They belong with her, and she felt she belonged in Vietnam. My only regret is that I have nothing of hers to touch, not a lock of hair or a ring or even a scarf—she had so many beautiful scarves, some of which she wore around her waist. But if my family had come with me, would they not in fact be a further difficulty in my becoming American? As it is, I have only myself to consider in this problem and that should make things simpler.

But there are certain matters in life that a man is not able to control on his own. My religion teaches this clearly. For a rich man, for a man with the gift to become rich even a second time, this is a truth that is sometimes difficult to see. But he should realize that he is human and dependent on forces beyond himself and he should look to the opportunity that his wealth can give him.

I do not even know John Lennon's music very well. I have heard it and it is very nice, but in Vietnam I always preferred the popular singers in my own language, and in America I like the music they call easy-listening, though sometimes a favorite tune I will hear from the Living Strings or Mantovani turns out to be a song of John Lennon. It is of no matter to a man like John Lennon that I did not know his music well before I possessed his shoe. The significance of this object is the same. He is a very important figure. This is common knowledge. He wrote many songs that affected the lives of people in America and he sang about love and peace and then he died on the streets of New York as a martyr.

I touch his shoe. The leather is smooth and is the color of teakwood and my forefinger glides along the instep to the toe, where there is a jagged scrape. I lift my finger and put it on the spot where the scrape begins, at the point of the toe, and I trace the gash, follow the fuzzy track of the exposed underside of the leather. All along it I feel a faint grinding inside me, as if this is a wound in flesh that I touch. John Lennon's wound. I understand this scrape on the shoe. John Lennon fell and his leg pushed out on the pavement as he died. This is the stigmata of the shoe, the sign of his martyrdom.

With one hand I cup the shoe at its back and slide my other hand under the toe and I lift and the shoe always surprises me at its lightness, just as one who has moments before died a martyr's death might be surprised at the lightness of his own soul. I angle the shoe toward the light from my window and I look inside. I see the words Saville Row on the lining, but that is all. There is no size recorded here and I imagine that this shoe was made special for John Lennon, that they carefully measured his foot and this is its purest image in the softest leather. I am very quiet inside but there is this great pressure in my chest, coming from something I cannot identify as myself. This is because of what I will now do.

I wait until I can draw an adequate breath. Then I turn in my chair and gently lower the shoe to the floor and I place it before my bare right foot. I make the sign of the cross and slip my foot into John Lennon's shoe, sliding my forefinger into the loop at the back and pulling gently, just as John Lennon did on the day he joined the angels. The lining is made of something as soft as silk and there is a chill from it.

I stand up before my desk and the shoe is large for me, but that's as it should be. I take one step and then another and I am in the center of my room and I stand there and my heart is very full and I wait for what I pray will one day be mine, a feeling about what has happened to me that I cannot even imagine until I actually feel it. I have asked the man in New York to look for another of John Lennon's shoes, a left shoe. Even if it is from some other pair, I want to own just one more shoe. Then I will put both of John Lennon's shoes on my feet and I will go out into the street and I will walk as far as I need to go to find the place where I belong.

Andrei Codrescu

A BAR IN BROOKLYN

My search for anonymity took me all the way to Brooklyn. I saw a Happy Hour sign in the window of a teeming watering hole and went in. I took the only stool in the sea of suits and imagined myself to be a slim sloop maneuvering the straits between the bulky tankers in the Gulf of Aqaba. A bubbling office siren to my right was emptying the contents of a coconut shell into her hold through a pink straw. But at my left—I had to do a double take. At my left was a priest.

His left hand, next to me, was planted on the bar at the elbow and a smoking cigarette bloomed from its fingers. Next to his other hand, which lay limply and ecclesiastically (as in "a holy hand") on the bar, was a Manhattan in a tall glass. The cigarette hand had a ring on the matrimonial finger. His fingernails were rosy and well clipped.

I ordered another (it was two drinks for the price of one) in order to steel myself for conversation with the man of the cloth. But as I involved myself in ordering, another floozie, born no doubt from the ground oyster shells that littered the floor of the establishment, took the father on. I say another floozie because when I search for anonymity _I'm_ a floozie.

She was a chestnut-haired, ruby-lipsticked nymph with a bottle of Bud in her hand. The business suit gave in to all kind of topography.

"Taking refuge from the sanctuary?" was what I had planned to ask him.

"Seeking asylum from the eternal verities?" was what she asked him.

That wasn't bad. And then she said: "I don't mean to impose," And that *was* bad. Quite plainly, she was imposing.

The priest was young. Forty at most, blond, pale, handsome and sensual, if not downright corrupt around the mouth.

"Not at all," he said. "The thing is, God is fairly indulgent. He's forgiven people for more than a Manhattan."

"And cigarettes?" the floozie asked.

It's exactly what *I* would have said. Maybe floozies are generic. I looked a little closer at my competition. Her sneer reminded me of one similar in a pic of myself, taken at Ocean City, Maryland, when I was fifteen and had just lost my cherry.

"That's a sin, I admit," the father said sadly. "Tried to kick it several times but every time it gains on me again. I wake up at night and see a little glowing tip inches from my face, tempting me." He half-closed his pale, weary lids in the likeness of a suffering man.

"The fathers of the desert should've had it so hard," laughed the hussy.

Father opened one eye, then the other, and switched gears. His voice took on the upper edge of the pulpit basso. "And you? Have you no vices, friend? Are you not stereotyping me in your mind, right now, quicker than I can dissuade you?"

"I try not to," she said, allowing a kind of velveteen chill into her voice. I felt it, and people must have felt it three stools away, because there was suddenly that silent bubble in the place, that sometimes opens abruptly in a noisy room and everybody can hear clearly the last thing said. Everybody looked at the priest, and then at the girl, and the understanding that surpasses all knowing gripped everyone, and then the noise resumed.

I was most intrigued by her at this point. I took her proportions mentally, using my palms to measure her in my mind from her moderately high high-heels to the part in her hair. She was about my height, and built similarly if one allowed for exaggerations and costume differences. It was a little spooky, and I decided to play avant-echo, to see if we did resemble each other all that much. I decided to say quickly to myself whatever seemed appropriate, before she made her replies.

The father, embarrassed by the silence but now relieved by the noise, and on his second Manhattan as well, said, "Any man's reputation can be ruined here, leave alone that of a servant of the Lord."

"Let's get back to your sins," I said to myself.

"We left off at the glowing tip," said she.

"Now, now," teased the priest, "Let's not get carried away. I'm a man, I have feelings."

"What kind of feelings?"

"What kind of feelings?"

I shifted uncomfortably. I said: "Jinx. You owe me a Coke."

"What?" said the floozie.

"Nothing," I mumbled. "Just thinking."

"Seriously though," she said to him. "Don't you find any contradiction between this bar and your duties?"

That was quick, I hadn't had time to get in an avant-echo.

"Not to delve too deeply, dear, but God is bigger than His contradictions. He really does forgive. He may in fact preside equally over picket-fences and tanks, over His Left and His Right, if the truth were known."

"Thanks," I said, because I was his left.

"I'm Episcopalian," he continued, "but in the Catholic Church God is divided between the rich and the poor, and between men and women. The clergy, the theologians, the wealthy prefer Jesus, while the poor and women and most of South America worship the Virgin of Perpetual Sorrow. The strong wield theology like a nightstick, the poor yield their tears like little bombs of grief. In any case, it's bound to end badly."

The father stopped short. Emotion had crept into his voice about halfway through this speech, and he'd surprised himself. I don't think he meant to say all that. He flushed and a number of freckles appeared like a strange constellation beneath the pale skin.

"That's some kind of revolutionary Manichaeism," I said to myself.

"You sound like a leftwing Nicaraguan," said she.

Now that was definitely out of her league. She just wasn't dressed the part for those words. Where would a lipsticked bimbo working in an office in Lower Slobovia get that kind of quick grasp? I looked closely at her, and as I looked I thought that I discerned dark lines under her eyes, barely covered by makeup. Her hands were shaking a little too, and on the wrist of one of them, just under the flowered sleeve of her blouse was a black mark. It could have been a speck of dirt or it could have been the outermost edge of a tattoo that began on one of her breasts and went down her arm to end just below the sleeve.

"And I didn't mean to upset you," she was saying.

Her bluster turned quickly into an apology. I was beginning to lose interest, and was just turning toward my right where, for the past few moments I had become aware of a massive bulk of horny meat, when I saw the father reach under his tunic.

From under there he extracted a Pelikan fountainpen. He took off the top and the gold nib glinted for a moment in the light refracted through my whiskey. He pulled the half-soggy napkin between us quickly toward him and scribbled a few words in rapid cursive. He handed it to her.

She put it in her skirt pocket without reading it, and held the priest's gaze in her own. Between them, ionized particles and magnetized atoms rushed to form an intense field. It was blinding. My heart fluttered like a dove.

"OK, then," I said to myself, but she said nothing.

Michael Martone

BLUE HAIR

Mister Pepe lowers the clear plastic canopy over my head, flicks a few switches. The engines throb to life. My blue hair, woven into whistling rollers, a snug helmet, bristles with bobby pins. The women on either side of me thumb through their magazines, but I am flying, flying over the checkerboard of friendly fields. The leafy woods below look like mats of hair on a linoleum floor. The engines roar. My wing men tuck in beside me, our staggered flight piecing together the formation of the whole bomb group. Now the contrails peel off our leading edges. We bank together, coming to the heading that will take us back to the Ruhr. The sky, severely clear. Mister Pepe pokes a puffy cloud with his rattail comb. The starched white cliffs of Dover drape away below us. The flashing sliver of shears dart in and out. Nimble pursuit planes. Escorts with belly tanks nipping at our stragglers.

It was my hair, after all, that won the war.

Years ago, I knew the war was beginning to come to an end when the bombers left the plants with their aluminum skins unpainted. No need to camouflage the Boeings with that European forest green. It was only a matter of time.

Hair, too, a matter of time. My hair would grow back. I watched as wave after wave of silver Forts lumbered over, climbed above the sound, the pounding of their engines rattling the bones in my head, my bare neck chilled by the breeze blowing in off the water.

"The hair, it is dead," Mister Pepe whispered in my ear. This was later when I first came here. He rinsed my hair of color, the tarnished yellow coiling down the drain. He had me peer into a microscope in the backroom of his salon. Curling in behind me, he tweezed the knobs on the machine. I saw the shaft of the hair he had plucked from my scalp rip apart then reassemble, watched as my sight dove right through the splitting hair, my vision melting then turning hard.

"There," I said when it came into view, kinked and barked like a tree limb, blue as ice.

"Let me see," Mister Pepe said, wedging in to look. "It is damaged, no? The over-treated hair. The frazzled ends. You need my help, yes?"

And years before that the general had said, "You cannot tell anyone why you cut your hair." I was a young girl in Seattle. My parents stood in the doorway of our kitchen, hugging each other as they watched the WAC snip a few locks. She held them up to the light, then draped the strands across the outstretched arms of a warrant officer. He slid the hair through his fingers, stretched it out straight, and lowered it into a box like the one florists use for long-stemmed roses.

I was a blond, and my hair had never been crimped or permed or ironed. I never knotted it up into braids, only trimmed the fraying. It was naturally straight. I brushed it every night a hundred times and shampooed it with eggs and honey. When I slept, my hair nestled in behind me like another person slipping up against my back as I breathed, a heavy purring weight.

"It's a secret," the WAC had said, evening the ends. "Let me look at you." She held my chin in her palm, her fingers squeezing my cheeks. "You look all grown up now. Not a word until the war is over. Tell people it was too much bother, a waste of water washing it." She plucked one single strand that clung to my sleeve as if she were pulling a stitch through me. She pulled until the other end swung free, and then she placed it with the rest in the box.

And only last week with my hair all done up, I was flying. From the air, the Rockies looked flattened down. The way the shadows fell fooled me into thinking the peaks were really craters. Then the clouds piled up below, and the jet climbed to evade the weather. The Air Force had bought the seat next to me for the bombsight. It was in its crate sitting there.

The cadets in Colorado had given it to me. An honor guard had marched across a checkerboard courtyard. And now it is home on the coffee table with the magazines, a conversation piece. It looks as if it should be potted with some viny plant, its tendrils hooking on to the knobs and buttons. Flying home after the ceremony, I wrestled it out of the box and plunked it down on my lap. It had the heft of a head, a lover gazing up at me and me stroking his hair. I leaned forward, lowering myself to the cold metal. It smelled of oil and polish. I squinted through the lens as the plane bumped beneath me, riding the turbulence over the mountains. There was just enough light, a white dime-sized hole of light. I saw the cross-hairs, crisp and sharp, my dead hair, half a century old, sandwiched between the glass deep within the machine. Outside the clouds broke apart, and in the Great Basin, the lights of each tiny city lit up as the sunset fell on each of them.

And now I have been staring at this *Redbook* spread on my lap, and my eyes won't see the words. The dryers want to lull me to sleep. From up here, the letters on the page look like the ruined walls of buildings, remains of burned foundations, blocks of pitted houses, alleyways that lead to nowhere. I follow the footprints of bombs. I was reading about hair, about its history, about its chemistry, about how we know more about it now than ever before. Below me, the words explode as I read them. One after the other. There is the roar in my ears. I sit here waiting. Soon it will be my turn again.

Sylvia Watanabe

EMIKO'S GARDEN

Mr. Ah Sing, the Vegetable Man, told the Koyama Store Lady that Doc McAllister had finally gone *pupule* as they watched him come out his front gate at quarter to six on Saturday morning. Dressed in Day-Glo orange shorts, a kelly-green T-shirt, and a yellow baseball cap, McAllister paused on the sidewalk in front of his house to perform a few sets of calisthenics before setting off.

"That crazy old man is pushing fifty already," Mrs. Koyama observed. "Where's he going that he has to run?"

"Looks like he's aiming to reach a hundred." The Vegetable Man laughed and continued unloading his truck. His arms moved rhythmically, balancing the weight of the produce crates.

"Ai ya." Mrs. Koyama laughed too. "He'd get there faster if he stayed home and slept."

Emi McAllister turned in an embrace of half sleep toward the sound of her husband's footsteps disappearing up the road. Without opening her eyes, she drew the warm sheets close and pressed her face against his pillow. The morning smelled of lavender from the garden, and rain.

As she lay drowsing, she thought of how familiar she'd become with all the different views of McAllister's backside—driving off in the middle of the night to deliver babies, walking away toward waiting airplanes, retreating out the back door to avoid her anger, paddling after the perfect wave on the rolling back of the sea. He had taken up running two years before, on his forty-fifth birthday, when he'd decided that he was going to live forever.

McAllister's mother claimed that anyone who ran that much couldn't be up to any good; she was suspicious of an excess of anything, except orneriness, which she described as "character." Emi wasn't entirely inclined to disagree. But whether McAllister was in retreat or pursuit, she'd never decided; it all seemed part of his singular struggle to attain what he'd once called a kind of grace—moments lived so intensely that all of one's passion and skill were brought to bear on them.

McAllister splashed through rain puddles up the center of the village, past the giant mesquite on fire with bougainvillea. Past the Buddhist temple and the Paradise Mortuary. He snatched a glimpse of himself in the window of the Sakamoto Hardware; YOU'RE NOT GETTING OLDER, the cigarette ad behind his reflection said.

It was coming easily now. The sleep was gone from his limbs, and the old stiffness in his right calf had worked itself out. The salt air felt good on his face and neck. He remembered the girl. Her hands, her bold yes-look, her black hair spilling upon the sand. His blood sang. Five miles out. Five miles back. He'd run his fastest mile his last year in college during the Regionals. There'd been a lap and a half to go, and Joey O'Day was in first; he was in second. He kept pushing the pace, but O'Day wouldn't break. Then they were in the final stretch, and McAllister passed him. The crowd was yelling.

"Cockadoodledoo!" McAllister's mother shouted out her bedroom window. She'd been wakened by the crowing of the fighting cocks, as McAllister ran past the Filipino camp.

Emi got out of bed and hurried down the hall.

"Get up! Get up!" the old woman yelled.

"Hush, Mother," Emi said, coming into the room. "You'll wake the Tamayoshis." Mr. Tamayoshi, the Japanese schoolmaster, lived with his spinster daughter in the cottage next door. But Emi was too late. The lights were already blazing in their windows. She could hear bewildered voices calling to each other. "Are you all right?" "What's happened?"

"Mack! Mack mack mack!" Sammy Lee's ducks joined in from several backyards away.

The light was changing quickly now as the sun rose, burning away the rain. McAllister wiped his eyes with the back of his hand and struggled upward against the hill. His chest burned.

"Slowpoke!" He remembered how the girl had called from the raft, her hair flowing over her brown shoulders. She'd dangled her legs in the water, sending sparks of sunlight rippling across the surface. Just as he'd been about to reach her, she'd risen and plunged, laughing, into the sea.

McAllister crested the top of the hill and began to descend the other side. He resisted the flow at first, as he always did, until he was sure. "Come," she said, pulling him down. He yielded to the downward slope, and it was easy again. Her arms around him, her warmth like a gift.

When Emi got home from handing out apologies and rice cakes to the neighbors, she gave her mother-in-law a dish of mountain apples and settled her in a lawn chair within sight of the garden. It was nearing seven, but McAllister wouldn't be back for another half hour.

She walked down the gravel path between the herb bushes, stopping now and again to scoop up a handful of soil or to pinch off a leaf and turn it over in her hand. She noted the mint sprawling toward the marjoram beds and the new siege of caterpillars attacking the basil. She pulled out the carrots her mother-in-law had planted under the allspice, the tomatoes in the potted laurel, the cucumbers among the sage. "Why don't you grow some real vegetables?" the old woman always chided her.

Emi stopped to weed under the lavender. The herb breathed its scent into the air, reminding her of photographs in gilded frames and camphorwood trunks filled with hand-made lace, like she'd seen at the Parmeter Estate where she worked on the housekeeping staff years before. She dug deeper, and the fragrance rose from the damp ground and clung to her hands, her skin, her clothes. She went deeper still into the clayey subsoil where the roots of the plant reached tenaciously down. Under the mango tree, the old woman was singing. Emi thought of fresh-scrubbed young women in white linen dresses. She thought of the girl. . . .

. . . It had just been one of those things, McAllister decided all over again, as he turned onto the coast road leading back to the village. He smiled. A sense of well-being spread through him. Two miles to go. Underfoot, the puddles were beginning to evaporate, and the road felt familiar and sure. The sky was luminous with sun. . . .

. . . as it had been that morning, when Emi had driven his mother to the new shopping center across the bay. On their way through the mall, they'd passed a young Filipino evan-

168

gelist with pomaded hair and a green and orange plaid jacket, shouting in the middle of the plaza. "Brothers and sisters, He is waiting with open arms!" His shouts echoed off the concrete walls. Emi had turned to hush her mother-in-law, who was beginning to mutter about people making spectacles of themselves in public places, when she glimpsed McAllister in the crowd.

"Hey, Doc!" Freddy Woo called from across the road. He was polishing his powder-blue Cadillac out on the parking strip in front of his house.

McAllister slowed and came over. He asked, "How's it going—the back okay?"

"Not bad. But now I get headaches," Freddy answered. He glanced at Haru Hanabusa watering the chrysanthemums in her yard next door, then leaned over and whispered, "My neighbors give them to me."

The two men laughed, and McAllister started on his way again.

His back had been to her, but Emi recognized the tilt of his head, the attentive, listening stance. She knew if she'd looked a little harder she could not have missed the girl. She no longer heard the preacher's shouting; she'd felt only the huge, prying hunger to *see*.

McAllister had moved away from the crowd, still bent toward his companion. Was he putting his arm around her? Emi had moved to follow. Suddenly, she'd become aware of his mother tugging at her sleeve. "What are you looking at?" the old woman demanded. "What do you see?"

Emi closed her eyes and breathed in. "Nothing," she said, willing the trembling in her voice to stop. "Nothing." She repeated the word firmly, then turned and placed herself, deliberately, in the old woman's line of vision. "I was looking for that new sushi place Mrs. Koyama is always talking about."

"But I saw you looking *at* something," her mother-in-law persisted.

"I think the restaurant's in that direction," Emi continued, without looking back. "They have all kinds of good things—yellowfin, squid, salmon roe . . ."

Her mother-in-law's face had lighted up, and she'd said, "I don't suppose they'd have some steak tartare?"

Now, McAllister's mother sang. Emi made one last thrust at the soil, then pulled. The lavender came out of the ground with a tearing sound. She laid down her trowel and went into the house to put on the coffee.

McAllister approached from the opposite direction than he'd set out. Already, the sun seemed too hot, and he was glad for the newly installed air conditioning in his office. He thought of hot coffee, slices of cold papaya, and biscuits melting with butter, then looked at his watch to make sure he had time to eat before getting to work.

When he arrived home, he greeted his mother, who was digging in the garden, then went around to the back of the house and called, "What's for breakfast?"

Emi was at the kitchen door, waiting. Her cotton frock had been bleached white in places by the sun and did not conceal the gentle sagging of her flesh beneath. As he climbed the steps toward her, he could smell the lavender on her skin.

"You running fool," she said, but her voice was soft. "Hurry and change out of those wet things before you catch your death of cold."

Fernando Sorrentino

THE VISITATION

When I was twenty-three, I was training as a teacher of Spanish language and literature. Very early one morning at the beginning of spring I was studying in my room in our fifth-floor flat in the only apartment building on the block.

Feeling just a bit lazy, every now and again I let my eyes stray beyond the window. I could see the street and, on the opposite side, old don Cesáreo's well-kept garden. His house stood on the corner of a site that formed an irregular pentagon.

Next to don Cesáreo's was a beautiful house belonging to the Bernasconis, a wonderful family who were always doing good and kindly things. They had three daughters, and I was in love with Adriana, the eldest. That was why from time to time I glanced at the opposite side of the street—more out of a sentimental habit than because I expected to see her at such an early hour.

As usual, don Cesáreo was tending and watering his beloved garden, which was divided from the street by a low iron fence and three stone steps.

The street was so deserted that my attention was forcibly

drawn to a man who appeared on the next block, heading our way on the same side as the houses of don Cesáreo and the Bernasconis. How could I help but notice this man? He was a beggar or a tramp, a scarecrow draped in shreds and patches.

Bearded and thin, he wore a battered yellowish straw hat, and, despite the heat, was wrapped in a bedraggled greyish overcoat. He was carrying a huge, filthy bag, and I assumed it held the small coins and scraps of food he managed to beg.

I couldn't take my eyes off him. The tramp stopped in front of don Cesáreo's house and asked him something over the fence. Don Cesáreo was a bad-tempered old codger. Without replying, he waved the beggar away. But the beggar, in a voice too low for me to hear, seemed insistent. Then I distinctly heard don Cesáreo shout out, "Clear off once and for all and stop bothering me."

The tramp, however, kept on, and even went up the three steps and pushed open the iron gate a few inches. At this point, losing the last shred of his small supply of patience, don Cesáreo gave the man a shove. Slipping, the beggar grabbed at the fence but missed it and fell to the ground. In that instant, his legs flew up in the air, and I heard the sharp crack of his skull striking the wet step.

Don Cesáreo ran on to the pavement, leaned over the beggar, and felt his chest. Then, in a fright, he took the body by the feet and dragged it to the kerb. After that he went into his house and closed the door, convinced there had been no witnesses to his accidental crime.

Only I had seen it. Soon a man came along and stopped by the dead beggar. Then more and more people gathered, and at last the police came. Putting the tramp in an ambulance, they took him away.

That was it; the matter was never spoken of again.

For my part, I took care not to say a word. Maybe I was wrong, but why should I tell on an old man who had never done me any harm? After all, he hadn't intended to kill the tramp, and it didn't seem right to me that a court case should embitter the last years of don Cesáreo's life. The best thing, I thought, was to leave him alone with his conscience.

Little by little I began to forget the episode, but every time I saw don Cesáreo it felt strange to realize that he was unaware that I was the only person in the world who knew his terrible secret. From then on, for some reason I avoided him and never dared speak to him again.

When I was twenty-six, I was working as a teacher of Spanish language and literature. Adriana Bernasconi had married not me but someone else who may not have loved and deserved her as much as I.

At the time, Adriana, who was pregnant, was very nearly due. She still lived in the same house, and every day she grew more beautiful. Very early one oppressive summer morning I found myself teaching a special class in grammar to some secondary-school children who were preparing for their exams and, as usual, from time to time I cast a rather melancholy glance across the road.

All at once my heart literally did a flip-flop, and I thought I was seeing things.

From exactly the same direction as four years before came the tramp don Cesáreo had killed—the same ragged clothes, the greyish overcoat, the battered straw hat, the filthy bag.

Forgetting my pupils, I rushed to the window. The tramp had begun to slow his step, as if he had reached his destination.

He's come back to life, I thought, and he's going to take revenge on don Cesáreo.

But the beggar passed the old man's gate and walked on.

Stopping at Adriana Bernasconi's front door, he turned the knob and went inside.

"I'll be back in a moment," I told my students and, half out of my mind with anxiety, I went down in the lift, dashed across the street, and burst into Adriana's house.

"Hello!" her mother said, standing by the door as if about to go out. "What a surprise to see you here!"

She had never looked on me in anything but a kindly way. She embraced and kissed me, and I did not quite understand what was going on. Then it dawned on me that Adriana had just become a mother and that they were all beside themselves with excitement. What else could I do but shake hands with my victorious rival?

I did not know how to put it to him, and I wondered whether it might not be better to keep quiet. Then I hit on a compromise. Casually I said, "As a matter of fact, I let myself in without ringing the bell because I thought I saw a tramp come in with a big dirty bag and I was afraid he meant to rob you."

They all gaped at me. What tramp? What bag? Robbery? They had been in the living room the whole time and had no idea what I was talking about.

"I must have made a mistake," I said.

Then they invited me into the room where Adriana and her baby were. I never know what to say on these occasions. I congratulated her, I kissed her, I admired the baby, and I asked what they were going to name him. Gustavo, I was told, after his father; I would have preferred Fernando but I said nothing.

Back home I thought, That was the tramp old don Cesáreo killed, I'm sure of it. It's not revenge he's come back for but to be reborn as Adriana's son.

Two or three days later, however, this hypothesis struck me as ridiculous, and I put it out of my mind.

And would have forgotten it forever had something not come up ten years later that brought it all back.

Having grown older and feeling less and less in control of things, I tried to focus my attention on a book I was reading beside the window, while letting my glance stray.

Gustavo, Adriana's son, was playing on the roof terrace of their house. Surely, at his age, the game he was playing was rather infantile, and I felt that the boy had inherited his father's scant intelligence and that, had he been my son, he would certainly have found a less foolish way of amusing himself.

He had placed a line of empty tin cans on the parapet and was trying to knock them off by throwing stones at them from a distance of ten or twelve feet. Of course, nearly all the pebbles were falling down into don Cesáreo's garden next door. I could see that the old man, who wasn't there just then, would work himself into a fit the moment he found that some of his flowers had been damaged.

At that very instant, don Cesáreo came out into the garden. He was, in point of fact, extremely old and he shuffled along putting one foot very carefully in front of the other. Slowly, timidly, he made his way to the garden gate and prepared to go down the three steps to the pavement.

At the same time, Gustavo—who couldn't see the old man—at last managed to hit one of the tin cans, which, bouncing off two or three ledges as it went, fell with a clatter into don Cesáreo's garden. Startled, don Cesáreo, who was half-way down the steps, made a sudden movement, slipped head over heels, and cracked his skull against the lowest step.

I took all this in, but the boy had not seen the old man nor had the old man seen the boy. For some reason, at that point Gustavo left the terrace. In a matter of seconds, a crowd of people surrounded don Cesáreo's body; an accidental fall, obviously, had been the cause of his death.

The next day I got up very early and immediately stationed myself at the window. In the pentagonal house, don Cesáreo's wake was in full swing. On the pavement out in front, a small knot of people stood smoking and talking.

A moment later, in disgust and dismay, they drew aside when a beggar came out of Adriana Bernasconi's house, again dressed in rags, overcoat, straw hat, and carrying a bag. He made his way through the circle of bystanders and slowly vanished into the distance the same way he had come from twice before.

At midday, sadly but with no surprise, I learned that Gustavo's bed had been found empty that morning. The whole Bernasconi family launched a forlorn search, which, to this day, they continue in obstinate hope. I never had the courage to tell them to call it off.

Translated from the Spanish by
Norman Thomas diGiovanni and Susan Ashe

Lynn Grossman

CARTOGRAPHY

The streets in Paradise-by-the-Sea were all named flower names, sweet-smelling places-for-mothers-to-live names like Magnolia Lane, Honeysuckle Boulevard, Lilac Place, Gardenia Street. Mother used to live on Gladiola Avenue in a house that smelled the way mothers' houses smelled then—face powder and grocery bags and mothballs and brewed coffee gone too long in the brewing.

Daughter is driving mother to where mother lives now.

Mother smells.

The smell of mother floats over from the backseat where mother is sitting. Daughter is certain mother's smell is being re-odored around the car again and again by the air conditioner, going smell-in through the low vents, around and into whatever is behind the dashboard and coming out the front vents cold and mixed up with the smells of the engine.

Daughter cracks the no-draft for fresh freeway air and looks in the rearview mirror at mother's face facing out the side window. "Paradise-by-the-Sea," daughter says to mother and daughter points to the exit they are passing. Mother continues to look out the side window, but daughter is not sure if mother sees the exit for Paradise-by-the-Sea.

Paradise-by-the-Sea is not on the sea or near the sea, the sea being ten miles to the west, and that being only an inlet. Paradise is more by the freeway.

Mother's house had a screened-in porch where mother used to sit at night if the wind was up, in the hope of smelling a sea breeze. Daughter would sometimes sit with mother on a wind-up night. "Smell the sea," mother would say to daughter. Daughter would not tell mother that what daughter smelled smelled to daughter like the rubbery smell of cars on a freeway going too fast.

When mother lived in Paradise-by-the-Sea, mother used to ride in the front seat. There was a time before that when mother used to be the driver.

Mother would drive daughter to the real sea past the inlet. Mother would pick up shells from the beach which mother said were dead but smelled the way they did to make you think something was still alive in them. Mother would hold the shells under the bubbling edge of the water and let the water go around and into the shells and when the shells were dripping with the wet sea, mother would hold the shells up to daughter's nose so that daughter would smell the sea smell.

Mother used to say a thing that is wet smells more of what it is than when it is dry.

At the real sea, mother smelled of sun and of seaweed and of coconut lotion she would drip on her body in white curlicues, and she would rub the lotion in and in until the white and the smell went into her body, and then mother would rub what was left on her hands of the coconut smell into daughter's back. Mother would put a sea-cracked rubber cap over her hair and go deep into the water to the place where mother told daughter the sea had no more smell, but tasted, instead.

Daughter thinks mother's smell today is a wet smell, not a dry smell. Daughter opens the front windows so that the air rushing into the car warm and oily and thick will be strong enough to carry the mother smell away with it.

Daughter off-ramps at the next exit, which is not the exit where mother lives now. Daughter opens all of the windows all the way down and she drives west to the real sea past the inlet.

In the rearview mirror, daughter can see mother's hair blowing away and off of mother's face, and daughter can see the shape of mother's skull beneath her face.

When daughter gets to the real sea, daughter drives the car off of the road and into the sand. Daughter smells the sea breeze coming into the car through all of the windows all at once, re-odoring around and around, bringing with it the smell of the sun and the smell of the seaweed and the rotten rowboat wooden smell of the almost wreck of a hull near where daughter has stopped in the sand.

Daughter gets out of the car and pulls the boat across the sand to the edge of the sea where the sand is not sandy, but dark and wet.

Daughter takes mother out of the car and helps mother onto the sand. Mother takes slow steps beside daughter, and the heels of mother's shoes sink down deep into the sand until mother cannot walk forward anymore, and mother cannot walk backward to where she has been.

Daughter lifts mother up high in her arms. Mother seems to daughter to be heavier than a child, but not to be as heavy as what daughter thinks a mother ought to be.

Daughter can smell mother in her arms and the mother smell surrounds daughter like a hug from mother, then the mother smell mixes with the smell of the world outside of the car.

Daughter carries mother to the boat at the edge of the

sea. Daughter looks out far to the deep place in the sea where mother used to say things did not smell anymore, not when you were out there that deep.

Daughter holds mother so that daughter can smell more of the mother smell, and what daughter smells when mother is close to her this way is the warm and deep mother smell mixed with the smell of perspiration coming strongly from daughter's own body.

Daughter carries mother into the rowboat and turns mother in her arms so that mother can see the edge of the sea coming up around the boat.

"Paradise," daughter says to mother. "Smell the sea."

Sherman Alexie

THE FUN HOUSE

In the trailer by Tshimikain Creek where my cousins and I used to go crazy in the mud, my aunt waited. She sewed to pass the time, made beautiful buckskin outfits that no one could afford, and once she made a full-length beaded dress that was too heavy for anyone to wear.

"It's just like the sword in the stone," she said. "When a woman comes along who can carry the weight of this dress on her back, then we'll have found the one who will save us all."

One morning she sewed while her son and husband watched television. It was so quiet that when her son released a tremendous fart, a mouse, startled from his hiding place beneath my aunt's sewing chair, ran straight up her pant leg.

She pulled her body into the air, reached down her pants, unbuttoned them, tried to pull them off, but they stuck around the hips.

"Jesus, Jesus," she cried while her husband and son rolled with laughter on the floor.

"Get it out, get it out," she yelled some more while her husband ran over and smacked her legs in an effort to smash the mouse dead.

"Not that way," she cried again and again.

All the noise and laughter and tears frightened the mouse even more, and he ran down my aunt's pant leg, out the door and into the fields.

In the aftermath, my aunt hiked her pants back up and cursed her son and husband.

"Why didn't you help me?" she asked.

Her son couldn't stop laughing.

"I bet when that mouse ran up your pant leg, he was thinking, *What in the hell kind of mousetraps do they got now?*" her husband said.

"Yeah," her son agreed. "When he got up there, he probably said to himself, *That's the ugliest mousetrap I've ever seen!*"

"Stop it, you two," she yelled. "Haven't you got any sense left?"

"Calm down," my uncle said. "We're only teasing you."

"You're just a couple of ungrateful shits," my aunt said. "Where would you be if I didn't cook, if my fry bread didn't fill your stomachs every damn night?"

"Momma," her son said. "I didn't mean it."

"Yeah," she said. "And I didn't mean to give birth to you. Look at you. Thirty years old and no job except getting drunk. What good are you?"

"That's enough," her husband yelled.

"It's never enough," my aunt said and walked outside, stood in the sun, and searched the sky for predators of any variety. She hoped some falcon or owl would find the mouse and she hoped some pterodactyl would grab her husband and son.

Bird feed, she thought. *They'd make good bird feed.*

In the dark my aunt and her husband were dancing. Thirty years ago and they two-stepped in an Indian cowboy bar. So many Indians in one place and it was beautiful then. All they needed to survive was the drive home after closing time.

"Hey, Nezzy," a voice cried out to my aunt. "You still stepping on toes?"

My aunt smiled and laughed. She was a beautiful dancer, had given lessons at the Arthur Murray Dance Studio to pay her way through community college. She had also danced topless in a Seattle bar to put food in her child's stomach.

There are all kinds of dancing.

"Do you love me?" my aunt asked her husband.

He smiled. He held her closer, tighter. They kept dancing.

After closing time, they drove home on the back roads.

"Be careful," my aunt told her husband. "You drank too much tonight."

He smiled. He put his foot to the fire wall and the pickup staggered down the dirt road, went on two wheels on a sharp corner, flipped, and slid into the ditch.

My aunt crawled out of the wreck, face full of blood, and sat on the roadside. Her husband had been thrown out of the pickup and lay completely still in the middle of the road.

"Dead? Knocked out? Passed out?" my aunt asked herself.

After a while, another car arrived and stopped. They wrapped an old shirt around my aunt's head and loaded her husband into the backseat.

"Is he dead?" my aunt asked.

"Nah, he'll be all right."

They drove that way to the tribal hospital. My aunt bled into the shirt; her husband slept through his slight concussion. They kept him overnight for observation, and my aunt slept on a cot beside his bed. She left the television on with the volume turned off.

At sunrise my aunt shook her husband awake.

"What?" he asked, completely surprised. "Where am I?"

"In the hospital."

"Again?"

"Yeah, again."

Thirty years later and they still hadn't paid the bill for services rendered.

My aunt walked down her dirt road until she was dizzy. She walked until she stood on the bank of Tshimikain Creek. The water was brown, smelled a little of dead animal and uranium. My cousins and I dove into these waters years ago to pull colored stones from the muddy bottom and collect them in piles beside the creek. My aunt stood beside one of those ordinary monuments to childhood and smiled a little, cried a little.

"One dumb mouse tears apart the whole damn house," she said. Then she stripped off her clothes, kept her shoes on for safety, and dove naked into the creek. She splashed around, screamed in joy as she waded through. She couldn't swim but the creek was shallow, only just past her hips. When she sat down the surface rested just below her chin, so whenever she moved she swallowed a mouthful of water.

"I'll probably get sick," she said and laughed just as her husband and son arrived at the creek, out of breath.

"What the hell are you doing?" her husband asked.

"Swimming."

"But you don't know how to swim."

"I do now."

"Get out of there before you drown," her husband said. "And get some clothes on."

"I'm not coming out until I want to," my aunt said, and she floated up on her back for the first time.

"You can't do that," her son yelled now. "What if somebody sees you?"

"I don't care," my aunt said. "They can all go to hell, and you two can drive the buses that get them there."

Her husband and son threw their hands up in surrender, walked away.

"And cook your own damn dinner," my aunt yelled at their backs.

She floated on the water like that for hours, until her skin wrinkled and her ears filled with water. She kept her eyes closed and could barely hear when her husband and son came back every so often to plead with her.

"One dumb mouse tore apart the whole damn house. One dumb mouse tore apart the whole damn house," she chanted at them, sang it like a nursery rhyme, like a reservation Mother Goose.

The delivery room was a madhouse, a fun house. The Indian Health Service doctor kept shouting at the nurses.

"Goddamn it," he yelled. "I've never done this before. You've got to help me."

My aunt was conscious, too far into delivery for drugs, and she was screaming a little bit louder than the doctor.

"Shit, shit, fuck," she yelled and grabbed onto the nurses, the doctors, kicked at her stirrups. "It hurts, it hurts, it hurts!"

Her son slid out of her then and nearly slipped through the doctor's hands. The doctor caught him by an ankle and held on tightly.

"It's a boy," he said. "Finally."

A nurse took the baby, held it upside down as she cleared his mouth, wiped his body almost clean. My aunt took her upside-down son with only one question: *Will he love to eat potatoes?*

While my aunt held her baby close to her chest, the doctor tied her tubes, with the permission slip my aunt signed because the hospital administrator lied and said it proved her Indian status for the BIA.

"What are you going to name it?" a nurse asked my aunt.

"Potatoes," she said. "Or maybe Albert."

When the sun went down and the night got too cold, my aunt finally surrendered the water of Tshimikain Creek, put clothes on her damp and tired body, and walked up her road toward home. She looked at the bright lights shining in the windows, listened to the dogs bark stupidly, and knew that things had to change.

She walked into the house, didn't say a word to her stunned husband and son, and pulled that heaviest of beaded dresses over her head. Her knees buckled and she almost fell from the weight; then she did fall.

"No," she said to her husband and son as they rose to help her.

She stood, weakly. But she had the strength to take the first step, then another quick one. She heard drums, she heard singing, she danced.

Dancing that way, she knew things were beginning to change.

Allen Hibbard

CROSSING TO ABBASSIYA

Mostafa Abd el-Salaam set out that morning, very pleased with himself. After all, he had been charged by his superiors with a special responsibility. The day before, his boss informed him a group of madmen were to be taken from the station at Imbaba, on the west side of the city of Cairo, to the central asylum at Abbassiya, on the other side of the city. He—Mostafa Abd el-Salaam—would drive the truckload of madmen across the city. It was a simple job, one which others no doubt would judge unimportant, but nonetheless Mostafa felt very proud.

The twelve men were there behind him. He could feel their weight in the truck as he accelerated. Even through the metal and glass partition separating him from them, he could hear their odd, repetitive chirpings. Rather like birds in the first days of spring, he thought. Perhaps they thought they were being taken somewhere to be released from their captivity. In fact, come to think of it, he didn't know what they'd been told. They had been in the truck when he arrived, and the station supervisor simply greeted him very warmly, asked how his family was, reminded him what he was to do, and wished him God's speed.

The traffic was heavy, as usual, at midmorning. The truck crawled across the 6th of October Bridge. Mostafa Abd el-Salaam could feel the heat rising. Sweat ran down his brow and he felt himself breathing with greater difficulty. What hope was there but to continue, placing his hope in God?

His mind wandered, directionless, from fragments of childhood memories, to the faces of those driving along, slowly, beside him, to little reminders to himself of things he had to do, to his family—two young boys, a baby girl, and his wife—back at their small apartment near Sayida Aisha. By the time he had gotten across the bridge and begun to head northeast toward Ramses Station, he had, in the heat and fantasia of revery, completely forgotten his mission. The men behind him, doubtless also affected by the heat, were silent, and Mostafa felt a wonderful kind of freedom.

As he was driving, he noted the landmarks along the way and thought of a certain cafe near Ataba where he would sometimes go and sit with his friends. He knew some of them would be there this morning. There was nothing else for them to do. They wanted to get out of their homes and this was where they went to meet and talk and smoke the hours away. Unconsciously Mostafa found himself turning off the main road and heading toward the cafe.

He double-parked the truck and explained to a few men sitting on chairs outside the building on the sidewalk that he would only be an hour or so and, if there was any trouble, he could be found at the cafe around the corner. They knew the place. In any case, he thought, it was a government truck and so the police weren't likely to bother it.

It was an hour and a half later, while he was talking with his friends, that Mostafa remembered what he was supposed to be doing that day. "Well, shouldn't you be going back to work?" one of the men joked, slapping him on his knee. "What are you doing over here anyway? We don't see you here very often this time of day." A look of amazement and horror came over Mostafa. He jumped up from his chair without explanation and ran out of the cafe. His friends looked at one another, shrugged, and chuckled.

The truck was where he had left it. One of the men with whom he had talked earlier was seated as he had been before. He had been there the whole time and never taken his eyes off the truck, he said, and everything was fine. "Thank you, thank you, a thousand thanks!" Mostafa said, greatly relieved. It was now twelve o'clock and very hot. He could always say the traffic had been very bad, so the trip had taken much longer than expected.

Mostafa was about to get into the cab and drive off, when it occurred to him he should check in on the nuts in the back. He went round to the rear of the truck. When he opened the door and looked inside he found it empty. At once he felt the weight of his body double and his mind frantically raced through dozens of horrifying scenarios. How could he explain it? It had, he knew, been his own fault, but he couldn't admit that.

He shut the door, composed himself, and turned again the man on the sidewalk. "You didn't notice anything strange while I was gone? I mean, you didn't see anyone ... ?"

"What? No. Are you missing something?" the old man replied. Perhaps he guessed the truck was carrying supplies of flour or sugar (which were much in demand in the city) and some had been stolen. "No. I didn't see anything," he insisted.

Mostafa Abd el-Salaam, on his side, didn't want to let anything out. So he said, *"Malesh,"* got into the cab, and drove off. What would he do now? Time wasn't a problem. He could say he had to stop for something to eat. Besides, nobody expected things to be done very quickly in Cairo. An idea, a plan, gradually began to form in his mind. All he had to do was deliver twelve crazy people. There was no list of names. What he had to do now, he thought to himself, was convince twelve people to get into his truck. That shouldn't be hard. If Cairo has nothing else, it at least has plenty of people. He even imagined many people had never ridden in a truck in their lives. Perhaps he could just park his truck near one of the popular districts of the city and ask if anyone would like to take a ride. The truck would fill up in no time.

By now he was heading toward an area of town where a lot of construction was going on. Sitting along the streets, their heads wrapped with scarves, their bodies covered with long brown *gallabiyyas*, shovels and picks lying beside them, were groups of poor villagers who had come to Cairo hoping for work.

Mostafa Abd el-Salaam pulled up his truck near a group of men, got out, and began to address them. His hands on his hips, he tried to act as authoritative as possible. "Do you want work?" he asked. Their eyes all lit up.

"Yes! Yes!" they cried, each voice competing with the others, rising and falling like the clamorous cackling of chickens.

"I need twelve good, strong men. I can give them work for as long as they want." He began to enjoy the role he was playing, particularly when he felt the eager desperation of the response. "You will have beds to sleep in and food to eat." With this, he knew he would be able to gain recruits. "I need just twelve today—perhaps more tomorrow. Who will go?"

He selected twelve of the most insane looking peasants (they all looked a bit crazy, he thought), promising the rest he would *in cha'allah* return for them the next day. He only had room for twelve in his truck. They would not, he told them, need their picks and shovels.

The men were still chirruping away excitedly when he pulled up to the gates of the mental hospital. "Ah, yes, we have been expecting you," the guard said, opening the iron gates. Once he got to the main building and his arrival had been announced, Mostafa Abd el-Salaam was greeted by the hospital administrator, who came out smiling and embraced him profusely, asking him how his family was and about the trip across town.

"Oh, very hot!" Mostafa replied. As he expected, the administrator seemed not to have noticed the long time it had taken him to cross the city. It was now two-thirty and he had left Imbaba at ten o'clock. "I stopped for lunch, then prayed, and the traffic was awful."

"Yes, yes. Praise be to God! The traffic is getting worse every day, isn't it? But you are here now and you have the men."

"Oh, yes, I have the men. They are all here. All twelve of them. And they're mad as hell. I've been listening to them scream and shout all across town. I thought at times I'd lose my head as well. I'm glad to give them over to you."

The administrator gave an order for the men to be taken from the truck into a nearby room where they would be processed. Mostafa watched the men, a little dumb-founded, as one by one they hopped out of the truck. They seemed to be taking in the new setting. They followed the orders and no one resisted. Mostafa tried as well to assess the reaction of the hospital staff as they led the men into the building. No one seemed to notice the difference.

"Well, it is getting late," Mostafa said to the chief administrator.

"Won't you have some tea?"

Mostafa agreed and they sat down together to talk of life, their jobs, their families, and the state of the country. During their conversation, they heard piercing shrieks and sounds of scuffling in the air.

"Ah, the new inmates!"

"Naturally they are resisting."

"But they seemed so docile when they got out. What did you do to them?"

"I told them I was going to give them work."

"Ah, that was very clever of you!"

And their burst of laughter rose, for a moment or two, above the shrieks and screams.

Mitch Berman

TO BE HORST

The man stood in the cafe's doorway staring openly and with no expectation of recompense at a girl who sat three paces away from him. His monochrome, leonine face, bracketed between curly hair and beard of that shade called red only because it is not what is usually called brown, was covered so contiguously with freckles that the places where flesh tones broke through were the real freckles. It was a face puzzled, stymied, suddenly decisive, wrongly decisive: a face full of error, of error simple and compound, error seen and missed, error mourned and error dreaded, error unerased. A single heavy Cyclopean eyebrow bore down on his eyes like a frown. He wore a collection of baggy, bulbous, but untorn plaids; he had a regular table in the window of the cafe where he would sit for hours, never reading. Nobody who worked there had ever seen him with anybody.

The girl, about twenty, raised to him a well-arranged and blank white face. The man pointed to his sternum and lofted his brow as high as it would go. Pushing against the thick brunt of shock, he began toward her in small slow steps, anxious not to disturb whatever delicate balance in the atmosphere made pretty girls look back at him today.

"Are you Horst?" she asked him.

"Horst?" He squeezed out the word on a long exhalation, an exhaustion: his chest caved, his shoulders folded in around it, and his clothes seemed to loosen as he shrank inside them. "No, I'm not Horst," he said, almost inaudibly. "But I'd like to be."

His hand fell away from his chest, as if it could no longer resist the pull of gravity; he broke at the waist and sagged into a chair. From there, ten feet away, he watched the girl steadily, his fingers spreading and contracting on the marble tabletop. Presently a man came in, introduced himself to the girl, and sat down with her.

Horst was a striking young man with dark brown hair, tanned olive skin and blue eyes. In or around the eyes was a weary ease that did not change when he saw the girl: he knew—approached her with the knowledge—that he could have her if he cared to. The eyes said *Hello, I am tired, Try to wake me up, I may be awakening, No, I am sorry, You tried, It is me, I cannot feel, I am a wanderer, Hello, I am tired, Try to wake me up.*

The red-haired man's eyes moved from the girl to Horst, and did not move from Horst. He was imagining what it might be like to be Horst. He could taste the drink that Horst drank, could see what Horst saw, breathe the air Horst breathed. He had forgotten entirely about the girl: she was merely a Horst-induced mirage; a manifestation, a byproduct, a proof of Horstness in a universe of Horstlessness; she was just one of many things that would happen to him in a life, the life ahead of him, of being Horst. Horst was the answer; the girl had been only the question. He stared inquisitively, to penetrate the mystery of being Horst; acquisitively, to wrench from Horst all of the Horstian secrets; he stared as if receiving an encrypted radio signal, as if this stare, so close by, could not possibly intrude upon the privacy of Horst, as if Horst, returning the stare, would look only into a mirror.

Horst into Horst equals Horst: something seemed to take hold of his nose, jerk it Horstward; something gently pinched the skin around his eyes into small weary crinkles. He held himself absolutely still as a sort of carbonation foamed up along the surface of the table and etched new whorls and eddies into his fingerprints. As his eyes changed, a smile stole into them. Soon now, very soon, the admirers would begin to come.

Judy Troy

TEN MILES WEST OF VENUS

After Marvelle Lyle's husband, Morgan, committed suicide—his body being found on an April evening in the willows that grew along Black Creek—Marvelle stopped going to church. Franklin Sanders, her minister at Venus United Methodist, drove out to her house on a Sunday afternoon in the middle of May to see if he could coax her back. Her house was ten miles west of Venus—seven miles on the highway and three on a two-lane road that cut through the open Kansas wheat fields and then wound back through the forest preserve. The woods at this time of year were sprinkled with white blooming pear trees.

Franklin had his radio tuned to Gussie Dell's weekly "Neighbor Talk" program. Gussie was a member of his congregation, and Franklin wanted to see what embarrassing thing she would choose to say today. The week before, she had told a story about her grandson, Norman, drawing a picture of Jesus wearing high heels. "I have respect for Norman's creativity," she had said. "I don't care if Norman puts Jesus in a garter belt."

Today, though, she was on the subject of her sister, whom
Franklin had visited in the hospital just the day before. "My
sister has cancer," Gussie said. "She may die or she may not.
My guess is she won't. I just wanted to say that publicly."

Franklin pulled into Marvelle's driveway and turned off
the radio too soon to hear whatever Gussie was going to say
next; he imagined it was something unfavorable about her
sister's husband, who, for years now, had been sitting outside
in his chicken shed, watching television. "One of these days
I'm going to dynamite him out of there," Gussie liked to
say. She was generally down on marriage, which Franklin
couldn't argue with—his own marriage being unhappy, and
that fact not a secret among his parishioners.

Franklin parked his new Ford Taurus between Marvelle's
old pickup and the ancient Jeep Morgan had driven. Hanging from the Jeep's rearview mirror were Morgan's military
dog tags. He'd been in the Vietnam War, though Franklin
had never known any details about it. Morgan Lyle had
never been forthcoming about himself, and the few times
Franklin had seen him at church, Morgan had spent the
length of the sermon and most of the service smoking outside. "You have to accept him as he is," Marvelle had once
told Franklin. "Otherwise, well, all I'm saying is he doesn't
mean anything by what he says and does."

Also in the driveway—just a big gravel clearing, really,
between the house and the garage where Morgan had had
his motorcycle repair shop—was the dusty van their son,
Curtis, drove. He was thirty-one and still living at home.
Franklin, who was sixty-three, could remember Curtis as the
blond-headed child who had once, in Sunday School,
climbed out of a window in order to avoid reciting the Lord's
Prayer. Now the grownup Curtis, in faded pants and no shirt,
his thinning hair pulled back into a ponytail, opened the

door before Franklin had a chance to knock. "Well, come on in, I guess," Curtis said. Behind him, Marvelle appeared in the kitchen doorway.

The house was built haphazardly into a hill, and was so shaded with oak and sweetgum trees that the inside—in spring and summer, anyway—was dark during the day. The only light in the room was a small lamp on a desk in the corner, shining down on iridescent feathers and other fly-tying materials. Curtis sat down at the desk and picked up a hook.

"I'll make coffee," Marvelle told Franklin, and he followed her into the kitchen, which was substantially brighter. An overhead light was on, and the walls were painted white. "I thought Sunday afternoons were when you visited the sick," Marvelle said.

"It was, but I do that on Saturdays now. I find other reasons to get out of the house on Sundays." Franklin sat at the kitchen table and watched her make coffee. She was a tall, muscular woman, and she'd lost weight since Morgan's death. Her jeans looked baggy on her; her red hair was longer than it used to be, and uncombed. "You could stand to eat more," Franklin told her.

"You men complain when we're fat and then worry when we're thin."

"When did I ever say you were fat?" Franklin said.

Marvelle turned toward him with the coffeepot in her hand. "You're right. You never did."

Franklin looked down at the table. This afternoon, with his mind on Morgan, and not on himself or his marriage, he'd managed to push aside the memory of an afternoon years ago, when he and Marvelle had found themselves kissing in the church kitchen. "Found themselves" was just how it had seemed to him. It was, like this day, a Sunday afternoon in spring; Marvelle and his wife and two other parishioners had been planting flowers along the front walk.

Marvelle had come into the kitchen for coffee just when he had. He wasn't so gray-haired then or so bottom-heavy, and they walked toward each other and kissed passionately, as if they had planned it for months.

"You've always been an attractive woman," he said quietly.

"Don't look so guilty. It was a long time ago." Marvelle sat down across from him as the coffee brewed. "The amazing thing is that it only happened once."

"No," Franklin said, "it's that I allowed it to happen at all."

"Where was God that day? Just not paying attention?" Marvelle asked.

"That was me not paying attention to God," Franklin told her.

Curtis had turned on the radio in the living room, and Franklin could faintly hear a woman singing. Louder was the sound of the coffee brewing. The kitchen table was next to a window that overlooked a sloping wooded hill and a deep ravine. These woods, too, Franklin noticed, had their share of flowering pear trees. "It looks like snow has fallen in a few select places," he said.

"Doesn't it? I saw two deer walking down there this morning. For a moment, I almost forgot about everything else."

Franklin looked at her face, which was suddenly both bright and sad.

"That's interesting," he said carefully, "because that's what church services do for me."

"Sure they do. Otherwise, you'd lose your place," Marvelle said.

"You don't realize something," Franklin told her. "I'd rather not be the one conducting them. I feel that more and more as I get older. I'd like to sit with the congregation and just partake."

"Would you? Well, I wouldn't. I wouldn't want to do either one." She got up and poured coffee into two mugs and handed one to Franklin. "How do you expect me to feel?" she asked him, standing next to the window. "Do you see God taking a hand in my life? There are people in that congregation who didn't want to see Morgan buried in their cemetery."

"You're talking about two or three people out of a hundred and twenty."

"I bet you felt that way yourself," Marvelle told him.

"You know me better than to think that," Franklin said.

Marvelle sat down and put her coffee on the table in front of her. "All right, I do. Just don't make me apologize."

"When could anybody make you do anything you didn't want to do?" Franklin said to her.

Franklin left late in the afternoon, saying goodbye to Curtis after admiring his fly-tying abilities. Marvelle accompanied him to his car, walking barefoot over the gravel. "You'll be walking over coals next," Franklin said, joking.

"Are you trying to sneak God back into the conversation?" Marvelle asked him. She had her hand on his car door as he got in, and she closed the door after him.

"I'm talking about the toughness of your feet," Franklin said through the open window. "I don't expect that much from God. Maybe I used to. But the older I get, the easier I am on him. God's getting older, too, I figure."

"Then put on your seat belt," Marvelle said. She stepped back into a patch of sunlight, so the last thing he saw as he drove away was the sun on her untidy hair and on her pale face and neck.

The woods he passed were gloomier now, with the sun almost level with the tops of the tallest oaks; it was a relief to him to drive out of the trees and into the green wheat fields. The radio was broadcasting a Billy Graham sermon, which Franklin found he couldn't concentrate on. He was wondering about Gussie's sister and if she'd live, and for how long, and what her husband might be thinking, out in that chicken shed. When Franklin was at the hospital the day before, Gussie's sister hadn't mentioned her husband. She'd wanted to know exactly how Franklin's wife had redecorated their bedroom.

"Blue curtains and a flowered bedspread," he had told her, and that was all he could remember—nothing about the new chair or the wallpaper or the lamps, all of which he took note of when he went home afterward.

He was also thinking, less intentionally, about Marvelle, who was entering his thoughts as erratically as the crows flying down into the fields he was passing. She was eight or nine years older than when he'd kissed her, but those years had somehow changed into days. When Franklin tried to keep his attention on her grief, it wandered off to her hair, her dark eyes—to every godless place it could. It wasn't until he heard Billy Graham recite, "He maketh me to lie down in green pastures: He leadeth me beside the still waters," that Franklin's mind focused back on Morgan lying in the willows. From that point on he paid attention to the words, falling apart a little when he heard, "Surely goodness and mercy shall follow me all the days of my life," because he didn't know anything more moving, except maybe love, which he didn't feel entitled to; he never had.

William deBuys

DREAMING GERONIMO

On the first night, this was the dream:

We surprised Geronimo's camp, destroyed his goods, and were chasing him deeper into Sonora when we ran into the Mexicans. They refused to believe we were white men because we were riding with Apaches. Since they got paid by the scalp and were more than us, they drew weapons and attacked.

Crawford, whose mystic eyes won devotion from the scouts, believed it was his destiny to catch Geronimo, and he believed his destiny was near. He climbed a rock waving his arms and shouting, *"¡Somos soldados Americanos! ¡Estamos tambien enemigos de Geronimo!"*

But the Mexicans cared nothing for that. One of them—we found out later it was the same 'breed who murdered Victorio, and he did it with the nickel-plated rifle he got for that job—blew off the top of Crawford's head, and then we all got into it with Crawford's body lying out there in the open between us, its brains spilled on the rock and cooking like an omelet in the sun.

We fired hot and steady, confusing the Mexicans. They

knew Apaches would not stand and fight with the numbers against them, so in minutes up comes their white flag, and they want to talk.

We held our fire, hoping it was a trick and that we'd have another chance for blood. Our dead captain had been the best of Crook's Apache scouts, and Geronimo had slipped away again.

On the second night, another dream:

The Apaches had no food and no rest from either the Mexicans or us, so finally they agreed to parley. I rode out with Crook and Bourke and a few others, including the idiot mayor of Tucson. Nana and Natches and Geronimo were already there, squatted down, each of them facing a different direction as though unaware the other ones existed. I recognized Geronimo by the lipless slash of his mouth across the hide of his face. He had long ago abandoned laughter.

Nana gave the tired-of-many-battles-and-the-Great-Spirit-weeps-in-Oklahoma speech, and Natches said he was fed up too, and he'd go in. So General Crook turned to Geronimo and asked what about him, and Geronimo said, "Keep the agents away."

Geronimo did not look at Crook. He seemed to speak to the dead wasp an ant was dragging through the dust in front of him. He said, "Promise there will be no agents like the blowflies that live in Tucson, and I'll drink rotgut and eat corn wherever you send me."

Then at last he turned to Crook and fixed him with a stare that caused a sound in my chest like a wagon wheel breaking on a rock. The flinty chief looked the general in the eye and said, "Piss on what you call your civilization. I am not as tired as you, but my people are few and dying. We will have to find another way to cut your throats and watch you bleed."

The third night's dream was this:

We sent each group a wagon to haul their blankets and other goods. We were the first party heading out. Next came Nana with his little clan, then Natches, and last Geronimo. Halfway to Bowie we overtook some Arizona whiskey traders, and Crook sent me back with Charley Meat-On-His-Eye to see what the liquor was doing to the Indians.

I rode past the groups of Nana and Natches. When I reached Geronimo, I found him lying in the back of the wagon with his squaw driving. He was unconscious and drooling. The rest of his bunch were no better. Occasionally a brave toppled from his horse and we'd stop and pick him up and load him belly-down across the saddle.

Shortly before sundown Geronimo awoke and jabbered to the squaw. She stopped the wagon, and Geronimo got out. He pissed like a horse for a few minutes, looking at the red stripe of sky above the western mountains, then he jabbered something more and the squaw began to turn the wagon, and all the others turned their horses.

I said, "Geronimo, what are you doing?"

He said, "I'm going back to Mexico."

Then and there, they went. They had their rifles and knives. Crook didn't believe in disarming Indians. He said it showed you were afraid of them.

Charley and I could not have stopped them if we tried. Charley said he'd trail them and rode off. I watched until he disappeared behind a ridge, then rode my horse to some rocks and shot him, and broke his leg too, in case of questions. Then, with the saddle on my shoulder, I started walking toward Fort Bowie.

On the fourth night, another dream:

My wife was as soft as the dough of rising bread. She was nothing to look at but she was a lake with deep waves in bed. She filled me up.

I rode with the scouts, weeks on the trail, and when I came in, I lay with her. I slept like wet clay.

Sheridan dismissed Crook when Geronimo escaped, but Crook never suspected me. I stayed on after his discharge and rode for Miles, who was without grace. I used to weep for Crook.

Miles finally got Geronimo, as any plodder with ten thousand troops had to do, and we hauled the bunch to the siding at Holbrook and loaded them on. I stood by the door of the boxcar as Geronimo climbed in. He was so close I could smell his smell of creosote and horse. He said to me, "Use a rough rock to wipe with."

And I said, "Do the same." When the train moved off, the Apaches' dogs followed it and disappeared howling into the desert.

Then came a dreamless night, the fifth.

Next, on the sixth night:

I dreamed of myself as an old man, after my wife had run off with the missionary. My heart was the clapper of a broken bell. It wasn't long before I took the train to Oklahoma.

Geronimo was outside his shack beside a fire of willow twigs. He spat when he saw me and looked away.

I squatted at the fire across from him, and finally he said, "What do you want?"

"I come for forgiveness," I said.

"Ha!"

"Time has passed, Geronimo. Can you see that even history was against you? There was no other way."

"Ha!"

"We did not do it for spite. In our way we admired you. Given the chance, I'd have helped you get away again."

Geronimo added sticks to the fire, and blew them into flame. "What do I care about forgiveness?" he said.

"Apachería is dust. You choke the rivers and make the land a withered tit where only ghosts can suck. Then you want forgiveness. Ha!"

"There are places we have left alone," I pleaded. "Much of the mountains where you used to hide. They would look the same to you now."

"Ha! Look at the air that blows over them. You turn the wind into a fart. You leave nothing alone."

I was silent as the fire of twigs burned down. Finally I stood: "Well then, Geronimo, is there nothing to be done?"

"Maybe something," he said. His voice took on the slightest edge of friendliness, and I felt it draw me in. "Maybe there can be a way," he said, with his eyes still fixed upon the embers.

Geronimo spoke: "Here is my forgiveness, for a price. We trade places, you and I. I become the dreamer and you become the thing that's dreamed. When you wake up, I have your life, and you stay here, where I am.

He looked at me closely, and in his eyes I saw reflections of the fire's smoking coals.

"Well," I paused. And then: "Tell me, Geronimo, can the quiet of this place feed an ordinary sorrow?"

On the seventh night, and every night thereafter:

From El Paso to Tucson and from Albuquerque down to old Chihuahua, children awake screaming in their beds, and men and women thrash in tortured dreams, sure that dark rough hands press icy blades upon their sleeping throats.

Mario Roberto Morales

DEAD WEIGHT

Matrimony emerged in ancient times as a punishment imposed on those couples who violated the endogamy taboo. Jailed in the home, the guilty suffered the mercilessness of absolute intimacy, while outside, their neighbors threw themselves into the irresponsible pleasure of free love.

—J. J. Arreola

Oh my God, it was too much, I swear. And yet I don't think I can ever forgive myself. At the same time, I wonder what I could have done? A woman has her pride and her own way of thinking. I couldn't just fold my arms and do nothing. My mother always warned me. But I loved him. I always loved him regardless of everything else. Deep down—I realize now—I believe he loved me too.

It was eight years—certainly no mere pittance. Eight long years of courting and at the end—nothing. His attitude was always the same. I did what I did because I began to despair. My mother and her terrible advice probably had a lot to do with it, too.

Gustavo was always like that. A drinker and a womanizer. He could never hide his addiction to skirts. He would stare at women insistently, without even being aware of my presence. It was like an uncontrollable urge within him. And the drinking, my God, that was the worst. Especially those early mornings when he'd arrive with mariachis or when he'd bang on the door just to declare his love for me. I would stop seeing him for weeks at a time. A few times I found out about some of his flings with women both my mother and I knew. He could beg forgiveness as easily as he had the affairs. My mother began to despise him but, charmer that he was, he'd win her over again come her birthday or Christmas or Mother's Day. He had a zest for life, I can't deny that.

But I could no longer bear his evasions. It had been eight years. So one night in the midst of one of his drinking bouts, I broke up with him. Proud as he was, he didn't come around the house for six months. I decided then—out of spite and to make him jealous—to accept Alfredo's proposal. He had always had my mother's approval. We were co-workers at the office, and he showed me his affection even in the simplest everyday gesture. During the days when Gustavo would lose himself in friends and women, Alfredo did all he could to raise my spirits. He'd accompany me wherever I wanted to go.

I knew Gustavo found out about my engagement to Alfredo because his sister works at the same company I do. He phoned one day to say it was urgent that he talk to me. And I, believing that the jealousy was having the desired effect, stupidly told him we had nothing to talk about. So then he spit out his horrible threat—if I got married he was going to kill us both, Alfredo and me—and hung up. Like a frightened child, the first thing I did—which was the biggest mistake of my life—was to tell Alfredo. Very calmly he told me not to pay attention to the threats, that they were childish tantrums, and that, on the contrary, we should speed up the wedding date. At this point my behavior started to get peculiar. First I agreed with what he said and set the wedding date for two weeks from that night. My thoughts of Gustavo became distant and dreamlike but filled with panic. When the night before the wedding arrived, I was still in this mental miasma. Then the nightmare happened. I was trying on the wedding gown when, without warning, my sister burst into the room, spilling the news. Gustavo had been shot at close range in a bar. He had six bullet holes in his chest and was in the hospital in serious condition. He had muttered my name and address so I could be notified. Without a second thought I threw the wedding gown in a corner of the room and took a taxi to the hospital. I don't know why, but my mother did nothing to stop me. At the hospital the doctor informed me that Gustavo was in bad shape; the chance of a fatal outcome was great. I thought to myself, I'll stay here until he gets better.

At three in the morning they managed to drag me away from there. My sisters, cousins, and aunts had arrived, as well as some of Alfredo's relatives, who begged me almost in tears to return to the house so Alfredo wouldn't find out. They repeated incessantly that I was to be married that morning at nine. At the exact instant that I was rethinking my marriage plans, Gustavo's sisters and mother appeared in the hospital room. We stared at one another intensely and broke down crying together. I won't get married, I said to them. I love him and I won't get married.

They hugged me tenderly, resignedly. Finally, my family was able to yank me from the chair where I was waiting to hear about the miracle of my beloved's recovery. That morning at eight, while everyone was still beseeching me to be sensible, to think of the scandal, that the guests would now be arriving at the church, I received the notice. Gustavo had died an hour before.

On our honeymoon at the hotel, Alfredo and I spoke with a strange coldness. Suddenly he started putting our things in the dressers and closets. I went to the window and stared out at the street. After a bit I felt his hands on my shoulders. I want you, he whispered in my ear. Right now the coffin is being lowered into the grave, I thought. The wreaths and flowers must be falling on top of Gustavo (like Alfredo on top of me). His relatives open the casket to see him for the last time and they see my bouquet. What faces they must have made when my sister went to place it in his hands so that everyone would know I wanted to give him and only him my heart, so that he could take it with him to infinity. It must have been like the silence that descended on everyone when, instead of turning around and throwing my bridal bouquet so one of Alfredo's sisters could catch it, I gave it to my sister to take to the funeral. Alfredo understood my gesture and kissed my forehead. I can feel the shovelfuls of earth, the flowers on top of Gustavo like Alfredo on top of me, sticky, grasping, moving above me like a worm on the earth, among the flowers, heavy like the dirt falling on Gustavo, on me, on the flowers of the coffin, heavy. *You got your wish, Alfredo. But it's a wish that will cost you dearly: first, because I despise a man who wins a woman's love through patience—it's degrading—and second, because we all know that in this country anyone can have a person killed for twenty-five pesos and think nothing of it.*

Oh my Lord, with this weight of flowers and earth on me, knowing deep in my soul I will never forgive myself, I think, what could I have done? No, who could have told me that from one day to the next my love would leave (with my bridal bouquet in his hands) forever and I'd be married, on a honeymoon, and thinking so much nonsense, holy virgin, without being able to say that one day I am going to throw away this dead weight.

Translated from the Spanish by Tina Alvarez Robles

Allen Woodman

WAITING FOR THE BROKEN HORSE

There always remained the doing of things.

Nathan put on his hat. It was an unfashionable felt hat that occasionally he chose to wear. "I'm going out for coffee," he said to Ann, his wife. "Do you have the keys?"

Ann held her face away from his. She was looking at a slick circular that advertised magazines at 50% off and touted a chance to win a vacation home at the beach. They had already retired to a vacation home at the beach.

She decided to subscribe to a magazine called *Farm Wife News,* even though she had never lived on a farm, even though she couldn't think of any future different from her past.

Nathan waited for the silence to break. Silence was part of their relationship.

Nathan dug around again in his pockets. He found the keys. "I've got them," he said.

Once he caught her in an unguarded moment. She was looking in the bathroom mirror. Her mouth was making an occasion out of it. Her lips were the color of ripe red peppers. The color was important to him because he was always

afraid of going blind. She was practicing an exercise she had
read about in one of her magazines. Her mouth was exaggerating the shape of vowels. It was a positive act, attempting to
postpone the haggard skin of long years.

And for a moment he wished that he could place his head
down next to hers and mime the gestures that her face was
making. And, as if by magic, their faces would laugh together
in a kind of toast to the way things can be put back together
after they have quietly fallen apart.

At the coffee shop, he ordered the Bottomless Cup. The waitress did not make any other suggestions. The price of coffee
did not carry any overwhelming need for exchanged
remarks.

He looked into the cup and tried to read its dark contents.
He set the coffee back down on the table to cool. He wished
that there had been a newspaper in the box out front. The
Thursday paper sold according to the cents-off food coupons.

The couple at the table next to him had ordered the *Barnyard Bonanza Buffet*. It was $3.95 and carried the slogan
"all-you-care-to-eat."

Nathan found the system in their numerous trips to the
food bar. Their first plates were loaded with protein. The
man's plate carried an equal number of bacon strips and sausage links, twelve pieces in all. The woman started to select
the links, but changed her mind in mid-air, and picked up
several sausage patties with a pair of silver tongs. Between
their plates, Nathan estimated a scrambled egg count of nine
eggs. It was enough to empty any small farmyard of life.

Their next plates were for the carbohydrates: hotcakes,
French toast, and biscuits, all covered in cane syrup; grits
and butter, and hash-brown potatoes and ketchup. And these
were followed closely by the fruits of the season plates laden
with orange slices and melon plugs.

As the couple were asking the waitress whether the soup

of the day came with the *Barnyard Bonanza*, Nathan looked outside the window. He was a little embarrassed that he didn't have anything better to do than to see how much food people could eat. It kind of reminded Nathan of something a radio-preacher had said once over the airwaves late at night about fast days. "Yes," he said, "keep them when there's neither bread nor bacon in the cupboard."

In the vacant lot next to the coffee shop, a young man had posted a sign that read *Merry-Go-Round Rides $1.00.* It was not the brightly painted and ornamented apparatus of the circus that played every year beside the state fair. It was reduced to bare bones, to wooden poles without a touch of paint. And the sculpted wooden horses were replaced by one broken nag pulled along by a frayed rope.

Nathan gave up his right to the Bottomless Cup of coffee. He walked over to the lot. He longed for something beautiful.

There was no music. The wood creaked as it turned in a tight circle. With a stick and shouts the young man drove a grey horse. The horse's once smooth coat was sliced by the plain shape of bones.

Nathan watched a boy that seemed far too heavy jumping up, now and again, upon the horse's sloped back. The horse moved stiffly around the ring in an absent-minded way.

Nathan looked at the multiplicity of half-ring shapes that the animal's hoofs had made in the sand.

"Care for a turn?" the young man asked.

Nathan was startled. "That horse," he said, "looks like it's ready for the pasture."

"Just a pure waste of space. It wasn't even worth shooting when I got it."

"It looks like it's starving," Nathan continued.

"It's just *lean*. You know, *a horse is a horse, of course, of course....*"

Nathan didn't understand the man. He had never watched *Mister Ed* on television. He had never seen any talking-horse shows. But once he had seen a movie about Francis, The Talking Mule, who managed to cause a great deal of trouble for his innocent sidekick, Donald O'Connor. What Nathan did next he understood even less.

"Why not sell it and get a *real* horse?" Nathan asked.

The man swatted the horse's back with the stick. He felt that special feeling of value for an unwanted item that someone else covets.

Nathan offered the man three hundred dollars for the horse. It was a high price, but Nathan had never bought a horse before. In fact, Nathan hadn't bought much of anything in years outside of a few irreclaimable items picked up at garage sales.

Nathan went home and waited in his backyard for the man to deliver the horse. It was a small yard, even by beach house standards. Nathan had never been one to want to putter around in a garden or trim shrubs to look like things other than shrubs.

Inside, the house had dwindled to a single room where his wife sat stacking and restacking magazines. She thought about buying an early American magazine rack to go beside the couch.

Outside, Nathan imagined her discovering the horse. She would stand beside it. She wouldn't say a word. There comes a point where there's no more virtue in words. Then her hand would brush the fuzzy hairs that radiated about the horse's eyes. She would not know why she did this. She would feel the hot flushing of her face, and strain to say, "Good boy." And without touching, it would be like Nathan and his wife were holding hands.

"It won't be long," thought Nathan, as he waited in the yard.

THE MONUMENT

I don't know why people talk in other towns and not in ours. I don't know why everything here is silent. The lawns around our house, for instance, are as green and silent as pools of water, except, at night, for the sound of the crickets in them, which I sometimes mistake, as I fall asleep, for the sound of old people rocking in wicker chairs on the front porch—a sound from my childhood.

Sometimes I forget and think my childhood was here, in this town. Certainly the grass in this town is the same color as the grass of my childhood; the green of sea glass on its underside, a color I cannot describe on top.

You may wonder how, in our silent town, we get by, day after day, without a word. The secret, I believe, is in our strict adherence to habit. For instance, whenever we—this other and myself—go to the diner in town, the counter man always brings us the same thing—black coffee—without our having to say a word. Perhaps he knows to bring us coffee because long ago, once, or perhaps several times, we might have ordered it with words, as people do in other towns. But if that were the case, then surely I would remember saying words, and I remember saying nothing.

Our adherence to habit also makes talk unnecessary in matters of household logistics. We—this other and myself—do not need to tell each other where we have put something, keys say, or at what time a certain domestic ritual will occur, supper say, because our habits are so exactly the same every day, every year, that nothing is left to chance.

I often feel that this pattern we follow—the trail of our feet through the house, the amount and placement of our cigarette ashes, the rhythm of our breathing even—corresponds in some way I cannot exactly express to the map of the town we have hung on our wall. Perhaps it is that we have learned our routine from the layout of our town's buildings and roads; or perhaps it is the other way around. Perhaps the town depends on our silence for its own silence, and if we were to talk, the spell that binds him and me and holds the town all around us would be broken.

When I say the word "spell" I am thinking of the old men in the diner. There is nothing about these old men to suggest that they are anything other than old farmers; nothing about their behavior is out of the ordinary, each hunched over a plate of food or a newspaper, each a lump of worn denim. Still, I often get the feeling that there is a silent communion between them, that they are a secret society or a council of elders, that it is these old men who hold our town to its silence. Then, when I look down into my black coffee, that my own reflection should be there, that my coffee should be a kind of mirror, seems like something they have arranged.

I wish I could say I don't miss talking, that it serves no purpose. But to tell you the truth, even in all this silence, my mind is never quiet; I am always talking to him inside. Always keeping it in is not pleasant, for when something is thought and not said, a pressure builds.

Perhaps because of this pressure, I am always imagining what we might say to one another if we lived in a town where people do talk. We might say, for instance, "I will never leave you; I would not exist without you." We might even say it in French. But after all, we moved to this town to avoid such things.

Did I tell you I grew up in this town? Back then, I had a rag doll with a piece of abalone shell sewn over its face. The shell looked like a winter sky or oil spilt on water.

When she gave me the doll, my mother told me—not with words, but with implication, or perhaps not with implication either, and it was only something I imagined—that there is a painless place where one can live and can expect peace; where, if nothing's very good, it's never very bad either.

When I looked into the shiny shell that was my doll's face all I could see was a vague shadow, the shadow of my own head. I used to imagine what her face might look like— whether it was painted on or blank under that shell—but I never bothered to cut the shell off.

In the summer, at night, we lie on top of the sheets, smoking, until it is time to sleep. Because of the moon, I suppose, the light at these times is strange. The smoke, rising silently from the cigarette in my hand, illuminated, looks like a veil hanging between us.

It is then, through that veil, that I really look at him. His skin is so pale that it glows a little in this strange light. He has little black hairs all over him. These hairs are like letters from an alphabet I don't know. There he is, spread out before me, like a page of a book written in a language I can't read.

When I see him like that, I think, for some reason, of the monument in the center of town. It is a rock, as tall as I am, with no words written on it. Perhaps it is not a monument at all, but just a rock that was too big to move.

In the summer, during the day, I walk down to the road to watch the cars that pass every once in a while. Mostly, these cars come from other towns, and so I am hoping to see the people inside, to see them talking. But for some reason cars always pass through our town with their windows rolled up. When I try to look in through the windows as the car drives toward me, all I can see is reflection—of trees, of fields, of the few, far-flung buildings of our town, of myself—sliding over the surface of the car.

It is the same with the stream that runs by our house, and farther down, past the town. I try to look down into the water, for although I am so familiar with the stream that it is like a thing from my childhood, I have the feeling that something quite unfamiliar is living under its surface. In that green world, something hovers, something darts around.

All I can see of the stream is its surface. No, that's wrong, I can't see the surface either; what I see is my own world reflected back—the trees, the sky, a shadow that's my head—a reflection that's hiding, like a veil laid on the water, that other world below.

These past seven nights I have had the same dream. We—this other and myself—are lying on the grass under the monument, or rock, at the center of town.

In this dream there is something I must say to him that I can't hold in any longer. As I open my mouth, as I draw my breath, as I make the first sound, the town around me grows blurry, warped, puckered. As I say what I must say to him, I know that what I had taken to be a town is really only a reflection, sliding over the surface of I don't know what.

THE BIRTHDAY CAKE

The air was cold and the daylight was draining from the sky. The street smelled of rotten fruit left in the carts and although this was a sour smell it was not altogether unpleasant. Lucia was accustomed to this odor, and because it reminded her of the feast days when she was a girl she enjoyed it, the way she imagined people on farms enjoyed the smell of manure.

It was past six and the shops on Newbury Street were closed, but she knew that Lorenzo would stay open for her. She did not hurry: she was an old woman, and age had spoiled her legs. They were thick now, and water heavy, and when she walked her hips grew sore from the effort of moving them.

She stopped by a bench, wanting to sit but knowing that to stoop and then to rise would be more difficult than simply to lean against the backrest. She waited for her breathing to slow, then walked the last block to the bakery. Lorenzo would be there. He would wait. Hadn't she come to the bakery every Saturday since the war? And hadn't she bought the same white cake with chocolate frosting, Nico's favorite?

"Buona sera, Signora Ronsavelli," he said as the chime clanged and the heavy glass door closed behind her. "You had me concerned."

Lorenzo Napoli was too young to be so worried all the time. She wondered about him. She did not trust him the way she had trusted his father.

Standing before the pastry case was Maria Mendez, the little Puerto Rican girl who worked at the laundry. "Este es la señora," Lorenzo said to her. They were everywhere now, these Puerto Ricans, all over the neighborhood with their loud cars and shouting children and men drinking beer on the sidewalk. Now the rents were increasing and the real estate people wanted the Italians to move to nursing homes. Even Father D'Agostino was helping them. "Lucia," the priest had told her, "you'd have company there."

This Maria from the laundry had a child but no husband. She smiled at Lucia, then peered down into the glass case.

"Miss Mendez needs to ask you a favor," the baker said.

Lucia removed her leather gloves and put them into her purse. "A favor?"

"My little girl," Maria said. "Today is her birthday. She's seven years old today."

"You must know little Teresa," Lorenzo said.

"Yes," Lucia said. She had indeed seen the child, out with her friends tearing up the vegetable gardens in the back-yards.

"And I was so busy today at the laundry, so busy, all day long there was a line, and I couldn't get out to buy her a birthday cake."

"Yes." Lucia remembered that it had taken her two days to fix the stakes for her tomato plants.

"Let me explain," Lorenzo said. "Miss Mendez needs a cake, and I have none left, except yours. I told her that you were my best customer, and of course we'd have to wait and ask you."

"All the other bakeries are closed," Maria said. "It's my little girl's birthday."

Lucia's hands began to shake. She remembered what the doctor had said about getting angry; but this was too much. "Every week I buy my cake. For how many years? And now this *muli* comes in and you just give it away?"

"Lucy." Lorenzo held out his hands like a little boy. "Don't get angry. Please, Lucy."

"No. Not Lucy." She tapped her chest with her finger. "Lucia."

"Lucy, please," he said.

"No 'Please, Lucy.' No parlare Inglese. Italiano."

"I could give you some sugar cookies," he said. "Or some cannolis. I just made them. They're beautiful."

"Once a week I come here and I buy Nico's cake."

Lorenzo tipped his head to the side. He seemed to be about to say something, but then he stopped. He waited another moment.

"Lucia, think of the poor little girl," he said. "It's her birthday."

"Then bake her a cake. You do the favor, if you like her so much."

"Lucia, there's no time." The party was going to begin in a few minutes, he said. Besides, he had already cleaned his equipment and put away his flour and eggs and sugar.

"Lucia," he said, "it's the right thing. Ask yourself, what would Nico do? Or my father?"

"I know what they wouldn't do. They wouldn't forget who their people were. They wouldn't start speaking Spanish for the *mulis*."

She stared at him until he looked away. Outside, the wind

had lifted a newspaper from the sidewalk and was pressing the leaves against the front window of the bakery. From somewhere on Common Street came the sound of a car's engine racing. She thought of Nico, how when he lay sick in bed during his last days she had gone outside and asked the children not to make noise and they'd laughed and told her to go on back inside, crazy old lady.

Without looking up, he spoke in a voice that was almost a whisper. "Lucia," he said, "it's just this once."

"No," she said. "No. I want my cake."

Maria began to cry. "Dios mio," she said. "My little girl."

Lorenzo leaned on his hands. "I'm sorry, Miss Mendez."

Maria turned to her. She was sobbing. "It's my daughter's birthday," she said. "How will she forgive me? Don't you have children?"

"I have three children," Lucia said. "And I never forgot their birthdays. I never had to rush out at the last minute."

"I was working," Maria said. "I'm all by myself with Teresa. I have to raise her alone."

"And whose fault is that?" Lucia waved at Lorenzo. "Pronto," she said. "Box up my cake."

Lorenzo eased the cake out of the display case and placed it into a white cardboard pastry box. His hands were soft and white. He drew a length of twine from the dispenser, tied off the box, then snapped his wrists and broke the string from the leader.

Lucia put on her gloves. As she turned for the door Maria took her arm. "I'll beg you," she said. "Please, I'll buy the cake from you. I'll pay you ten dollars."

Lucia pulled her arm free. "I don't want your money."

"Twenty dollars, then." She pulled a folded bill from the pocket of her dress and placed it in Lucia's hand. "Please, Mrs. Ronsavelli, take it."

Lucia tried to push the bill back into her hands, but Maria

curled her fingers into fists and began to cry. "You can't do this," she said.

Lucia threw the crumpled bill to the floor and opened the door. Maria fell to her knees and picked up the bill. "You witch!" she screamed. "Puta! Whore!"

Lucia did not look back. She moved slowly down Newbury Street, being careful to avoid the spots of ice. What did that laundry girl, or even Lorenzo, understand about her? What did they know about devotion?

From the alley behind her building she heard the screaming, a terrible choked wail that rang from the street and into the alley and echoed off the walls and trash cans. She imagined Maria the laundress stumbling home to her daughter, and she imagined the red, contorted face of the little girl when her friends arrived and there was no cake.

Still, what would they know about suffering, even then? They would know nothing. The light was poor in the staircase, and she held the railing with her free hand. After each step she paused; she let the flicker of pain ease from her hips, then lifted again.

Inside the kitchen she raised the glass cover and took out last week's cake. The air that had been under the glass smelled sweet and ripe. The cake had not been touched; it might have been a clay model of the new one. As she carried it to the trash, tips of chocolate frosting broke off and scattered on the floor like shards of pottery.

She swept up the pieces, washed the smudges of frosting from the cake stand with a sponge, then opened the bakery box, removed the new cake and put it under the glass cover. It was dark outside, and in the hills around the city the lights in the windows of hundreds of houses glowed like the tiny white bulbs in the branches of a Christmas tree. She thought of her children; they were up in those hills, eating dinner with their own children—those little light-skinned boys and girls who shrank from their nana's hugs, kept their jackets on, and whispered to each other until it was time to leave. It was cold near the window; she shivered and stepped away.

She sat at the kitchen table, beneath the photos of Nico and the children. She looked at the door, wishing, as she did each time, that there might be a knock, or that it might just swing open, and one of them, just one of them, might be there.

THAT CHANGES EVERYTHING

I

This feeling that something is deeply wrong. Not basically, as some people might say, but deeply, as in to the core. Blood and bone. As in this is the stuff we're made of and there's no getting away.

II

Brush one hundred times before you go to bed. Rise at eight and scrape cornflakes off the counter. Put your makeup on in a different order and the day may hold surprises.

III

"Be thankful for what you've got," he says, spreading mustard on his bun. He means two eyes, of course, 'cause he lost one in Vietnam. He means two of everything that's supposed to come in twos, like heartbeats, and footsteps, and yes, even people.

And I want to tell him it's different than that. But how do you say this to a man who's stared down shrapnel?

I V

When he lost his eye, he lost his depth perception. He'd reach for a beer and grab thin air. He once cracked his forehead on a doorway. "It comes back," he told me. "It takes a while, but the brain relearns to see things in perspective."

V

Each morning I make a list of things to do. At night, whatever is left undone I transfer to another list which I keep in a bedroom drawer. This other list is ten pages long. At the top it says, "Box baby clothes." I have them all in boxes, but they aren't the right boxes for storing clothes you want to save for your grandchildren.

V I

You can tell which one isn't real by the way it sits in its socket, staring blankly into the world like the eye of a gaffed mackerel. I like to look at it, this ball of sightless glass. When the light is right, I can see myself in its reflection.

V I I

I lie in bed after midnight and count stars through our open window. They arc slowly across a cloudless sky. Last night there were fifty-seven.

V I I I

Years ago he wore a patch, but gave it up when he saw the women it attracted. "Earth mothers," he told me. Women who wiped soup from his beard and clipped the dead skin from around his toenails. In bed, they rode him like a stick pony.

He chose me, he said, because I seemed indifferent.

IX

Some mornings, after the kids have gone to school, I sit in bed and watch steam rise from my coffee. It has purpose, steam. It knows what to do.

X

He bites hard into his burger. Hunches close to the table. Looks up at me with half an eye.

And I want to tell him I know I am loved. And that that changes everything.

And it would be such an easy lie.

Dagoberto Gilb

THE SEÑORA

The view from the señora's building was handsome. Below its height on the Franklin Mountains sat a wide, manly expanse of land, from the buildings downtown, over the river to Juarez, past its colonias, to the emptiness of the Chihuahua Desert. In the day, in the summer, the land below never budged, and the blue sky would hang above it without end, everywhere, while in the evening the same sight was an ocean mirroring a black, starry air above. No doubt it was this which attracted the señora to the spot here on the mountain so many years ago when she was young, when she and her husband, who survived only a year back on this side, moved north, wealthy from Mexican mines. So maybe her building wasn't the most plush in the city, but expenses weren't spared either. This could have been a matter of chance—that is to say, a matter of history, because it was built in the days when property and labor were especially easy to come by—though it could equally be argued that for someone of her wealth and position, life has always been cheap in El Paso.

Maybe cheap, but never easy. Anyone who had lived here knew this. Jesus knew, and Jesse had come to. They both knew that this woman—the señora was all they ever called her—wouldn't for one moment let them think it could have been another way. Not that they would mention this to her, not that she'd have to remind them of it, or even bring it up once. Not that they thought about it at all.

They thought about her, though. Maybe for the obvious reasons. Like that Jesus, a national without documents, often got work from her, both here and on her ranch in New Mexico, and that his wife, who was also undocumented, was her maid. Like that Jesse rented one of the guest houses (in these times called a "furnished apartment") for practically nothing, even when he paid, which he hadn't every month because the señora didn't always notice. But there was more to it than that. They thought about her because it would be impossible not to.

In the four months he was a tenant, Jesse seldom came out of his apartment. When he did, he always had his shirt off and dark glasses on. There was no one around to ask him what he was doing in El Paso, why, how; no one but Jesus made a question of anything, and his only one had been where Jesse was from. California, Jesse told him, the Bay Area. And even that was answered with a caution Jesus could read. But despite first appearances, Jesse was gentle and soft-spoken, friendly toward Jesus, who was as kind as the name of the village he'd come from, La Paz.

"Coffee?" Jesse asked with a leg outside his screen door. His shirt was not on, and a blue tattoo of an eagle spanned his hairless chest.

"Of course," said Jesus, pleased. He rested his roller in the bucket of white paint and wiped his hands on his brown cotton work pants. Then he adjusted the paint-splattered Houston Astros baseball cap, and waited at the steps near Jesse's door.

Jesse came back and stepped outside with two mugs of hot instant coffee he'd already sweetened. "You keep going as fast as you are and you'll paint yourself out of the money." The arm with the black widow tattoo held out a mug for Jesus.

"The señora told me when I finish with this she has more for me, like the rooms inside, and some other things too." Jesus had been defensive ever since he perceived that Jesse didn't approve of the wage he'd accepted for the work.

"It's a little hot," said Jesse.

"I think it's just right," Jesus said, referring to the coffee.

"I'm talking about the sun, the heat. That it's already hot."

"Oh. Yes. A little." He hadn't thought about it.

They drank the coffee under the wooden eaves of the building while the chicharras, the cicadas, clicked on and off like small motors.

It was always quiet when the señora wasn't there. She wasn't physically loud when she was around, but even her unseen presence filled what was silence otherwise. So the noise she made the day she died wasn't surprising. Both Jesus and Jesse heard it from the beginning and neither thought anything peculiar about it. She was throwing a tantrum at a nurse—the woman, anyway, who wore a white uniform. The señora fired her, screamed at the woman as she was helping the señora into the wheelchair. The señora told her to get back in her car and to go and to not come back. The nurse obliged and drove down the unpaved alley, popping her tires off the rocks, dusting the air. The señora rolled herself across the rocky path until she got to the smooth cement sidewalk. Neither Jesus nor Jesse moved to help her, instinctually knowing better. When the señora got to her door she began screaming about that nurse still having the keys. She stood with her cane, then standing on her old legs, heaved that cane into the glass panes of the door. That's when Jesus came over. He couldn't understand all she was wailing about in English, but he broke out a square of glass and reached inside and turned the deadbolt. When the door still didn't open, the señora tensed again and screamed more. She was not sweating, but she was breathing with a loud hiss. Jesus couldn't get it opened, and the señora hollered. That's when Jesse came over. He positioned himself, then kicked the door. It splintered the jamb and sprang into an arc. The señora did not thank them as she went inside and left behind the wheelchair and the two men. She screamed and complained from within her home. Jesus and Jesse returned to what they were doing after a few moments, which is to say Jesus rolled white paint onto the plaster walls and Jesse went to the other side of the screen door where he couldn't be seen.

It got hugely quiet. Jesse stepped out of his apartment, and Jesus looked over to him.

"We better see," Jesse told Jesus.

"Yes. It's what I'm thinking."

They entered the señora's home, the mahogany and crystal and silver sparkling with cleanliness. She was sprawled on her rug, the stem of a rose in the carpet's pattern seeming to hook between her teeth. Her eyes were closed, but an ornery scowl kept the señora from looking peaceful. The combination suited her death. There was nothing at all sad about seeing her like this, and neither man felt a twinge of sentimentality. They simply respected the finality of it.

Later, after people had come for her body, Jesus tried to finish the section of wall he'd started, while Jesse went back to his apartment. In those hours, the chicharras, hundreds of them, drilled without pause at the sky. They were the reason the memory of that day became so inexhaustible, and they were what both men, in their separate lives, talked about from the moment they moved on and told this story.

Traci L. Gourdine

GRACEFUL EXITS

My daughter teases me. She says I have no friends. This is because the phone never rings for me. Only the relatives and creditors can rouse me to the phone or to lick an envelope. The rest I have discouraged, preferring my silence, that long pause between dusk & dawn. I like to unplug the phone, shove it in a drawer, pretend the doorbell is broken and the shower too loud. I have learned how to raise my eyebrows, frown perplexed when acquaintances say, "I called & called you." "Oh" is my response. I don't promise to call them. I can't promise something like that. I prefer to meet people by chance on sidewalks or in cafés. There are escape routes all around me. I know how to get alone. I know how to nod & nod & back away grinning, until it is time to shout good-bye from a far distance. I'm polite that way. It's only polite.

Sometimes, in this solitude, horniness creeps in. It's hard to avoid. Some type of neediness rises to sprint throughout my veins. This has nothing to do with being social. I have recognized the animal in this. Sex is part of the grocery list. When I feel myself moan & hunger for touch, I begin to search faces. Hands & lips become interesting. I peruse; I browse what's available. I recall what's been tried, what's spoiled too fast. I remind myself about hasty decisions. I should be careful. I know how I am. People should be warned.

There was a boy. A very young boy. His dark eyes, his soft lips, his agile touch made us both innocent & eager. My hard edges, my unexpected soft spots, intrigued him. At night he taught me languages where silence used to fall. He took me on. He wore me out. He gathered in strength, eclipsing the moon, shielding me from the expanse of night skies. Soon he was too much wind. He wouldn't go away. He didn't know how to be quiet. I imagined phones ringing constantly as we made love. Sometimes I'd find the front door hurled open, banging against the wall. Leaves hurried down the hall. I didn't know young boys were expensive. Daughter said I looked tired. The boy was wrapped around my neck like a toddler. He said he was in love. He wanted me pregnant. He said I was his Barbie & he was my Ken. He said I slept like a virgin. Oh god, oh god, oh god. . . .

The bathroom is the chamber of solitude. People will leave you alone there. All kinds of excuses can be called from the other side of that door. Usually people believe you. In the bathroom a person can figure things out, plan a means of escape, work out the logistics in the mirror. Sometimes you can feel the line beginning to form on the other side. The boy waited like a lonely dog. I could see the shadow of his shoes. I couldn't hear what he was saying; the shower was too loud, my fingers were in my ears. While he waited, I found a gray hair. I thought it was lint from my underwear. I thought I was going to die. He was aging me in places I thought would never grow old. He was reminding me of my mother's words when I found a gray hair above my brow.

"Daughter," she said with her thick West Indian accent.

"You worry when you find the gray in the coochie. Then you are moving toward old woman. Gray on the head means wisdom, gray in the coochie means old coochie. Not'ing be worse for a woman than finding her coochie old. You worry then."

I sent the boy away. I sent the boy away & turned on the answering machine. I sent the boy away & drilled a peep hole in the front door. He comes through the mail now. He is prerecorded messages of love that I play back with my coat on. I am busy signals & dial tones. I am the Barbie with frayed hair, twisted clothes & limbs in impossible positions. I cannot speak, except to lower my eyes & smile politely.

Richard Plant

FLATLAND

How did we come to be there, my wife waist-deep in grass while I sat quiet, waiting for the dark? We were driving home from Colorado. The real mountains were 150 miles behind us, only hinted at here by great rock patches. Every couple of miles these would jut out of the prairie's flat like the bony plates of buried dinosaurs. Soon I figured even these would shrink away and leave the horizon open. This was the Oklahoma panhandle and Carol was driving. After Samantha's funeral we had gone west, the two of us, to stay with Carol's parents. They had treated us gently there, our adult voices humming softly in their big old house. They had tried to make us happy. Now we were going home.

It was about an hour before sunset, and although I was resting my eyes, I wasn't asleep. I was thinking how the house would be dark when we arrived. I wondered what we would do when we went inside, and tried to imagine us turning on lights, unpacking our things, taking ourselves to bed. I was trying to picture us performing these acts when I heard my wife speak.

"This is a National Park," Carol said. "Did you know this

was here?" I opened my eyes in time to see a green sign race by the window. "Can you imagine anybody coming to see this?"

This was just grass, is what she meant. You couldn't see any mountains or trees. It was a national grassland, maybe a national prairie. It looked like a monument to emptiness.

"You have to admit it's different," I said. "You can see for miles out here."

"But there's nothing to see. No trees, no houses. Not even cows. Don't you think it's spooky?" I could feel the car surge forward as she pressed the accelerator. I watched the speedometer hit 70. Then 75. Why not? There was nobody there but us. The grass must have been four feet high. The road seemed like a narrow trail through these green walls of grass. Driving through such a landscape you couldn't help but think of the places behind you, the places ahead.

Our daughter died of a fever. That's all I can tell you. First she was a healthy two-year-old, then she got the shivers. Somehow she became this white little face looking up at us from her ice bath at the hospital. Then she was dead. All of this happened in two days. The doctors couldn't even give it a name. There's no preparation for a thing like this.

I rolled my window down. My eyes stung, but that was just the wind from the car. There wasn't any wind over the land, the grass itself didn't seem to be moving. But the air smelled warm and rich, like pasture.

"I've got the air conditioner on," Carol said, and I rolled up my window. I could still smell the grass a little through the air conditioner vent.

Now the sky behind us was getting red. The road was a straight line, and we were making good time. Every so often a small flock of birds would break into the sky ahead of our car. First nothing, then a flutter of brown wings against the sky. I couldn't tell you what kind of bird this was living in the national prairie.

Then we saw three or four birds ahead of us on the highway itself, walking around on the asphalt. Carol slowed down a little. Just in time, she swerved to the other lane, and the birds flew off.

"Good lord," she said. "Did you see that?" She brought it back down to 65.

A couple miles later there was another small group of birds walking around on the highway, and I could feel the car slow down. "It's okay," I promised, "they'll get out of our way." She was doing about 50 now. But she didn't change lanes and sure enough, the birds fluttered out of the road a few yards ahead of the car.

Of course, I thought. I never knew anybody to hit a bird.

This kept on happening. Half a dozen brown birds would be pecking at the highway in a cluster, sometimes right down the yellow stripe. Did these birds strut around on the road all the time, I wondered, or did they just come out at evening to eat the bugs left by cars? There wasn't any other traffic and the sun was going down, but there was still plenty of light to see by.

Then we hit one. At least we thought we did. There was a group of four or five, and when the car passed over I saw only a couple fly safely over the hood. Carol was really slowing down now.

"I killed one," she said.

"No, I don't think you did."

"I did. I saw it in the rear view mirror. There was this one little bird standing behind us on the road, then I saw it fall over. John?"

"They always get out of the way," I told her. "Nobody hits a bird."

"Well congratulations," she said. "Apparently I have."

I could see it upset her. I said, "If you really hit one, there must have been some reason. It was probably sick or old. It couldn't get out of the way."

"Sure," she said. "A reason. I guess that makes it okay."

She had really slowed down now, braking at the first sign of birdlife, and doing only 45 in between. I didn't say anything, but I wondered what she would do if somebody came up behind us. I wondered how we might look to a cop, jerking along this way, going under the limit on this lonely road in the national prairie. How long would it take to get out?

At one point we passed a couple of farms. A slight elevation allowed us to spy them laid out neatly in the distance, their houses and barns, their plowed fields and silos, their scraggly windbreaks. I'm not a farmer myself, but I thought I could smell the plowed earth mixed in with the odor of grass. Or maybe they just had cows. Anyway I pointed these buildings out to Carol. I hoped this evidence of life and order might help my wife relax, maybe forget the little bird left in the road.

Then it happened again. I know she lifted her foot from the gas, she tried to swerve left, but we both felt the slightest bump of a bird beneath the tires.

"Oh Christ," she said. She was slowing down and pulling off to the right. I wasn't sure where we would end up. This was just a two-laner without much of a shoulder. "You promised me they couldn't get hit," she said, and she flung out her hand and struck me on the chest. I didn't say anything for a minute, not until we stopped. I rolled my window down and took a deep breath.

"I don't understand it," I told her. "You'd think they would move out of the way. I mean this is a state highway."

My wife snapped back at me. "It's a national grassland. They ought to be safe here. They ought to have protection."

The smell of the grass was heavy in the car. There was grass just outside my door, and I thought of the grass bent over beneath us. "I don't know," I said, trying to find a good reason, one we could both believe. "Maybe there's not enough traffic on this road. Maybe they're not used to cars."

"Well I don't think I can keep going," she said. "I don't want to be responsible for any more." Carol was looking out her window, and at first I thought she might be crying. But she wasn't. She wasn't going to cry about the loss of these two birds. Then my wife got out of the car, slamming the door as if she were mad. She waded a few yards into the grass.

I didn't say anything. The car was well enough out of the road and like I've said, we hadn't seen anybody for it seemed like hours. So I sat there in the car and waited for it to turn dark. At night, I figured, the birds would go back into the grass, huddle up, go to sleep. Then we could go on our way.

I could see my wife's back and shoulders floating above the grass. Her hair looked red in that sun. Who knows what she was looking at, standing there in the tall grass out on the flatland of the Oklahoma panhandle? I couldn't tell which sad thoughts she was thinking. I wasn't sure what was being resolved. But it seemed quiet as the moon there, peaceful, and the two of us were in no hurry to get home.

While I waited I heard noises in the silence. The car's hot engine ticking beneath the hood. The bent or broken grass hissing against the car's hot chassis. Insects chirruped as the night came on. When Carol turned back to the car, we could talk if she wanted. And when it got dark I would offer to drive us from there.

Barry Peters

ARNIE'S TEST DAY

Arnie Watson, facing five tests on a spring Friday of his junior year at Riverdale High School, sat in his bedroom at five a.m. and wrote all over his clothes. Beneath the bill of his Chicago Bulls cap, Arnie wrote in Spanish twenty of the vocabulary words from a list that he was provided with by Señora Martin on Monday and told to memorize by Friday. Certainly Arnie would have memorized those words, just as he had done with vocabulary lists all year, had he not been on the phone for two hours Thursday night trying to convince Marilou Spencer not to break up with him. Dismayed when Marilou slammed the phone in his ear, Arnie couldn't concentrate on his Español the rest of the night. Exasperated, he rose early on Friday and meticulously wrote those twenty words and shorthand definitions in fine black ink on the underside of the cap's red bill.

Frankly, Arnie didn't have the chance to study history, either, that week. Gus Finley and Arnie were going to meet at the Riverdale Library on Tuesday and study the amendments to the Constitution, but Arnie got stuck in the house after a fight with his parents. How are you going to get into a real college, they yelled, a Michigan or a Duke or a Stanford, if you fall out of the top five percent of your class, if you bring home any more eighty percents in your honors classes? Just you wait and see, Arnie retorted, storming upstairs to his bedroom. It won't be possible, they said.

Knowing that he couldn't leave the house after such a scene, Arnie didn't meet Gus at the library, which is why on that Friday morning before school, Arnie wrote abbreviated versions of the amendments on the inside collar of his Reebok polo shirt, actually needing to write on the inside of the shirt itself, repealing Prohibition just above his heart.

Luck ran against Arnie that week in English, too. Mr. Phelan, the Riverdale basketball coach, told his players they had better be at spring conditioning OR ELSE. Naturally, Arnie wanted to stay on Phelan's good side for his senior season, so Arnie ran and lifted weights with the rest of the team after school that week, precluding him from reading all but the first chapter of *The Great Gatsby*. On Friday morning, then, Arnie wrote "Jay Gatsby" and "Nick Caraway" and "Tom Buchanan" and "Daisy Buchanan" on the tanned inside of his belt along with a very brief synopsis of their literal and metaphorical roles in the novel; on the pale blue inside waistband of his jeans, Arnie elaborated on Fitzgerald's symbolism, even drawing a pair of spectacles overlooking a map of East Egg and West Egg, Gatsby's mansion, a heap of ashes and a skyscraper representing New York City, praying that the information he had gleaned from *Cliff's Notes* would be useful on Mrs. Schenck's in-class essay.

Possibly the most difficult test for Arnie would be physics. Quantum theory was hard enough for Arnie to understand during lectures and labs; finding time to memorize formulas for Friday's test was another problem.

Right when he opened his notebook on Wednesday night, Arnie's grandmother called to say that Grampa had been admitted to Riverdale Hospital with chest pains. So Arnie and his parents spent three hours at the hospital, where Arnie read *People* magazine instead of *Introduction to Physics* while waiting for the doctors to report Grampa's condition. They said Grampa would have surgery on Friday—Arnie's test day—only a few hours after Arnie wrote quantum physics formulas on the outside of his polyester white socks.

Unusual as it was, Arnie faced a fifth test that Friday in trigonometry. Vindicating himself for being required to attend Riverdale Lutheran Church choir practice last night—after basketball conditioners and before his devastating phone call to Marilou Spencer, after lying to his parents that no, he did not have any tests on Friday, after answering countless questions from other choir members about his grandfather's impending heart operation—Arnie wrote trigonometry notes on the bottom white soles of his Air Jordan basketball shoes. Why me, Arnie thought, and next to the silhouette logo of Michael Jordan flying above the world, Arnie charted trigonometic patterns. X-axis: the function of pressure is on the rise. Y-axis: the probability exists that Arnie will be forced to use his crib notes. Z-axis: the arc of trouble in Arnie's life increases at an extremely sharp angle, the black line speeding unheeded toward infinity.

Merrill Gilfillan

F. O. B. FLICKER

Aboy walked through town, cutting along the swayback dirt alleys. Some days he took the alleys to avoid the townspeople on the streets; sometimes he took the streets to avoid the snarling backyard dogs in the alley—a half-breed boy. Either way, it was the end of July and the town was full of dusty hollyhocks and late afternoon pools of shade and young flickers cried all day from their nest holes.

He walked along until he saw the circus poster on a telephone pole. He had forgotten all about that. He read the poster, then cut three blocks over to where the circus was just setting up on a vacant lot at the edge of town.

It was a small outfit for sure—half a dozen stubby house trailers and two large trucks with Texas and Florida license plates. The boy walked shyly around the doings. The people he saw looked foreign and distant. Even though busy at their work they seemed angry and unhappy. A lone man smoking a cigarette behind the big animal truck glanced at the boy when he turned the corner, but never acknowledged him—just looked off over his head.

The boy walked completely around the edge of the camp

243

and then sat down on a slope fifty yards away. He watched a circus woman staking out a pony and a fancy horse. A baby elephant stood near a truck, eating from a pan on the ground. The best thing he saw was three men driving the stakes for the large tent, the way they got their sledges going in rapid-fire order on the same stake—*clink-clink-clink, clink-clink-clink*—as fast as they could go.

Next morning the boy walked back to the circus grounds and sat on the same slope. By now the big tent was up and people were moving about getting things ready for the mid-day performance. The woman was saddling the fancy horse. She got on and warmed up the horse for its dance routine: sideways, backwards, round and round in a rocking, pretty-boy canter. None of the circus people seemed excited; they had done all this 500 times across Nebraska and Kansas, all the way from Texas. A juggler was strolling around tossing colored balls in the air.

Then the boy saw Crow coming across the field. He watched him coming across, his long braids bouncing, and knew his friend had seen him sitting there. Hé. Hé.

"You going to the circus?"

"No."

"You doing anything now?"

"No."

"Come on then. I want to show you something."

"Show me what?"

"Something you've never seen before."

They walked off. Crow's step was quicker than usual, the boy noticed that. They walked three blocks and cut in through the bushy backyard of an old house. Crow led the way, in through the back door and across the yellow kitchen.

In the next room, Crow's cousin, Hill, was sitting at a cluttered table. There were lots of beer cans. Hill was just sitting there bleary-eyed and smoking. He looked up at the boys. Hé.

On the mattress against a wall, a large blond woman was lying, asleep. She was naked. A corner of bedsheet hid her loins. The rest of her body was uncovered, in the sprawl of deepest sleep. After a moment, there was the smell of wine rising from her deep, slow breath.

Crow whispered to the boy. "She works at the circus."

Hill looked over at them. "Florida." He smoked and his gaze fell back to the ashtray.

The boy looked at the unconscious woman—her large splay breasts, the mottled pink and white thighs, the shaved armpits. He took a short step toward her, out of politeness to Crow, and looked again at the breasts and the full belly, then stepped back by the table.

Another boy came quietly in the door with a friend. They sidled into the room, glancing quickly at Crow and at Hill, then gaped at the sleeping woman. Hill looked at them after a while, then got up heavily. He walked quietly over to the woman and crouched by her feet. He reached out a finger and gently tickled the sole of one foot. The woman hardly stirred, but on some convoluted reflex cue her loins pumped halfheartedly three or four times, far removed, ventriloquial, ghostly.

No one said a word. Hill sat down heavily without a look. Crow and the boy sat across from him and made baloney sandwiches on the cluttered table and ate them. Now and then another schoolboy would materialize and tiptoe into the room and peek at the mattress.

Then there were four old men, wrinkled and thin. They arrived in a group—the boys heard the four car doors slam softly out front—and walked in very slowly, very formally and respectfully.

They removed their Stetsons and walked in a silent line past the mattress. In the dull gloaming light of the room, it was like a line of well-wishers filing reverently by a casket. And that is what the boy remembered for many long years: the eerie decorum, the slight shuffle of feet and clothing and a trace of guarded, proprietous public breathing above the heavy, oblivious, shore-like breaths of the girl.

THE FISH

Come daybreak, Ida knew what they'd find—Jake standing over one hundred and twenty of his cattle he'd managed to pen and shoot, one by one. She knew full well that he'd lost his mind and she'd never have him back. She knew that she was now a widow.

Her porch light showed two cows that had escaped the pen standing in the black morning near the ranch house and looking out toward Jake's hissing kerosene lantern, the only other light for five miles. She clicked off her light and sat in her porch rocker.

She'd called the sheriff, but by the time he got there Jake was two-thirds finished and they couldn't see him in the dark and besides, as the sheriff said, "They're his cows anyway. No point in pushing a man into taking a shot at you." So he parked his patrol car up the dirt road and decided to wait for daylight.

A gunshot sounded from the pen and echoed off a mountain bluff a mile away. In the silence that followed, Ida heard the sheriff's radio crackle once, and then his voice calm and quiet, saying he'd presently be bringing Jake in. There was a garbled and mechanical reply, then the radio was turned off. The only indication of the sheriff in the darkness was the red pinpoint of his cigarette where he stood waiting outside his car. "He'll simmer down," he'd told her, "after he finishes."

But she knew there'd be no simmering down. It was the way Jake had said, "Good night, Ida," as he stepped out the screen door with his gun. On those words, whatever bond that had held them together for forty-seven years snapped. And she saw Jake drifting into space like an astronaut who gets his cord to the mother ship cut in one of those sci-fi movies. She was on the mother ship. The mother ship was earth, and Jake was gone.

Her own calmness surprised her. But she'd known nights like this before. She'd been through the deathwatches of both her parents, and was there and awake when the trembling took her father and he opened his eyes, knowing what was coming. And she remembered when she was a girl and her neighbors, the Ramseys, lost their house to fire and had no insurance. Her mother gave their two little girls cookies and read them stories while the men dug through the ashes.

All her years had taught her that no matter how horrible the night, the next day the world would always be different; maybe not better, but changed and set off on a new course. And all you had to do was let the world take you that way. Her mother once told her that you can't let your heart break if no good can come of it.

With her toe, she pushed against the porch floor of the house and the rocker creaked back and forth. She knew the sun would be breaking through any moment to the east behind her. The fence had appeared in front of the house like a shadow, and a shrub or two on the other side of it were dark blurs. Each morning from the porch she watched the first light come up from the ground across the ranch like mist, objects crystallizing before her. Now she could see three tumbleweeds pressed against the fence and remembered the tumbleweed snowmen she had made each Christmas since she got the idea thirty years ago.

She leaned back in her chair and thought of Florida and her sister and realized that that was more than likely where she was headed. Good, she thought. Someplace different. Her sister had warned her against marrying Jake, said any man that would try and raise milk cows instead of beef cows in west Texas was crazy. "Jake's interested in milk," she'd heard herself say and regretted it the instant she said it. No way her sister was going to understand. Ida didn't understand herself, but she knew whatever made Jake want to raise milk cows against all common sense was tied in with the thing that made her love him.

To everyone's surprise, Jake somehow managed to turn a profit from his little dairy. The milk cows certainly weren't made for long-range, west Texas grazing, but he was able to cut a couple of good deals with local farmers for feed, and by irrigating was able to raise a few acres of alfalfa himself. And he sure didn't have to worry about competition for his milk.

Only when they first married did he say anything about the cows. He explained that he just liked the idea of feeding babies, of them going from their mother's breast to him and his cows, then growing up and into the world. He liked being a part of that.

Ida wondered how many gentle and fragile people lived full, happy lives because the one event that could have pushed them over the edge never occurred. For Jake, that event was the test the people from Texas A&M ran on his milk. It showed traces of lead and arsenic, just within legal limits, and more than likely on the rise. What Jake could not get from his mind for the next three days was the thought that babies had been drinking his milk. Today was the fourth day.

Some young people had approached them about it, pointing fingers toward groundwater pollution and a toxic dump site. They wanted to take it to court. But for those three days after the test it was all Ida could do to take care of Jake, and now it was too late to matter. With Jake gone, she was surprised how easily everything fell from her shoulders, how easily she could let go of the burden of this beautiful, desolate land. This was Jake's country, and she could not bear witness to it without him. And without Jake, it lost its claim on her. It would be easy enough to leave this house.

She remembered driving down the dirt driveway that Friday afternoon the doctor told them that Jake couldn't father any children. She hated the doctor for that. He should've never said whose fault it was because it didn't matter. *They* couldn't have children, not Jake alone. Driving home he didn't say a word, and in the silence she became gripped by the fear he'd leave her. She knew he was thinking that he wasn't good enough for her, wasn't enough of a man. In bed that night she insisted he love her. Demanded it. And when he couldn't, and the coldness and distance swept into her, some dark part of herself opened and she did something she never thought she could do, then things she'd never even heard of. She was so shameless it scared him, but it woke him up and brought him to her. "It's not for babies," she told him. "It's for me. It's so you can please me."

A shot rang out, and she blushed, having been caught remembering *that*, then slowly began pushing those memories away. They didn't go easily. They seemed to flutter inside her like birds, frightened, insistent, white. She imagined opening a window and setting them free; watched them fly over the desert until the curves of their wings shrunk to pinpoints, then disappeared altogether into the sky.

There was nothing she could do to bring him back this time. She had nothing new to show him. He was through, and that was all. She knew him well enough to let him be.

"Accept, accept," she whispered as she slowly rocked. This part of her life was simply over. She told herself to count her blessings for forty-seven years with a man like Jake. And if her sister, Mae, brought it up, then Ida'd have to point out that her husband had only lasted twenty-five.

She thought again of Florida: she could get fresh seafood, and she remembered riding with Mae in the back seat of their Chevrolet the summer before the war when their folks took them to Galveston. Ida ordered flounder almost every meal. It infuriated Mae, who could see no point in eating a fish so silly it had both eyes on the same side of its face. But Ida explained that it simply wanted to see the sky. And Jake when he was courting her—she caught him lying on his back in a field in the middle of the morning. She walked out to him and asked him what he thought he was doing. "I reckon I'm just looking up," he told her. She watched him, then lay beside him. When he reached out and took her hand, she knew she was married.

Ida hadn't thought about the flounder since she was a little girl. She'd have to tell Mae, and Mae would tell her she was as crazy as Jake. Ida was surprised the thought could make her smile. It was daylight now, quiet, and she could see the sheriff ambling toward the pen.

Yahya Gharagozlou

A SIMPLE DEATH

Mr. Hosseini was asleep when a small artery in the right hemisphere of his brain burst, signaling the start of his slow death. His unconscious promptly began informing him of that fact, and he dreamt that he stood on the windowsill of his apartment looking down at a crowd. "Is my wife down there?" he asked. "No ... good." He relaxed and casually took a step into empty space. Still, the unconscious wasn't satisfied.

Mr. Hosseini used his small fingernail to pick at the sleep seeds which of late felt like pine needles. He opened his caked-up eyes. It was eight thirty-five, Sunday morning, and it was going to be his last day alive. Not that he felt sick or any worse than he would have felt any other day. It was more the case that, overnight, he had simply lost the will to live and couldn't figure out why. So clear was this awareness that he had an overpowering impulse to oversee his own death. Crazy, he thought. Old men don't commit suicide. Only young, mixed-up kids do that. You read about them in the paper. Eighteen-year-olds jumping off bridges. Imagine a seventy-year-old man throwing himself out of an apartment in Quincy. He could see the newspaper headline: Elderly Iranian immigrant jumps to death from third story. No, he would never create a scene. It wouldn't be fair to his wife and daughter. He could imagine them as they approached the crowd, chattering away after a weekend with relatives. Their eyebrows would arch, for an instant, with curiosity, and then, his wife's face would drop; she'd know something was wrong even when there wasn't anything wrong.

He rubbed his fists into both eyes and swung his legs down to put on his slippers. The right slipper was there beside the little red table. He bent over nearly double to look under the bed for the left one. The blood rushed into his head; ". . . three, four, five . . . ," said his temples, "you are still alive." He flipped the bedspread and the lint balls twirled momentarily around a common center. Underneath the bed there was the box for the electric blanket, his nephew's spring exerciser, and, far back, hung the fringed ends of the blue, cretonne bedspread. But the left slipper was not there. Everything was quiet with his wife and daughter away. Frowning, he went around to his wife's side of the bed. Smells changed (the odors a little richer, a little creamier). Her bright blue, fluffy mules pointed neatly outward from their place under the nightstand. He placed his feet carefully in them, then he got into his brown checked dressing gown and went to the kitchen to prepare tea.

He put the water on the stove and sat at the table waiting for the kettle to boil. Ungenerous life! he thought. Waiting this long to show its true face: the love of his life, his younger brother Esfand, army general, shot dead through his uniform by a flea-ridden mullah who couldn't wash his own asshole. Himself, standing behind the yellow immigration line, the image of a supplicant, to enter America, a world he wanted no part of. But why had he panicked and left? What would anyone have wanted with a retired pharmacist? He poured the boiling water in his glass. He missed his samovar. Of course none of this explained the urge to die. Not even an urge really. More a certainty. He wasn't some young boy confused about life or about himself. He knew what he felt. Today was going to be his last day alive. That was all that needed to be understood. Mr. Hosseini dipped the tea bag a few more times, then wrapped the soggy bag around the spoon squeezing it tight with the string to get the last bit of flavor. He liked strong tea. He could hang himself, he thought, but rejected the idea almost immediately. He had seen a few hangings in his time, years ago when it was performed as a kind of a word to the wise.

Reza, his cousin, had explained the way it worked in a matter-of-fact style, like a doctor explaining to his colleagues the onset of disease. As soon as the guard removes the support from under the prisoner's feet, the body falls rapidly under the force of its own weight. It comes to an abrupt halt at the taking of the rope's slack, and the neck breaks instantly. Crack. Reza had emphasized the "crack" with a simulated karate chop to his palm. And the prisoner, he said, dies painlessly. Mr. Hosseini poured some of the tea from the cup into the saucer and placed a sugar cube inside his right cheek. He drank noisily from the saucer, blowing and sucking to cool the hot tea. He kept the bitter liquid in his mouth long enough to mix with his sugary saliva. On the table, next to his wife's eyelash curler, lay her pocket-size cosmetic mirror. The double-sided mirror swung between a wishbone-shaped chrome holder. On one side was a concave mirror, the type which enlarged every pore. In it he saw a blurred image of the top of his head: it reminded him of the triplegic puppet village children held by the lone remaining limb, most of its hair loose. Showing through are the obscene pink patches of alopecia.

A surge of vanity almost made him fetch his dentures, but it was momentary. He moved his head back and forth, focusing the reflection of his unshaven cheek—now a lump around the sugar cube. The white hair bristled stiffly on his wizened face, each single hair visible and inches apart. Maybe a razor, he thought. He had heard that if you sit in a bathtub full of hot water, even the cutting is painless. Apparently, one drifted away comfortably. Then he remembered, with a little pride at his own sense of detail, that the bathtub didn't retain water very well. What an ugly sight that would be: wife and daughter returning to find his body in an almost empty tub; his thin flabby buttocks and thighs displacing the red small lozenge-like puddles; blood clotted around his white-haired chest and genitals. And the stench of blood, for he remembered his brother's room the time Esfand had nearly bled to death from an intestinal ulcer.

The sugar had melted. He shuddered from the bitter taste of the tea. No, he couldn't kill himself violently. Not by cutting, hanging or jumping. These were methods for the young, who were after effect and attention. He just wanted to die with the least trouble to his family and the people around him. Gas was not an unattractive option, but the house didn't run on gas. No one in the house used sleeping pills. He was beginning to perceive the problem. This wasn't going to be easy. He flicked at the mirror, making it spin. The reflected light beam bounced jerkily around the room. He remembered the famous French magician, Dr. Gastonier, who had entertained the people in his town one evening close to half a century ago. The good doctor would flick open his pocket watch and, using the small mirror inside, hypnotize certain individuals in the crowd. All he had to do was focus the reflection on their foreheads. And the way he used to move objects by merely concentrating on them. "The real trick is that it must not be a trick," the magician would tell his audience confidently. For weeks afterwards he tried to move objects. He'd concentrate for hours at a time on a glass of water until he'd drop from exhaustion and frustration. The glass never budged a hair.

The fascination with his own mind-over-matter faded over the years and was replaced by a skeptical and practical mind. He spent a lifetime weighing and measuring drugs. Most of his business was centered around the neighborhood Armenian ladies. He sold his own shampoo which he made from castor oil and camphor spirits mixed in a viscous coal-tar solution. He also offered a special face cream, a mix of salicylic acid powder and sulphur powder, which had been a good seller. Since the days of Gastonier, only one incident had crossed the indistinct borders of the supersensible. The old woman who brought with her, like a first cold wind, the winter of his life.

It was a spring evening, a week after his fifty-third birthday. Strolling outside the house, smoking his after-dinner cigarette, he noticed an old woman crossing the street toward him. As she drew near, he found himself absorbed in estimating her age, raising the figure as details sharpened in the dusk light. The skin on her face hung straight down, unwrinkled, like a stretched sheet of white dough. But the skin around her eyesockets was like the deep lunette folds of a theater curtain. The eyes themselves were colored a dirty pearl and dull. The hollow bones were so delicate, he knew they could be snapped between thumb and forefinger. So vivid was the dilapidated figure that his mind was over-whelmed with her impending death. She is going to die tomorrow, he thought he had thought. She had only passed him by a few steps when he felt the blow of her cane on his back. "Stop saying that I tell you," she said. Turning, he saw two eyes glowing with life and defiance. But only for an instant. The eyes reverted to their earlier lifeless gaze. What was she holding onto so desperately? When he had caught pneumonia the next day, in his mind it was she who was to blame.

And looking back, he could confidently point, as if to an old photograph in an album: there, that was the week I became an old man. Today he would hold her in his arms like a child and comfort her. There really wasn't anything to worry about. It was easy.

At that last thought, Mr. Hosseini was once again jogged into the realm of practicality. He straightened his back. What's easy? It's not easy at all. There must be some way. I must think of a way out. Must think of a way out. THINK OF A WAY OUT, he smiled, shaking his head.

Maybe I could concentrate on dying. Now that would be a clean way for everybody.

The possibility intrigued him. He had the rest of the day to himself. He'd lie on his sofa, close his eyes and concentrate on the job. It would be easier than those youthful extensive bouts of concentration. Besides, he was older and much more patient. He took a last sip of the lukewarm tea, rinsed the cup squeaky clean with his index finger and walked to the darkened living room. He removed the slippers and lay back on the sofa, closing his eyes gratefully. He began to concentrate.

His last two conscious thoughts before dying were that his left slipper was under the laundry bag in the corner of the room, and that this method of dying wasn't difficult at all. The trick was that it must not be a trick.

Madison Smartt Bell

THE NAKED LADY

This is a thing that happened before Monroe started maken the heads, while he was still maken the naked ladies.

Monroe went to the college and it made him crazy for a while like it has done to many a one.

He about lost his mind on this college girl he had. She was just a little old bit of a thing and she talked like she had bugs in her mouth and she was just nothen but trouble. I never would of messed with her myself.

When she thrown him over we had us a party to take his mind off it. Monroe had these rooms in a empty mill down by the railroad yard. He used to make his scultures there and we was both liven there too at the time.

We spent all the money on whiskey and beer and everbody we known come over. When it got late Monroe appeared to drop a stitch and went to throwin bottles at the walls. This caused some people to leave but some other ones stayed on to help him I think.

I had a bad case of drunk myself. A little before sunrise I crawled off and didn't wake up till up in the afternoon. I had a sweat from sleepin with clothes on. First thing I seen when I opened my eyes was this big old rat setten on the floor side the mattress. He had a look on his face like he was wonderen would it be safe if he come over and took a bite out of my leg.

It was the worst rats in that place you ever saw. I never saw nothin to match em for bold. If you chunked somethin at em they would just back off a ways and look at you mean. Monroe had him this tin sink that was full of plaster from the scultures and ever night these old rats would mess in it. In the mornin you could see they had left tracks goen places you wouldnt of believed somethin would go.

We had this twenty-two pistol we used to shoot em up with but it wasnt a whole lot of good. You could hit one of these rats square with a twenty-two and he would go off with it in him and just get meaner. About the only way to kill one was if you hit him spang in the head and that needs you to be a better shot than I am most of the time.

We did try a box of them exploden twenty-twos like what that boy shot the President with. They would take a rat apart if you hit him but if you didnt they would bounce around the room and bust up the scultures and so on.

It happened I had put this pistol in my pocket before I went to bed so Monroe couldnt get up to nothin silly with it. I taken it out slow and thew down on this rat that was looken me over. Hit him in the hindquarter and he went off and clamb a pipe with one leg draggen.

I sat up and saw the fluorescents was on in the next room thew the door. When I went in there Monroe was messen around one of his sculture stands.

Did you get one, he said.

Winged him, I said.

That aint worth much, Monroe said. He off somewhere now plotten your doom.

I believe the noise hurt my head more'n the slug hurt that

rat, I said. Is it any whiskey left that you know of?

Let me know if you find some, Monroe said. So I went to looken around. The place was nothin but trash and it was glass all over the floor.

I might of felt worse sometime but I dont just remember when it was, I said.

They's coffee, Monroe said.

I went in the other room and found a half of a pint of Heaven Hill between the mattress and the wall where I must of hid it before I tapped out. Pretty slick for drunk as I was. I taken it in to the coffee pot and mixed half and half with some milk in it for the sake of my stomach.

Leave me some, Monroe said. I hadnt said a word, he must of smelt it. He tipped the bottle and took half what was left.

The hell, I said. What you maken anyway?

Naked lady, Monroe said.

I taken a look and it was this shape of a woman setten on a mess of clay. Monroe made a number of these things at the time. Some he kept and the rest he thrown out. Never could tell the difference myself.

Thats all right, I said.

No it aint, Monroe said. Soon's I made her mouth she started in asken me for stuff. She wants new clothes and she wants a new car and she wants some jewry and a pair of Italian shoes.

And if I make her that stuff, Monroe said, I know she's just goen to take it out looken for some other fool. I'll set here all day maken stuff I dont care for and she'll be out just riden and riden.

Dont make her no clothes and she cant leave, I said.

She'll whine if I do that, Monroe said. The whole time you was asleep she been fussen about our relationship.

You know the worst thing, Monroe said. If I just even

thought about maken another naked lady I know she would purely raise hell.

Why dont you just make her a naked man and forget it, I said.

Why dont I do this? Monroe said. He whopped the naked lady with his fist and she turned into a flat clay pancake, which Monroe put in a plastic bag to keep soft. He could hit a good lick when he wanted. I hear this is common among scultures.

Dont you feel like doen somethin, Monroe said.

I aint got the least dime, I said.

I got a couple dollars, he said. Lets go see if it might be any gas in the truck.

They was some. We had this old truck that wasnt too bad except it was slow to start. When we once got it goen we drove over to this pool hall in Antioch where nobody didnt know us. We stayed awhile and taught some fellers that was there how to play rotation and five in the side and some other games that Monroe was good at. When this was over with we had money and I thought we might go over to the Ringside and watch the fights. This was a bar with a ring in the middle so you could set there and drink and watch people get hurt.

We got in early enough to take seats right under the ropes. They was an exhibition but it wasnt much and Monroe started in on this little girl that was setten by herself at the next table.

Hey there Juicy Fruit, he said, come on over here and get somethin real good.

I wouldnt, I told him, haven just thought of what was obvious. Then this big old hairy thing came out from the back and sat down at her table. I known him from a poster out front. He was champion of some kind of karate and had come all the way up from Atlanta just to beat somebody to death and I didnt think he would care if it was Monroe. I got Monroe out of there. I was some annoyed with him because I would have admired to see them fights if I could do it without bein in one myself.

So Monroe said he wanted to hear music and we went some places where they had that. He kept after the girls but they wasnt any trouble beyond what we could handle. After while these places closed and we found us a little railroad bar down on Lower Broad.

It wasnt nobody there but the pitifulest band you ever heard and six bikers, the big fat ugly kind. They wasnt the Hell's Angels but I believe they would have done until some come along. I would of left if it was just me.

Monroe played pool with one and lost. It wouldnt of happened if he hadnt been drunk. He did have a better eye than me which may be why he is a sculture and I am a second-rate pool player.

How come all the fat boys in this joint got on black leather jackets? Monroe hollered out. Could that be a new way to lose weight?

The one he had played with come bellyen over. These boys like to look you up and down beforehand to see if you might faint. But Monroe hooked this one side of the head and he went down like a steer in the slaughterhouse. This didnt make me as happy as it might of because it was five of em left and the one that was down I thought apt to get up shortly.

I shoved Monroe out the door and told him to go start the truck. The band had done left already. I thown a chair and I thown some other stuff that was layen around and I ducked out myself.

The truck wasnt started yet and they was close behind. It was this old four-ten I had under the seat that somebody had sawed a foot off the barrel. I taken it and shot the sidewalk in front of these boys. The pattern was wide on account of the barrel bein short like it was and I believe some of it must of hit all of em. It was a pump and took three shells and I kept two back in case I needed em for serious. But Monroe got the truck goen and we left out of there.

I was some mad at Monroe. Never said a word to him till he parked outside the mill. It was a nice moon up and thowin shadows in the cab when the headlights went out. I turned the shotgun across the seat and laid it into Monroe's ribs.

What you up to? he said.

You might want to die, I said, but I dont believe I want to go with you. I pumped the gun to where you could hear the shell fallen in the chamber.

If that's what you want just tell me now and I'll save us both some trouble.

It aint what I want, Monroe said.

I taken the gun off him.

I dont know what I do want, Monroe said.

Go up there and make a naked lady and you feel better, I told him.

He was messen with clay when I went to sleep but that aint what he done. He set up a mirror and done a head of himself instead. I taken a look at the thing in the mornin and it was a fair likeness. It looked like it was thinkin about all the foolish things Monroe had got up to in his life so far.

That same day he done one of me that was so real it even looked like it had a hangover. Ugly too but that aint Monroe's fault.

He is makin money with it now.

How we finally fixed them rats was we brought on a snake. Monroe was the one to have the idea. It was a good-sized one and when it had just et a rat it was as big around as your arm. It didnt eat more than about one a week but it appeared to cause the rest of em to lay low.

You might say it was as bad to have snakes around as rats but at least it was only one of the snake.

The only thing was when it turned cold the old snake wanted to get in the bed with you. Snakes aint naturally warm like we are and this is how come people think they are slimy, which is not the truth when you once get used to one.

This old snake just comes and goes when the spirit moves him. I aint seen him in a while but I expect he must be still around.

Bruce Holland Rogers

MURDER, MYSTERY

Okay, this is a murder mystery. The victim is lying in a field not far from U.S. 36. Face down.

It's early morning. Along the eastern horizon there's a band of clouds, though the sky overhead is blue. The sun is up, but still hidden. Here's what I want you to see: to the west, another cloud bank lies against the Flatirons, with just the jagged tops of the first and third Flatirons jutting through. I've already said the sky is blue, but I don't think you've really seen it. Brilliant blue? Piercing blue? At this distance, you can see the summits of Longs Peak and Mount Meeker, capped with snow and orange in the early light.

See it? See the bright orange mountains against the blue sky? See the clouds hugging the Flatirons? Can you sense what the light is like for someone standing in this field? (There is no one standing there, of course. There's just the body, and the body is lying down.) A western meadowlark sings. They only sing at certain levels of light, early in the day and early in the evening. The song is like this: three bright, slow notes, then a flurry of song too fast and complex to describe. You can hold the sound in your mind for only a moment, then the memory of it melts away.

I know what you're thinking.

We'll get to the body, I promise. But first I want to be certain you can see the light, the two banks of clouds, the orange mountains, the blue sky behind them. It's spring. The foothills are green. Soon the sun will rise a little more and burn those clouds from the Flatirons. You'll see just how green the hills are. The western meadowlark will stop singing.

There's heavy traffic on U.S. 36, but no one has seen the body. Cars swish by. Anyone could spot this body. It's right here in the field.

It looks as if the dead man was shot in the back and fell forward. There's not much blood around the hole in the back of his shirt. The exit wound is probably another story.

Was he killed here? Did he expect it? Were there two men holding his arms while another pointed the gun? What caliber of gun was it? Was he a drug dealer? Witness to another crime? Jealous husband? The lover? Maybe the wife killed him. Maybe he didn't expect it. Maybe he was killed somewhere else and brought here, dumped here.

The soil in the field is soft. There are footprints. Someone will be able to tell the story, or part of it, anyway, by looking at those footprints. They'll figure out the caliber of the gun. They'll identify the man and unravel his history, interview suspects.

But we won't.

This is not that kind of mystery.

His face is against the ground, but turned a little.

At this time of year, at this time of morning, there's something about the smell of earth and growing grass.

The man's lips are parted. His tongue juts a little between his teeth. It's as if he's tasting the dew on the grass.

That's not a symbol or anything. That's just the way it is.

I wish I had a word for the blue of the sky.

GIVING IT AWAY

All I wanted were dining chairs for the refectory table, something oak but not too precious, late teens or twenties maybe, t-backs, with new tapestry covered seats. But Xaviera was thinking bigtime, she was into Shaker and Stickley and Marxism, and thwarting industrialization. Capitalism was nosediving, there was an Arts and Crafts revival, all this and more she flung at me on Saturday mornings when we drove the valley, hitting yard sales and estate sales, hopefully ahead of the antique dealers; or, if the dealers beat us there, they would be after Depression glass or Roseville and not the chairs stacked high under the tarp in the garage, where I would spot them, and where I would measure their turned legs with my eye, flip them over one by one and check for planing, gouges, clucking at the sad state these lovely pieces had fallen into—white spiders nesting in the joints, the seats worn and faded.

"Don't give anything away," Xaviera said, meaning I looked too eager, meaning I should hold out for the real thing, meaning I have a face that anyone could read, and, after having done so, anyone would raise the price, or decide not to sell.

Every Saturday morning that spring she was at my door
by seven-thirty, classifieds in hand, the ads highlighted and
color-coded by location. Fluorescent orange, the Avenues.
Green, the east bench, from Holladay to Sandy. Hot pink,
Sugarhouse. I sometimes dragged Xaviera to Rose Park,
even though she had tried to educate me in the ways of
things, of antiques—that nothing good could be found west
of Trolley Square—but Xaviera, I said, these people have
grandmothers and great aunts who ordered mission furniture from the Sears catalogue and bought Fiesta place settings at Woolworth's, and she shrugged.

"Junk," she said, "is relative; but if all you have are grandmother's pearls and her turkey platter, would you let them
go?"

"Keeping a thing is also relative," I said. "Like that
woman in Sugarhouse who said her therapist told her that
selling her mother's oak sideboard might help her clean up
her internal house and live in the here and now.' "

"Might," Xaviera said. "Not that I haven't thought about
it myself, cutting everything loose and starting over—you
have to admit it's tempting. People start to expect certain
things from you after a while, like you only collect thirties
flatwear, or you would never wear black or vote a straight
party ticket or would drop everything and start over, wham,
just like that. Quicksilver, presto-changeo."

Right now, I thought, when Xaviera was snapping her
fingers and looking determined, right now is not the time to
be saying these things to me; right now I want chairs that
are not all business, chairs I can bring to life with orange oil
and steel wool; right now I want to look like I am putting
down roots, thinking of remodeling, maybe putting in a bay
window on the east side of the dining room or a skylight in
the bathroom—I want this now. Starting again, *(startling
again,* my mother once said, adding an *l,* propping the black

phone receiver up to her ear with her shoulder while she sprinkled the laundry on ironing day, *morning is always that way for me, a new beginning, rise and shine—so why should this be any different?)*, no thank you, not me—what I want is continuity.

"Think about it," Xaviera said, and I was, that was the problem, that's all I have ever done, my one big problem, *you think too much*—always I weighed possibilities and probabilities against each other. Until that spring with Xaviera I had shrugged it all off and kept on. Very much as always, with Xaviera saying turn here, don't turn there, and then that one day she yelled stop stop! and jumped out of the car before I had even complied, and I stopped thinking and took notice.

"Why here?" I asked, but Xaviera wasn't listening, she was heading for a house that sat back a bit from the street, a house with odds and ends stacked up high on the porch and on the lawn, a house that wasn't highlighted on our list.

Xaviera said, "Oh jeez, oh lord, sweetie look at this," and she unrolled a rug that was all over rose trellises and blue hyacinths and yellow birds, a Victorian copy from the twenties, I guessed, and Xaviera was crouched down, resting her chin on her knees, remembering something, from the look on her face.

"You're giving it away," I said, and the woman standing in the open doorway thought I was talking to her and jumped and called out a price that was too high, and Xaviera turned to me and whispered *please, please, how much can you help with this?*

Zip, I thought, zero, nothing will help this, but I gave her what she needed anyway.

Lee K. Abbott

HOW ONE BECOMES THE OTHER

This is the story Freddy Pease told me the afternoon he got ticketed up to Segregation. A classic type spooky felon, Mister Freddy McKinley Pease. Your basic habitual criminal, back in the joint for his fourth B & E. Interesting guy—about as predictable as flash flooding.

Seems like Freddy was in his house one day not long ago, listening to the Notre Dame game on his radio. Good match. Much to and fro.

"Catholics versus convicts," he tells me, "saints against sinners."

Anyway, late in the third quarter, a ruckus commences in the house next door—home of a junkie biker named Leon and his housebuddy, Clyde, who called himself Betty. You know the kind: unaffiliated meat in need of protection, dabs on a little non-reg Revlon lip gloss, and makes an acceptable sweetie if you're so inclined. Plenty are.

So: a disagreement develops. Domestic strife, according to Pease. That was his word, "strife." Something about money—scrip, not street. A quarrel erupts.

"It's after lock'n'count," he tells me.

This was Orient, our place in the world, us temporary roomies—him only a month up on the chain from declassification—and we were in the yard watching the population dance its usual hokey-pokey.

"The ruckus," I said.

Freddy was watching a couple of Muslims take direction from a hack named Wedge. Naked, Wedge might have resembled a root system.

"It's the hooting first," Freddy said. "High pitched squealing. Metal on metal."

"Where's the watch sergeant?" I say.

"Dentist," he says. "Man has teeth like a piano, gotta be played. Only one around is this new screw, name of Nellis."

I think the unthinkable vis à vis the scene: rookie hack, indifferent convicts, the effects of long-term incarceration. The possibilities, as my ex-wife used to say, boggle the brain.

"So there's shouting," Freddy says. He's curious, takes a peek. Walkway yo-yos everywhere. Lifers, ragheads, beaners, even an Indian with one of those high maintenance Krishna hairdos. The whole tier's lined up for the showdown.

"Take your time," I tell Freddy.

Pretty soon, according to Pease, there's debris.

"Debris?"

"Leon's throwing stuff," he says. "Knickknacks, a teeny-weeny Eiffel Tower made out of matchsticks. Some beads. They come flying out of there. Magazines, too. *Better Homes and Gardens*, old copies of *Silver Screen*."

"A flurry," I say.

"Then goodies," Freddy says. "Edibles from the canteen. Vienna sausages. Hydrox cookies, Diet Pepsi, salami sticks."

I consider telling him about my old lady, Ellen, what she could do in the kitchen—tamale roll, etcetera—but he is telling a story and, as with all dings, I am no more advised to get between it and him than between hell and high water.

"The whole time," Freddy Pease says, "Betty is screaming. Motherhumper–this, motherhumper–that. Sounds like a sixteen-year-old girl."

I was watching Wedge. Like Pease himself, he could be moved to meanness by the weather, I'd heard. Plus which, according to my ex-cellmate, Fat Willie the Forger, Wedge had a wife built like Olive Oyl with the go-get-em personality of a Doberman pinscher. God knows what Pease had outside. Maybe a Vegas showgirl, maybe an oak tree with hips.

"Seems Leon's been drinking pruno. It was an occasion."

"Raisins?" I wonder.

"Crushed seedless grapes," he says. "Lifer's Choice. Two pinches of pot and some Smucker's jelly. Leon's lost control, a couple of times Betty comes flying out of the cell. She's wearing State issue denim but with a zipper up the side. Flowered sneakers. Looks like a movie star."

I mention my favorite: Meryl Streep.

"Sally Field," he says.

Across the way, Wedge is writing a ticket for some Zapatista in a hairnet. Miguel or Jesus–one of those.

"I got a ringside seat," Freddy goes on. "Betty and Leon going back and forth like rats in a bag."

"You got a way with words," I tell him.

Here it is he talks literature, the good and bad of it. Danielle Steel, John Grisham. Most cons have a favorite. James Jones or whatever: any type of language from the far-away–lapping waters, buxom maidens in the throes, chases like you get in war. Me, I work over in Furniture. The rest of the time I'm reading, writing letters, writing stories, working on my critical faculties. I go for agony, ecstasy, how one becomes the other. Got an imagination the way Kellogg's has cornflakes.

"The rest of it goes like this," Freddy Pease says. "Leon wrecks the place. Curtains, little decorative items, pictures–the whole bit. Utterly trashed."

"Comes a moment, however?" I wonder.

"Exactamente," Freddy tells me. "Comes a moment when Betty goes flying out the door, grabs the rail. She's enraged, teary-eyed, flushed. Got her blouse ripped. Big bare nipples. Plus a tattoo."

"Pirate ship," I say, guessing. "Maybe a heart with blood."

Pease looks at me hard, like being watched by a dog that can talk English.

"You in a hurry?" he asks.

"Got a delivery to make," I tell him. "Over to Electrical." Freddy cracks a knuckle or two. Yonder, Wedge is doing deep knee bends, which would be comical but for the flesh going which-away.

"We're all jammed up," Freddy Pease says. "Even the new screw, Nellis, is—what?—mesmerized. Looks bug-eyed, like a frog. Betty's sporting a lump on one cheek. She's holding a bottle of Old Spice. Beautiful fingernails."

"Red?" I ask.

He nods.

"More details," I say.

"Exactamente," he says. Whereupon he uses my nom de pen: Switchboard.

I'm the messenger inside. Take, as has been said, the one to the other. Make the yon hither, and vice versa. Suppose you got a confidence needs to get to, oh, West Mess or Protective Custody. I'm your guy. You get assured delivery, I get a pack of smokes or some Ho-hos or your baked potato at dinner time. Your innermosts are safe with me. Alvie Patterson, semi-professional car thief.

"It's the quiet I remember," Freddy says, himself dreamylike. "Silence thick as wool," he says. "Cold, too. Quiet with color. Climactic, like."

Me and Ellen, we had a couple of those climaxes ourselves—lighting like you find in Boris Karloff movies, the smells to be smelled, heart hammering in the ears, maybe smoke or fog as a special effect—what I'd rather hear about than live through again.

"Then it's over," Freddy says. "Betty's standing there, all cried out. Leon comes out of the house. He's a big fella, arms like railroad ties. Got a face you don't want to read too much into. I figure Betty's going over the rail. Swan dive or something. Make a splat on the floor."

Pease has me in his gaze again, eyes about as life-affirming as bbs. Apparently, it's my turn to talk.

"Holy moly," I say.

"The holiest," he says, "the moliest." Leon takes a step, he tells me, then another. He's got scratches across his cheek, a little blood coming from the ear—a bite maybe. You can hear Betty breathing, gasping like she's been underwater. "You cold?" Leon asks. "Why you want to know?" Betty says, still on guard. Leon shrugs, "You're shaking, baby," he says. Betty brushes her cheeks, tries to huff up a little. Something's been settled, evidently. "You sorry, Leon?" she says.

"The scrip?" I ask Freddy Pease.

He's nodding. It was for a birthday cake. Leon's birthday. Plus, Betty had scored a pint of sour cream icing from the cook in East Mess. Plus a hand-tooled leather belt from some fish upcountry.

I wonder about Nellis, the new hack.

"About does a back flip," Freddy says. "Serious applause. He nearly craps his pants."

I'm standing now, casual-like. The four-thirty whistle has gone off, so it's time for me to chop-chop.

"Happy ending," I tell him. "That's sweet."

For a moment we watch Wedge. He'd been looking our way like we were stuff to step on. Out in the world, so we'd heard, Wedge yodeled country-western. Wore the outfits, too. Chaps, high heel boots, shirts with pearl buttons. Looked like a sissy.

"So they kiss and make up, Leon and Betty," Freddy says. "Ozzie and Harriet all over again."

So here it is: we cons are sentimentalists and proud of it. Patriotism, the handshake that seals the deal, what you can say about a mother—we take it all seriously. Hell, I've seen your average armed robber go mano mano over the Fifth, Eighth, and Fourteenth Amendments. Aside from evil, only difference between us and the Boy Scouts of America is maybe bad table manners.

"Look at that grease-dripping pig-sucker," Freddy says.

Wedge is on the move now—another climax I aim to avoid. I got a piece to write, plus my aforementioned delivery. After that is dinner (shepherd's pie and orange Jell-O: it is Wednesday), maybe a half-hour of pinochle with Fat Willie, then a call to make up in Rec. I got only one more question.

"So who won," I say, "the football game?"

Freddy Pease, on his way to Segregation for good reason no doubt, is humming anew, is eyeballing Wedge.

"Convicts," he says. "A cakewalk."

Peter Meinke

THE CRANES

Oh!" she said, "what are those, the huge white ones?"
Along the marshy shore two tall and stately birds, staring
motionless toward the Gulf, towered above the bobbing
egrets and scurrying plovers.

"Well, I can't believe it," he said. "I've been coming here
for years and never saw one ..."

"But what are they?" she persisted. "Don't make me guess
or anything, it makes me feel dumb." They leaned forward
in the car and the shower curtain spread over the front seat
crackled and hissed.

"They've got to be whooping cranes, nothing else so big!"
One of the birds turned gracefully, as if to acknowledge the
old Dodge parked alone in the tall grasses. "See the black
legs and black wingtips? Big! Why don't I have my binocu-
lars?" He looked at his wife and smiled.

"Well," he continued after a while, "I've seen enough
birds. But whooping cranes, they're rare. Not many left."

"They're lovely. They make the little birds look like
clowns."

"I could use a few clowns," he said. "A few laughs never hurt anybody."

"Are you all right?" She put a hand on his thin arm. "Maybe this is the wrong thing. I feel I'm responsible."

"God, no!" His voice changed. "No way. I can't smoke, can't drink martinis, no coffee, no candy. I not only can't leap buildings in a single bound, I can hardly get up the goddamn stairs."

She was smiling. "Do you remember the time you drank thirteen martinis and asked that young priest to step outside and see whose side God was on?"

"What a jerk I was! How have you put up with me all this time?"

"Oh no! I was proud of you! You were so funny, and that priest was a snot."

"Now you tell me." The cranes were moving slowly over a small hillock, wings opening and closing like bellows. "It's all right. It's enough," he said again. "How old am I, anyway, 130?"

"Really," she said, "it's me. Ever since the accident it's been one thing after the other. I'm just a lot of trouble to everybody."

"Let's talk about something else," he said. "Do you want to listen to the radio? How about turning on that preacher station so we can throw up?"

"No," she said, "I just want to watch the birds. And listen to you."

"You must be pretty tired of that."

She turned her head from the window and looked into his eyes. "I never got tired of listening to you. Never."

"Well, that's good," he said. "It's just that when my mouth opens, your eyes tend to close."

"They do not!" she said, and began to laugh, but the laugh

turned into a cough and he had to pat her back until she stopped. They leaned back in the silence and looked toward the Gulf stretching out beyond the horizon. In the distance, the water looked like metal, still and hard.

"I wish they'd court," he said. "I wish we could see them court, the cranes. They put on a show. He bows like Nijinsky and jumps straight up in the air."

"What does she do?"

"She lies down and he lands on her."

"No," she said, "I'm serious."

"Well, I forget. I've never seen it. But I do remember that they mate for life and live a long time. They're probably older than we are! Their feathers are falling out and their kids never write."

She was quiet again. He turned in his seat, picked up an object wrapped in a plaid towel, and placed it between them in the front.

"Here's looking at *you*, kid," he said.

"Do they really mate for life? I'm glad—they're so beautiful."

"Yep. Audubon said that's why they're almost extinct: a failure of imagination."

"I don't believe that," she said. "I think there'll always be whooping cranes."

"Why not?" he said.

"I wish the children were more settled. I keep thinking it's my fault."

"You think everything's your fault. Nicaragua, ozone depletion. Nothing is your fault. They'll be fine, and anyway, they're not children anymore. Kids are different today, that's all. You were terrific." He paused. "You were terrific in ways I couldn't tell the kids about."

"I should hope not." She laughed and began coughing again, but held his hand when he reached over. When the

cough subsided they sat quietly, looking down at their hands
as if they were objects in a museum.

"I used to have pretty hands," she said.

"I remember."

"Do you? Really?"

"I remember everything," he said.

"You always forgot everything."

"Well, now I remember."

"Did you bring something for your ears?"

"No, I can hardly hear anything, anyway!" But his head
turned at a sudden squabble among the smaller birds. The
cranes were stepping delicately away from the commotion.

"I'm tired," she said.

"Yes." He leaned over and kissed her, barely touching her
lips. "Tell me," he said, "did I really drink thirteen martinis?"

But she had already closed her eyes and only smiled. Outside the wind ruffled the bleached-out grasses, and the birds
in the white glare seemed almost transparent. The hull of
the car gleamed beetle-like—dull and somehow sinister in its
metallic isolation from the world around it.

Suddenly, the two cranes plunged upward, their great
wings beating the air and their long slender necks pointed
like arrows toward the sun.

Pam Houston

SYMPHONY

Sometimes life is ridiculously simple. I lost fifteen pounds and the men want me again. I can see it in the way they follow my movements, not just with their eyes but with their whole bodies, the way they lean into me until they almost topple over, the way they always seem to have itches on the back of their necks. And I'll admit this: I am collecting them like gold-plated sugar spoons, one from every state.

This is a difficult story to tell because what's right about what I have to say is only as wide as a tightrope, and what's wrong about it yawns wide, beckoning, on either side. I have always said I have no narcotic, smiling sadly at stories of ruined lives, safely remote from the twelve-step program and little red leather booklets that say "One Day at a Time." But there is something so sweet about the first kiss, the first surrender that, like the words "I want you," can never mean precisely the same thing again. It is delicious and addicting. It is, I'm guessing, the most delicious thing of all.

There are a few men who matter, and by writing them down in this story I can make them seem like they have an order, or a sequence, or a priority, because those are the kinds of choices that language forces upon us, but language can't touch the joyful and slightly disconcerting feeling of being very much in love, but not knowing exactly with whom.

First I will tell you about Phillip, who is vast and dangerous, his desires uncontainable and huge. He is far too talented, a grown-up tragedy of a gifted child, massively in demand. He dances, he weaves, he writes a letter that could wring light from a black hole. He has mined gold in the Yukon, bonefished in Belize. He has crossed Iceland on a dogsled, he is the smartest man that all his friends know. His apartment smells like wheat bread, cooling. His body smells like spice. Sensitive and scared scared scared of never becoming a father, he lives in New York City and is very careful about his space. It is easy to confuse what he has learned to do in bed for love or passion or art, but he is simply a master craftsman, and very proud of his good work.

Christopher is innocent. Very young and wide-open. He's had good mothering and no father to make him afraid to talk about his heart. In Nevada he holds hands with middle-aged women while the underground tests explode beneath them. He studies marine biology, acting, and poetry, and is not yet quite aware of his classic good looks. Soon someone will tell him, but it won't be me. A few years ago he said in a few more years he'd be old enough for me, and in a few more years, it will be true. For now we are friends and I tell him my system, how I have learned to get what I want from many sources, and none. He says this: You are a complicated woman. Even when you say you don't want anything, you want more than that.

I have a dream in which a man becomes a wolf. He is sleeping, cocooned, and when he stretches and breaks the parchment there are tufts of hair across his back and shoulders, and on the backs of his hands. It is Christopher, I suspect, though I can't see his face. When I wake up I am in Phillip's bed. My back is to his side and yet we are touching at all the pressure points. In the predawn I can see the line of electricity we make, a glow like neon, the curve of a wooden instrument. As I wake, "Symphony" is the first word that forms in my head.

Jonathan came here from the Okavango Delta in Botswana; he's tall and hairy and clever and strong. In my living room I watch him reach inside his shirt and scratch his shoulder. It is a savage movement, rangy and impatient, lazy too, and without a bit of self-consciousness. He is not altogether human. He has spent the last three years in the bush. I cook him T-bone steaks because he says he won't eat complicated food. He is skeptical of the hibachi, of the barely glowing coals. Where he comes from, they cook everything with fire. He says things against my ear, the names of places: Makgadikgadi Pans, Nxamaseri, Mpanda-matenga, Gabarone. Say these words out loud and see what happens to you. Mosi-oa-Toenja, "The Smoke That Thun-ders." Look at the pictures: a rank of impalas slaking their thirst, giraffes, their necks entwined, a young bull elephant rising from the Chobe River. When I am with Jonathan I have this thought which delights and frightens me: It has been the animals that have attracted me all along. Not the cowboys, but the horses that carried them. Not the hunters, but the caribou and the bighorn. Not Jonathan, in his infi-nite loveliness, but the hippos, the kudu, and the big African cats. You fall in love with a man's animal spirit, Jonathan tells me, and then when he speaks like a human being, you don't know who he is.

There's one man I won't talk about, not because he is married, but because he is sacred. When he writes love let-ters to me he addresses them "my dear" and signs them with the first letter of his first name and one long black line. We have only made love one time. I will tell you only the one thing that must be told: After the only part of him I will ever hold collapsed inside me he said, "You are so incredibly gentle." It was the closest I have ever come to touching true love.

Another dream: I am in the house of my childhood, and I see myself, at age five, at the breakfast table; pancakes and sausage, my father in his tennis whites. The me that is dreaming, the older me, kneels down and holds out her arms waiting for the younger me to come and be embraced. Jonathan's arms twitch around me and I am suddenly awake inside a body, inside a world where it has become impossible to kneel down and hold out my arms. Still sleeping, Jonathan pulls my hand across his shoulder, and presses it hard against his face.

I'm afraid of what you might be thinking. That I am a certain kind of person, and that you are the kind of person who knows more about my story than me. But you should know this: I could love any one of them, in an instant and with every piece of my heart, but none of them nor the world will allow it, and so I move between them, on snowy highways and crowded airplanes. I was in New York this morning. I woke up in Phillip's bed. Come here, he's in my hair. You can smell him.

Barry Yourgrau

SILVER ARROWS

I track a girl I fancy through the park. My little friend is
helping. It's slow going. The path veers up and down all the
time, and the stubby wings my friend sports are in fact just
ornamental, so I'm forced to lug him about on my back, so
he can keep up. The arrows in his quiver jab me in the neck.
I have to put him down repeatedly to make him rearrange
things.

But the girl is impeded also. She has bags of groceries and
shopping with her. We've gotten close enough once to
wound her—but naturally this has had the disadvantage of
putting her vehemently on guard.

We labor up a winding woodland section. We've lost sight
of her for several minutes. But now my friend gives a shout.
"Where?" I huff. "Over there!" he cries, pointing with his
little chubby hand. I spot the tawny blond head suddenly
against the autumn red and gold of the leaves. It disappears
behind the flank of a crest. "I'll cut her off!" I cry, wheeling
and lumbering off the path in pursuit. Almost immediately I
catch my foot and the two of us go sprawling. Cursing, we
hurriedly retrieve the petite silver bow and bright, scattered

arrows. We remount and hectically I plod up the steep-angled incline.

We're in luck. We crouch behind a rhododendron. On a bench in a clearing directly below us, the girl has had to pause with her bags to catch her breath. She looks right and left in great consternation. The silvery feathered shaft protrudes from the back of her shoulder. "Alright," I whisper, "this time make sure it's a good shot." "This breeze is kind of tricky," my friend mutters, glancing about with a screwed-up eye as he fits the arrow to its string. Suddenly we whirl around. A figure looms over us. It's a large woman, in tweeds. She grins, panting, leaning on her walking stick. "Hello there," she announces. She beams. "What a handsome child," she declares. She bends forward. "What is your name, little fellow? Are you going to shoot something?" she asks. "Beat it, Grandma!" my friend rasps savagely. "For Christ's sake, lady," I add, "he happens to be thousands of years old! Can't you see we're busy?" I demand. The woman looks shocked. She retreats. We wrench back around. "She's onto us," my friend cries. "She's bolting!" The girl is on her feet, backing away from the bench, looking wildly in our general direction. She turns to flee. "Shoot, shoot!" I yell, jumping up. The arrow flashes wide in the slanting light. The girl squeals and veers, fluttering her hands, and rushes across the leaf-scattered grass. "She's going for cover, over there," I shout. "The pond's back there, she won't have any way out—I'll go around and close her off, and drive her this way!" I make a hectic, breathless gesture. "When she breaks, you get her," I admonish fiercely.

I rush down into the clearing, past the bench and the abandoned, monogrammed shopping bags, and head over along the far side of the undergrowth. My heart soars with the thrill of the chase. I wheel about, and start in, tramping loudly and hollering stentorian endearments. "My sweetest of sweet, my beloved!" I shout. "My permanent rose! My autumn heart's golden apple!" At last I hear her wounded voice, quailing. "Please," it cries from somewhere not too far off. "I confess I do find you (unexpectedly) profoundly attractive, but my personal life has other priorities just now." "Oh but true love is merciless!" I bellow. "It won't take no for an answer!"

I crash toward her voice with redoubled violent stamping and thrashing. Suddenly there's a clamor in a rhododendron nearby. "She's breaking, she's breaking!" I shout hectically. I come swarming back out into the clearing. The girl bursts into the open not twenty feet away. She leaps across the clearing, gorgeous in full flight in the splendid gold of the afternoon. A whistling flash stuns her in her tracks. She flings her arms out magnificently wide, as if to the dying grandeur of the trees all around her. Then she twists, and sinks down to her knees, and pitches over sideways to the ground.

I come rushing up. I kneel over her. My little friend approaches unhurriedly, a wry, self-congratulatory smirk on his lips. He stops nearby, and we exchange a silent nod of acknowledgment of his archery. I gaze down at the girl. Carefully I reach around her shoulders, minding the brilliant dart there, and raise her up and support her against my chest. The second shaft protrudes its precious-wrought feathers just off-center out of her pullover. The shot struck her dead in the heart. She looks utterly beautiful. "Are you all right?" I inquire gently. She blinks up at me, her eyes slowly focusing in dewy radiance. "I don't think I've ... ever felt ... this wonderful ... in my life," she whispers haltingly, with a trembling little laugh. "You know ... you've always been ... the only one ... in the world for me," she adds. "Oh, my darling," I tell her. Our lips meet. We kiss, tenderly ... deeply ... extravagantly.

My little friend watches us, leaning on his bow, pink cheeked. He snorts with embarrassment. He ducks his head away, a snaggle-toothed, wincing grin on his childish face. Suddenly he pushes his bow aside, and turns and hoots, and with his pudgy legs bent he shoots a thin, celebratory arc of silvery water out into the afternoon light, over the glorious, windblown leaves.

Glen Weldon

THE CAT WAS DEAD

It was the kind of story he never finished reading, the kind he'd begin with the best intentions on long gray Sunday afternoons while Sharon read the Review and Opinion section, and the dull colorless light through their picture window made the room look sickly. It was drab fiction, passionless fiction, about a couple who lived on an island and whose marriage was, of course, not what it could be. The author described the shores of the island as being "fraught with gorse."

His eyes narrowed in pain. He wanted to put the story down and leave that couple to their gorse-choked island, as he'd abandoned so many couples before them, trapping them in his memory at mid-exposition, fixing them in a stasis before the first conflict or plot-point was introduced.

He steeled himself and continued on, desperately looking for a fresh, exciting image. But the woman's hair was honey-colored, her eyes steel-blue, and her calves both lean and sinewy. The man, he discovered as he plowed further, had an aquiline nose and a slim waist and said things like, "It's the damned war, it changed us, all of us."

A slight headache began to test the waters around his temples as he read on, through the couple's slow, inexorable dissolution. Too slow, too inexorable, he thought, and bit the inside of his cheek as the author returned yet again to the dominant metaphor of the piece, a rotting woodpile.

He looked up from the story, silently commanding his face to adopt an expression of earnest pleasure. "I like how you use the word *interstices*, in describing the woodpile," he said to the author, "I've always liked that word."

Sharon, his wife, shimmied slightly in the loveseat and said, "Thank you." She leaned forward. "What do you think of the woodpile itself?" she asked. "Do you get the symbolism?"

"Oh yes," he said.

"It's not too subtle, I mean, you see what I'm getting at."

" 'Too subtle.' No," he said, and was relieved to hear truth in his voice again.

"I mean," she continued, "it's been a search for the right metaphor, really it has."

"Oh, is that how it works?" he asked, trying to recall what a sincerely curious person looked and sounded like. More eye-contact, he thought, and maybe a follow-up question. "You start with the metaphor and work, uh, out?"

She laughed dismissively. "No," she said, "at least, that's not the way I work. But the right metaphor's real important, a writer could spend a lifetime looking for one that really *says it*, you know? All we can do is try to come up with our own green lights and ash heaps."

"Ah," he said, nodding. A Gatsby reference, he thought. Jesus Christ.

"But don't let me. . ." she said, and waved him to continue.

He read further and found that they had a dog, this fictional, listless, still-born couple, and a cat and a parakeet.

None of the pets had names, or none at least were mentioned. The dog was loved by both the man and the woman, the cat by neither one, and the parakeet flew away at the bottom of the second page in a tight one-sentence paragraph.

He knew as he read on that it would come down to a fight over who the dog loved more. He knew that the woodpile was meant to reflect the warmth of home and hearth, and that the spiders, worms, mildew and rot that slowly overran it as the story lurched forward were the author's comment about the loss of love, subtle as a whack in the face with a sea-bass.

He looked up from a passage about the island's trees whispering in the wind to see his wife staring at him. He stiffened. Had his lips been moving? She always made a big thing of that for some reason, such a stupid little thing to notice.

"Where are you now?" she asked.

"Nearly done," he said, too happily. "The trees are whispering."

Before lunging back into the story, he surreptitiously counted the pages remaining. Three. Three pages to go and nothing had happened besides the parakeet escaping, the woodpile rotting, a meandering dialogue about the war and another one about weather-stripping. Oh, and long, brooding looks. Lots of them, at least seven so far.

Onward. The parakeet came back, but that was hidden in the middle of a dense page-and-a-half paragraph composed almost entirely of adjectives like "sun-dappled," and he almost missed it completely.

The cat died as he turned the last page. It happened like this: at the bottom paragraph of the next-to-last page, the couple found the cat washed up on the gorse. There was a description of the cat's wet fur and bloated tongue, and then, at the very bottom, thrust against the right margin, were the words:

The cat was

He stared, knowing the word—the numbing sentence-halting predicate adjective—that waited for him at the top of the next and last page. And, dammit, he didn't want to see it.

The cat was the only thing he'd really liked. It had been mentioned only twice in the story, but the author had captured it perfectly, simply, flawlessly-well, nearly flawlessly. Flawlessly enough. There was that one part about the cat's "baleful stare," and he'd wondered, when he read it, why "stare" always followed "baleful," wasn't there any other kind of stare in the world, but he'd forgiven that; when considered against its environment, the cat, the wonderfully adjective-and-cliche-free cat, was sublime.

He knew the cat would fight tenaciously for life as long as the page remained unturned, and he let it struggle. When he did turn the page, he saw, up at the top, flush with the left margin, the word and punctuation that sucked the breath out of the noble, horribly mistreated creature:

dead.

He thought of the miserable thing as a martyr, trapped in a trite gray world of his wife's creation, where the women were fresh as daisies and men had eyes like hawks. Why did it have to die? Why couldn't it have been one of the whispering goddamn trees?

There were only two paragraphs left to the story, but his

vision started to blur and he couldn't make out much more than the woman saying something about seasons, and yet another spider skittering over the woodpile.

"George," his wife sounded astonished, elated, "Are you *crying?*"

Oh, the cat, he thought, the poor, poor cat.

NOTES ON THE AUTHORS

LEE K. ABBOTT is the author of five collections of stories, the most recent of which is *Living After Midnight* (Putnam, 1991). His work has appeared in *The Best American Short Stories*, the *Push-cart Prize* anthology, the *O. Henry Prize Stories*, and *Editor's Choice*. Twice a recipient of fellowships in fiction from the National Endowment for the Arts, he teaches at Ohio State University.

STEVE ADAMS is a playwright whose theater pieces have been produced in New York and Los Angeles. "The Fish" is his first published short story and was the winner of *Glimmer Train*'s 1994 New Writer Award. He lives in Austin, Texas.

SHERMAN ALEXIE is the author of the critically acclaimed collection of stories *The Lone Ranger and Tonto Fist Fight in Heaven* (Atlantic, 1993), and his first novel, *Reservation Blues* (Atlantic, 1995), is set on his own Coeur D'Alene Indian Reservation. He is a citation winner for the PEN Hemingway Award for best book of fiction and winner of a 1994 Lila Wallace-Reader's Digest Foundation Award. He lives in Seattle.

CATHRYN ALPERT's fiction has appeared in anthologies and magazines, including the 1989 and 1991 volumes of the *O'Henry*

Festival Stories, The Best of the West 5, ZYZZYVA, and *Puerto del Sol.* Her first novel, *Rocket City* (McMurray & Beck, 1995), has received wide critical acclaim. Formerly a stage director and teacher of theater, she lives in northern California.

MARGARET ATWOOD is the author of more than twenty volumes of poetry, fiction, and nonfiction. Her most recent novels are *The Handmaid's Tale* (Crest Fawcett, 1986), *Cat's Eye* (Bantam, 1989), *Wilderness Tips* (Bantam, 1993), and *Robber Bride* (Doubleday, 1993). "My Life as a Bat" first appeared in *Antaeus.*

CHARLES BAXTER lives in Ann Arbor and teaches at the University of Michigan. Three of the stories which appeared in *A Relative Stranger,* where "Scheherazade" was published (Viking Penguin, 1991), were selected for *Best American Short Stories* (1987, 1989, 1991). His earlier story collections are *Harmony of the World* (University of Missouri Press, 1984) and *Through the Safety Net* (Viking Penguin, 1986). He is the author of two novels, *First Light* (Viking Penguin, 1988) and *Shadow Play* (W. W. Norton, 1993).

MADISON SMARTT BELL is the author of eight novels, including *The Year of Silence* (Harcourt Brace, 1987), *Doctor Sleep* (Harcourt Brace, 1991), *Save Me, Joe Lewis* (Harcourt Brace, 1993), and *All Soul's Rising* (Pantheon, 1995). He is also the author of two collections of short stories, *Zero db* (Ticknor and Fields, 1987), and *Barking Man* (Harcourt Brace, 1990). He lives in Maryland and teaches at Goucher College.

MITCH BERMAN is the author of the novel *Time Capsule* (Putnam, 1987), and co-edited a book about China, *Children of the Dragon* (Collier / Macmillan, 1990). "To Be Horst" first appeared in *Michigan Quarterly Review.* Berman lives in New York City, where he is working on a new novel entitled *Jonestown.*

KENNETH BERNARD is the author of *From the District File* (Fiction Collective Two, 1992) and the long poem *The Baboon in the Night Club* (Asylum Arts, 1994). His plays have been performed by the Play-House Brooklyn Center of Long Island University. "Sister Francetta and the Pig Baby" first appeared in the anthology *The Maldive Chronicles* (PAJ Publishers, 1987). He lives in New York City.

MARGARET BROUCEK holds an M.F.A. in writing from Sarah Lawrence College. She lives in Chicago, where she is a project editor for *Encyclopedia Britannica*. Her screenplay "The Fifteenth Spaghetti" is currently in production and she is writing songs for the soundtrack. "Alvin Jones's Ignorant Wife" first appeared in *Tri-Quarterly*.

ROBERT OLEN BUTLER has published seven novels and a volume of short fiction, *A Good Scent from a Strange Mountain* (Holt, 1993), which won the 1993 Pulitzer Prize for Fiction. His stories have appeared in such publications as *The New Yorker* and *Harper's*, and have been chosen for three annual editions of *The Best American Short Stories*. He lives in Lake Charles, Louisiana, and teaches at McNeese State University.

RON CARLSON's fiction has appeared in many magazines, including *The New Yorker, Harper's, Playboy*, and *Story*. "The Tablecloth of Turin" is reprinted from his most recent collection of stories, *Plan B for the Middle Class* (W. W. Norton, 1992). He lives in Tempe, Arizona, where he directs the Creative Writing Program at Arizona State University.

ANDREI CODRESCU grew up in Romania. He is a regular commentator on National Public Radio, and has written and starred in the movie *Road Scholar*. His latest books are *The Blood Countess* (Simon & Schuster, 1995), *Zombification: Essays from NPR* (St. Martin's Press, 1994), and *The Muse is Always Half-Dressed in New Orleans* (St. Martin's Press, 1994). He teaches writing at Louisiana State University in Baton Rouge, and edits *Exquisite Corpse: a Journal of Books & Ideas*.

WILLIAM deBUYS is the author of two books of nonfiction, *Enchantment and Exploitation* (University of New Mexico Press, 1985) and *River of Traps* (University of New Mexico Press, 1991). He lives in Santa Fe, where he works as an editor and consultant for The Conservation Fund, a national land conservation non-profit organization. "Dreaming Geronimo" first appeared in *Story*.

DON DeLILLO is the author of numerous plays and books of fiction including *White Noise* (Viking, 1985), *End Zone* (Viking, 1986), and *Libra* (Viking, 1988) which won the National Book Award. His most recent novel is *Mao II* (Viking, 1991). "Videotape" appeared in the final issue of *Antaeus* (Autumn 1994) and was reprinted in *Harper's*.

STEPHEN DIXON is the author of eleven story collections, the last an omnibus entitled *The Stories of Stephen Dixon* (Henry Holt, 1994). He has also published six novels, the most recent of which is *Interstate* (Henry Holt, 1995). The story "Flying" is from his collection *Long Made Short* (Johns Hopkins University Press, 1994). He lives in Baltimore and teaches at Johns Hopkins University.

YAHYA GHARAGOZLOU grew up in Iran, went to secondary school in England, then studied in the United States before returning to his native country prior to the 1978 revolution. In 1984 he took an engineering degree from the University of New Hampshire and also began writing short stories about the plight of Iranian immigrants in this country. "A Simple Death" first appeared in *New Renaissance*.

DAGOBERTO GILB was born and raised in Los Angeles. He is the author of a novel, *The Last Known Residence of Mickey Acuña* (Grove Press, 1994), and a collection of stories, *The Magic of Blood* (University of New Mexico Press, 1993), which won the PEN Ernest Hemingway Foundation Award from the Texas Institute of Letters at the University of Texas. In 1995 he received a fellowship from The Guggenheim Foundation. He now lives in El Paso.

MOLLY GILES is the author of a collection of short stories, *Rough Translations* (University of Georgia Press, 1985), which won the Flannery O'Connor Award for Short Fiction, the Bay Area Book Reviewers Award, and the Boston Globe Award. Her regular book reviews in the *San Jose Mercury* won her the 1990 National

Book Critics Circle Citation for Excellence in Book Reviewing. "The Writer's Model" first appeared in *Mānoa*.

MERRILL GILFILLAN is the author of three books of poetry and two collections of essays, *Magpie Rising: Sketches from the Great Plains* (Random House, 1991) and *Moods of Ohio Moons: An Outdoorsman's Almanac* (Kent State University Press, 1991). "F.O.B. Flicker" is from his collection of stories, *Sworn Before Cranes* (Orion / Crown, 1994). He lives in Boulder, Colorado.

TRACI L. GOURDINE lives in Davis, California. She teaches at three state prisons and chairs the creative writing department for the California State Summer School for the Arts.

LYNN GROSSMAN's stories have appeared in *Story Quarterly*, *The Quarterly*, *TriQuarterly*, and the anthology *Hot Type: America's Most Celebrated Writers Introduce the Next Word in Contemporary Fiction*, edited by John Miller (Collier, 1988). "Cartography" first appeared in *TriQuarterly*. She lives in New York City.

JOY HARJO is a member of the Muscogee tribe of Oklahoma. Her most recent book, *In Mad Love and War* (Wesleyan University Press, 1990), won a William Carlos Williams Award from the Poetry Society of America. Other books include *She Had Some Horses* (Thunders Mouth Press, 1983) and *Secrets from the Center of the World* (University of Arizona Press, 1989). "The Flood" first appeared in *Grand Street*. She teaches at the University of New Mexico.

URSULA HEGI grew up in Germany. She has authored four novels, including *Salt Dancers* (Simon & Schuster, 1995) and *Stones from the River* (Simon & Schuster, 1994), which was nominated for the PEN Faulkner Award, and a collection of short stories, *Unearned Pleasures* (University of Idaho Press, 1988). "Doves," was first published in *Prairie Schooner*. She teaches at Eastern Washington University in Cheney.

ROBIN HEMLEY is the author of the short story collection *All You Can Eat* (Grove / Atlantic, 1988), a novel, *The Last Stude-*

baker (Graywolf, 1992), and a book of practical criticism, *Turning Life Into Fiction* (Story Press, 1994). His stories have appeared in such journals as *Ploughshares, Story, North American Review,* and *Mānoa,* and have been anthologized in *The Pushcart Prizes* and in *The Best in American Humor of 1994.* He lives in Bellingham, where he teaches at Western Washington University.

ALLEN HIBBARD has spent most of the last decade teaching at the American University in Cairo as a Fulbright lecturer at Damascus University. He is the author of *Paul Bowles: A Study of the Short Fiction* (Maxwell Macmillan International, 1993) and a collection of stories published in Arabic under the title *Crossing to Abbassiya and Other Stories.* He currently teaches at Middle Tennessee State University in Mulfreesboro.

PAM HOUSTON has published fiction and nonfiction in a wide range of magazines, including *Elle, Travel and Leisure, Allure, Mirabella, Mademoiselle,* and *The Gettsyburg Review.* "Symphony" first appeared in her collection of stories *Cowboys Are My Weakness* (W. W. Norton, 1992). She is the editor of *Women on Hunting: Essays, Fiction, and Poetry* (Ecco, 1994). She lives in northern California.

SHELLEY HUNT has published stories in *Utah Holiday Magazine* and *The Way We Live: Stories by Utah Women.* She is a graduate student at the University of Utah and has served as the executive director of Writers At Work, a summer writers' conference in Park City. "Giving It Away" first appeared in *What If? Writing Exercises for Fiction Writers,* edited by Pam Painter and Anne Bernays (Harper Collins, 1995).

DENIS JOHNSON was born in Munich and lived in Tokyo, Washington, Manila, and Munich by the time he was nineteen, when his first collection of poetry, *The Incognito Lounge* (Carnegie Mellon, 1982), was selected for the National Poetry Series. He has published four other books, including *Resuscitation of a Hanged Man* (Farrar, Straus & Giroux, 1991), and *Jesus' Son* (Farrar,

Straus & Giroux, 1992), which includes the story "Out On Bail." He lives in northern Idaho.

PAGAN KENNEDY has worked as a street preacher, cartoonist, Elvis impersonator, freelancer at the *Village Voice,* and restaurant reviewer. Her fiction has been published in such magazines as *The Quarterly* and *Story Quarterly.* "The Monument" first appeared in *Prairie Schooner.*

ANDREW LAM came to the United States at the end of the Vietnam War, when he was eleven years old. He is an associate editor with the Pacific News Service in San Francisco and has won numerous awards for his nonfiction, including the World Affairs Council Excellence in International Journalism award and the Society for Professional Journalists' Outstanding Young Journalist Award. He lives in northern California.

DAVID LEAVITT grew up in northern California. His collection of stories, *Family Dancing* (Knopf, 1984), was a finalist for both the National Book Critics Circle Award and the PEN / Faulkner Award. His fiction has appeared in *The New Yorker, Harper's,* and *Esquire.* His most recent novels are *The Lost Language of Cranes* (Bantam, 1987) and *Equal Affection* (Harper Collins, 1990). "We Meet at Last" first appeared in *Mississippi Review.* He lives in East Hampton, New York.

BRET LOTT grew up in Los Angeles. "I Owned Vermont" was his first published story (in *Writers Forum*), and later a chapter in his first novel, *The Man Who Owned Vermont* (Viking, 1987). His other novels include *Jewel* (Simon & Schuster, 1991) and *Reed's Beach* (Simon & Schuster, 1993). His collections of stories include *A Dream of Old Leaves* (Viking, 1989) and *The Difference Between Women and Men* (Anchor Books, 1994). He teaches at the College of Charleston.

DANIEL LYONS's story "The Birthday Cake" is taken from *The Last Good Man* (University of Massachusetts Press, 1993), a collection of short stories which won him the Associated Writing Programs award in short fiction. His stories have appeared in *Gentleman's Quarterly, Playboy, Redbook, Story,* and elsewhere. He is the recipient of a National Endowment for the Arts Fellowship and lives in Ann Arbor, Michigan.

MILOŠ MACOUREK, born in Czechoslovakia, is a poet, children's writer, playwright (including several plays co-written with Vaclav Havel), and screenwriter. A first collection of stories, *Love and the Cannonballs,* was published in Prague in 1989. A collection of stories, *Curious Tales* (Oxford University Press, 1980), has been translated into several languages. "Jacob's Chicken" was translated by DAGMAR HERRMANN and first appeared in *Prairie Schooner.*

CLARENCE MAJOR is the author of seven novels and nine books of poetry. His three most recent novels are *My Amputations* (Fiction Collective, 1986), *Such Was the Season* (Mercury House, 1987), and *Painted Turtle: Woman with Guitar* (Sun & Moon Press, 1988). His story collection, *Fun & Games* (Holy Cow! Press, 1990), was nominated for a Los Angeles Times Book Critics Award. He teaches at the University of California at Davis.

MARCEL MARIEN was born in Antwerp. He is one of the better-known surrealists in the visual arts. He has written some twelve books of poetry and prose. KIM CONNELL, the translator, teaches at New York University and has published his own fiction and poetry in *North American Review, The Southern Review,* and the *New England Review.*

MICHAEL MARTONE is the author of five books of fiction, the most recent of which is *Seeing Eye* (Zoland Books, 1995). An earlier book, *Pensees: The Thoughts of Dan Quayle* (Broadripple Press, 1994), brought him Midwestern fame. Martone teaches at Syracuse University and has taught previously at Harvard and at Iowa State University. "Blue Hair" first appeared in *Colorado Quarterly.*

WILLIAM MAXWELL has published six novels, including *So Long, See You Tomorrow* (Knopf, 1980), which won the American

Book Award and the Howells Medal of the American Academy of Arts and Letters. He is also the author of *Over by the River and Other Stories* (Godine, 1984) and *Billie Dyer and Other Stories* (Knopf, 1992). For forty years Maxwell was a fiction editor at *The New Yorker*. His most recent book is *All the Days and Nights* (Knopf, 1995).

THOMAS McGUANE is the author of four novels, *The Sporting Club* (Farrar, Straus & Giroux, 1974), *The Bushwacked Piano* (Random House, 1984), which won the Rosenthal Foundation Award of the American Academy and Institute of Arts & Letters, *Ninety-Two in the Shade* (Farrar, Straus & Giroux, 1974), and *Panama* (Farrar, Straus & Giroux, 1978). "War and Peace" first appeared in *The New Yorker*. McGuane lives in Montana.

PETER MEINKE's story "The Cranes" appeared in his book *The Piano Tuner* (University of Georgia Press, 1986), which won the Flannery O'Connor award. His work has appeared in *The Atlantic, The New Yorker*, and *The New Republic*. His latest book is *Liquid Paper: New & Selected Poems* (University of Pittsburgh Press, 1991). He has been writer-in-residence at the University of Hawaii and The University of North Carolina. He lives in St. Petersburg, Florida.

W. S. MERWIN has published more than a dozen volumes of poetry and several volumes of prose, including his memoir of life in the south of France, *The Lost Upland* (Random House, 1992), and a new book of poems, *Travels* (Knopf, 1993). He has been the recipient of a PEN Translation Prize, the Fellowship of the Academy of American Poets, the Bollingen Prize, and the Pulitzer Prize. He lives in Hawaii and is active in environmental causes.

MARIO ROBERT MORALES's story "Dead Weight" appeared in *Clamor of Innocence: Central American Short Stories*, edited by Barbara Paschke and David Volpendesta (City Lights Books, 1988). Morales is an exiled Guatemalan writer living in Costa Rica. He received the 1985 EDUCA Prize for his novel *El Esplendor del Piramide*. TINA ALVAREZ ROBLES, the translator, has contributed to *Volcan* (Editoria Nacional, 1965), *La Dabacle* (Editoria Istimo, 1969), and *Tomorrow Triumphant* (Night Horn Books, 1984).

CHARLOTTE PAINTER is the author of several books of personal narrative and fiction, including *Gifts of Age* (Chronicle Books, 1985). She was co-editor of *Revelations: Diaries of Women* (Random House, 1979). "Deep End" first appeared in *Witness*. Her new novel is *Conjuring Tibet* (Mercury House, 1996). She lives in Santa Cruz, California.

RICARDO PAU-LLOSA was born in Havana. He is the author of three books of poetry including *Bread of the Imagined* (Bilingual Press, 1992), and *Cuba* (Carnegie Mellon, 1993). He is a widely published art critic specializing in modern Latin American art, and his fiction has appeared in *New England Review, Fiction,* and *Prairie Schooner*. He lives in Florida and teaches at Miami-Dade Community College.

BARRY PETERS lives in Ohio. He received his M.A. from Wright State University in 1995 and teaches English at Centerville High School. "Arnie's Test Day" originally appeared in *What If? Writing Exercises for Fiction Writers*, edited by Pamela Painter and Anne Bernays (Harper Collins, 1995).

RICHARD PLANT, a native of Oklahoma, now lives in Virginia where he teaches writing at Mary Baldwin College. He has published stories in *The Cimarron Review* and *The Antioch Review*, as well as *Prize Stories: The O. Henry Award* and *Best Stories From New Writers*. "Flatland" first appeared in the *South Dakota Review*.

LUIS ARTURO RAMOS is a novelist, short story writer, and essayist born in Minatitlan. He is the author of three novels, *Violeta Peru, Intramuros,* and *Este era un gato,* and several books of stories, including *Del tiempo y otros lugares, Los viejos asesinos,* and *Domingo junto al paisaje*. ROBERT KRAMER is a translator and teaches German, English, and classical literature at Manhattan

College in New York. GLORIA NICHOLS was born in Havana. She has served as a translator and interpreter for the U.S. Department of State and for the United Nations.

MARK RICHARD grew up in Texas and Virginia. Before devoting himself to writing, he spent three years on oceangoing trawlers, coastal steamers, and fishing boats. He also worked as a radio announcer, a reporter, a bartender, a private investigator, and a teacher. "On the Rope" is from his collection of stories entitled *The Ice at the Bottom of the World* (Knopf, 1989). His most recent book of fiction, a novel, is *Fishboy* (Doubleday, 1994). He lives in New York City.

BRUCE HOLLAND ROGERS has published over fifty short stories for *Ellery Queen's Mystery Magazine*, *The Magazine of Fantasy and Science Fiction*, *Century*, and *Asylum*. His story "Enduring As Dust" was nominated for an Edgar Allen Poe Award by the Mystery Writers of America and his stories have appeared in *The Year's Best Mystery and Suspense Stories: 1994*. "Murder, Mystery" first appeared in *Quarterly West*. He lives in Illinois.

SALARRUÉ (Salazar Arrué), the late Salvadorean writer and painter, is one of Central America's most highly respected authors. His selected works have been published by the University of El Salvador. "We Bad," appeared in *Clamor of Innocence: Central American Short Stories*, edited by Barbara Paschke and David Volpendesta (City Lights Books, 1988). THOMAS CHRISTENSEN, a former editor at North Point Press, has also translated Julio Cortázar's *Around the Days in Eighty Worlds* (1988).

FERNANDO SORRENTINO was born in Buenos Aires. In his first book of short stories, *Zoological Regression* (Editores Dos, 1969), he says he made the error of trying to please hypothetical readers, while in his second collection, *Empires and Servitude* (Seix Barral, 1972), he began to write the stories he himself would like to read. "The Visitation" was translated by NORMAN THOMAS diGIOVANNI and SUSAN ASHE. Among Sorrentino's other story collections are *The Best of All Possible Worlds* (Plus Ultra, 1976), and *Sanitary Centennial and Selected Short Stories* (University of Texas Press, 1988).

TERESE SVOBODA won the 1994 Bobst Prize with her novel, *Cannibal* (New York University Press). She has also written three books of poetry: *Mere Mortals* (University of Georgia Press, 1995), *Laughing Africa* (University of Iowa Press, 1990, Iowa Prize), and *All Aberration* (University of Georgia Press, 1985). "Sundress" first appeared in *Mānoa*. She lives in Kāneohe, Hawaii.

MARY SWAN grew up in Southwestern Ontario, and attended York University. She now works in the library at the University of Guelph. She has published in the *Malahat Review* and *Best Canadian Stories* and is currently at work on a short story collection.

JUDY TROY's collection of stories, *Mourning Doves* (Scribners, 1993), was nominated for the Los Angeles Book Award for First Fiction. Her stories have appeared in *The New Yorker*, *Antaeus*, *American Short Fiction*, and other publications, as well as in several anthologies. She has just finished her first novel, entitled *Small Rain*. She lives in Alabama, where she teaches fiction writing at Auburn University.

ALICE WALKER, a native of Georgia, attended Spelman College and earned a B.A. from Sarah Lawrence College. She is the author of five books of poetry, three short story collections, and five novels, including *The Color Purple* (Harcourt Brace, 1982), for which she was awarded the Pulitzer Prize. "The Flowers" originally appeared in *In Love & Trouble* (Harvest Books, Harcourt Brace Jovanovich, 1974). Her most recent book is *Warrior Marks* (Harcourt Brace, 1993).

SYLVIA WATANABE was born in Hawaii on the island of Maui. "Emiko's Garden" is from her book *Talking to the Dead* (Doubleday, 1992). She is the recipient of a Japanese American Citizens League National Literary Award and a fellowship from the National Endowment for the Arts, and was a 1991 O'Henry Award winner. Several of her stories have appeared in anthologies and literary journals. She now lives in Michigan.

GLEN WELDON has received a John Steinbeck Writing Award, and a 1994 PEN Fellowship in the Arts for Fiction. His stories have appeared in *Story, Sundog, Confrontation*, and other magazines. "The Cat Was Dead" originally appeared in *Quarterly West*. He is a student at the Iowa Writers Workshop.

ALLEN WOODMAN's most recent work is a comic novella entitled *All-You-Can Eat, Alabama* (Apalachee Press, 1994). He is also the author of several children's picture books, with David Kirby, and a collection of short-short stories, *The Shoebox of Desire and Other Tales* (Livingston University Press, 1987). "Waiting for the Broken Horse" first appeared in *Carolina Quarterly*. Woodman lives in Flagstaff, where he teaches at Northern Arizona University.

BARRY YOURGRAU was born in South Africa and came to the United States as a child. An author, performance artist, and MTV personality, he has published three collections of stories and fables, *Wearing Dad's Head* (Peregrine Smith Books, 1987), *A Man Jumps out of an Airplane: Stories* (Sun, 1984), and *The Sadness of Sex* (Delta, 1995), from which "Silver Arrows" is taken. He lives in Los Angeles.

ACKNOWLEDGMENTS

Review. Copyright © 1987 by Madison Smartt Bell. Reprinted by permission of Gelfman Schneider Literary Agents, Inc.

Mitch Berman, "To Be Horst" from *The Male Body: Features, Destinies, Exposures,* edited by Laurence Goldstein (Ann Arbor: University of Michigan Press, 1994). Originally published in *Michigan Quarterly Review* 32, no. 4 (1993). Copyright © 1996 by Mitch Berman. Reprinted by permission of the author.

Kenneth Bernard, "Sister Francetta and the Pig Baby" from *The Maldive Chronicles.* Copyright © 1987 by Kenneth Bernard. Reprinted by permission of the author.

Margaret Broucek, "Alvin Jones's Ignorant Wife" from *TriQuarterly* 74 (Winter 1989). Copyright © 1996 by Margaret Broucek. Reprinted by permission of the author.

Robert Olen Butler, "Relic" from *Gettysburg Review* (Summer 1990). Copyright © 1990 by Robert Olen Butler. Reprinted by permission of the author and Witherspoon Associates.

Ron Carlson, "The Tablecloth of Turin" from *Plan B for the Middle Class.* First appeared in *Story.* Copyright © 1992 by Ron Carlson. Reprinted by permission of W. W. Norton & Company, Inc.

Andrei Codrescu, "A Bar in Brooklyn" from *Monsieur Teste in America & Other Instances of Realism: Short Stories by Andrei Codrescu* (Minneapolis: Coffee House Press, 1987). Copyright © 1987 by Andrei Codrescu. Reprinted by permission of the author.

William deBuys, "Dreaming Geronimo" from *Story* (Summer 1991). Copyright © 1991 by William deBuys. Reprinted by permission of the author.

Don DeLillo, "Videotape" from *Antaeus* (Autumn 1984). Copyright © 1984 by Don DeLillo. Reprinted by permission of Wallace Literary Agency, Inc.

Stephen Dixon, "Flying" from *Long Made Short* (Baltimore: Johns Hopkins University Press, 1993). Originally published in *North American Review* (March / April 1993). Copyright © 1993 by Stephen Dixon. Reprinted by permission of the author and Witherspoon Associates.

Yahya Gharagozlou, "A Simple Death" from *the new renaissance* 7, no. 1. Copyright © 1996 by Yahya Gharagozlou. Reprinted by permission of *tnr.*

Dagoberto Gilb, "The Señora" from *The Magic of Blood* (Albuquerque: The University of New Mexico Press, 1993). Originally published in *The Threepenny Review.* Copyright © 1993 by Dagoberto Gilb. Reprinted by permission of the author.

Molly Giles, "The Writers' Model" from *Side Show* (Somer Salt Press,

1993). Copyright © 1993 by Molly Giles. Reprinted by permission of Ellen Levine Literary Agency.

Merrill Gilfillan, "F. O. B. Flicker" from *Sworn Before Cranes*. Copyright © 1994 by Merrill Gilfillan. Reprinted by permission of the author.

Traci L. Gourdine, "Graceful Exits" from *ZYZZYVA*. Copyright © 1994 by Traci L. Gourdine. Reprinted by permission of the author.

Lynn Grossman, "Cartography" from *TriQuarterly* 74 (Winter 1989). Copyright © 1989 by Lynn Grossman. Reprinted by permission of the author.

Joy Harjo, "The Flood" from *The Woman Who Fell From the Sky*. Originally published in *Grand Street*. Copyright © 1994 by Joy Harjo. Reprinted by permission of the author and W. W. Norton & Company, Inc.

Ursula Hegi, "Doves," *Prairie Schooner* 65, no. 4 (Winter 1992). Copyright © 1991 by University of Nebraska Press. Reprinted by permission of the publisher.

Robin Hemley, "The Liberation of Rome." Originally appeared in *North Carolina Humanities* and *The Big Ear: Stories by Robin Hemley* (Blair). Copyright © 1995 by Robin Hemley. Reprinted by permission of the author and Sterling Lord Literary Agency, Inc.

Allen Hibbard, "Crossing to Abbassiya" from *Cimarron Review* (April 1992). Copyright © 1996 by Allen Hibbard. Reprinted by permission of the Board of Regents for Oklahoma State University.

Pam Houston, "Symphony" from *Cowboys Are My Weakness*. Copyright © 1992 by Pam Houston. Reprinted by permission of W. W. Norton & Company, Inc.

Shelley Hunt, "Giving It Away" from *What If?: Writing Exercises For Fiction Writers*, edited by Anne Bernays and Pam Painter (New York: HarperCollins Publishers, 1995). Copyright © 1995 by Shelly Hunt. Reprinted by permission of the author.

Denis Johnson, "Out on Bail" from *Jesus' Son*. Copyright © 1992 by Denis Johnson. Reprinted by permission of Farrar, Straus & Giroux, Inc.

Pagan Kennedy, "The Monument" from *Prairie Schooner* 63, no. 3 (Fall 1989). Copyright © 1992 by the University of Nebraska Press. Reprinted by permission of the publisher.

Andrew Lam, "Grandma's Tales." Copyright © 1996 by Andrew Lam. Reprinted with the permission of the author.

David Leavitt, "We Meet at Last" from *Mississippi Review*. Copyright © 1993 by David Leavitt. Reprinted by permission of Wylie, Aitken & Stone, Inc.

HarperCollins Publishers, 1995). Copyright © 1995 by Barry Peters. Reprinted by permission of the author.

Richard Plant, "Flatland" from *South Dakota Review* 30, no. 4 (Winter 1992). Copyright © 1992 by University of South Dakota. Reprinted by permission of *South Dakota Review.*

Luis Arturo Ramos, "Under Water," translated by Robert Kramer and Gloria Nichols. Copyright © 1996 by Luis Arturo Ramos. Reprinted by permission.

Mark Richard, "On the Rope" from *The Ice at the Bottom of the World.* Copyright © 1989 by Mark Richard. Reprinted by permission of Alfred A. Knopf, Inc.

Bruce Holland Rogers, "Murder, Mystery" from *The Quarterly* (Fall 1992). Copyright © 1992 by Bruce Holland Rogers. Reprinted by permission of the author.

Salarrué (Salazar Arrué), "We Bad," translated by Thomas Christensen, from *Clamor of Innocence.* Copyright © 1996 by Thomas Christensen. Reprinted by permission.

Fernando Sorrentino, "The Visitation," translated by Norman Thomas diGiovanni and Susan Ashe. Reprinted by permission of the author.

Terese Svoboda, "Sundress" from *Mānoa: A Pacific Journal of International Writing.* Copyright © 1996 by Terese Svoboda. Reprinted by permission of the author.

Mary Swan, "Where You Live Now" from *Malahat Review* (March 1991). Copyright © 1991 by Mary Swan. Reprinted by permission of the author.

Judy Troy, "Ten Miles West of Venus" from *The New Yorker* (June 27 / July 4, 1994). Copyright © 1994 by Judy Troy. Reprinted by permission of Georges Borchardt, Inc. for the author.

Alice Walker, "The Flowers" from *In Love & Trouble: Stories of Black Women.* Copyright © 1973 by Alice Walker. Reprinted by permission of Harcourt Brace & Company.

Sylvia Watanabe, "Emiko's Garden" from *Talking to the Dead.* Copyright © 1992 by Sylvia Watanabe. Reprinted by permission of Doubleday, a division of Bantam Doubleday Dell Publishing Group, Inc.

Glen Weldon, "The Cat Was Dead." First appeared in *Quarterly West* 36 (Winter 1992). Copyright © 1992 by Glen Weldon. Reprinted by permission of the author.

Allen Woodman, "Waiting for the Broken Horse" from *The Shoebox of Desire and Other Tales* (Livingston University Press, 1987). Copyright © 1987 by Allen Woodman. Reprinted by permission of the author.